WHAT IT TAKES TO FALL

C.R. ELLIS

Editor: Jennifer Archer @ Archer Editing & Writing Services

Proofreading: All Encompassing Books

Cover designer: Hang Le, ByHangLe

HarLex Publishing

E-book ISBN: 978-1-7323131-4-9

Paperback ISBN: 978-1-7323131-5-6

PROLOGUE
BRYCE

THEN
Bryce - 8, Elliot - 5

"Mom, do I have to go? I won't eat any junk food if I stay," I promised.

I really wanted the leftover Easter candy hidden in my closet, but I wanted to stay home more. Going with my parents to visit our neighbors, the Kincaids, was *bor-ing*. They were older than Mom and Dad and had no kids. Or they used to, but they didn't anymore. I couldn't remember which.

Mom pulled a pie out of the oven and set it down before turning toward me. "Honey, come here. We need to talk." I walked toward the island stools and plopped down. "Do you remember the time you asked me about the girl in the photo at the Kincaids' house, and I told you she was their daughter, but she didn't live with them anymore?"

I nodded.

"Well, she had two daughters of her own, and now both girls are going to live with Mr. and Mrs. Kincaid. It's a scary time for them as they adjust to their new life, so having you around might help them feel more comfortable. Plus, now you'll have friends within walking distance."

That could be fun, even if they were girls.

"How come they had to move in with their grandparents? Did their mom move in too?"

"No, she didn't. Their mom is having a tough time, so she brought the girls to live with their grandparents while she gets better."

"Oh. Okay. Do you think they'll want to swim? I could take my diving rings. I guess I could bring other toys too."

Mom leaned over and cupped my chin. "Don't ever let life harden your sweet heart, Bryce. The world needs more kind souls like you."

"*Mom,*" I groaned, making a face and squirming out of her grasp. She was *always* saying stuff like that to me.

She sighed and held up her hands. "Okay, okay. As far as swimming goes, I'm not sure, honey. I think they're both a bit younger than you, so they might not be able to swim yet. Tell you what, I'll finish with the pie while you get some toys together, then we'll get your dad and head over to the Kincaids' house. Deal?"

"Deal."

Thirty minutes later, I sat on the Kincaids' couch, but had only seen the younger sister. Elliot, the older sister, had run up the stairs as soon as we got here.

"I'm sorry, Bryce. Elliot's very shy. This is all still new for her," Mrs. Kincaid explained. Sophia, the younger one, hid behind Mrs. Kincaid's legs, but kept peeking her head out to look at me.

"That's okay. I have a friend at school who's like that." I pulled my backpack off and set it down. I wasn't sure what they liked, so I brought a little bit of everything—pool toys, Pokémon cards, Uno, Let's Go Fishin', Sorry, a Bop It, a Lego set, and my Superman figure.

I opened the bag, and that made Sophia come over to me. Her eyes were bugged out, like she couldn't wait to see what toys I had. I grabbed Superman and held it out to her. "Here. You wanna play with him?" She took him, and she was holding on so tight I just knew she wasn't going to give him back. "Um, how about we play Let's Go Fishin' instead?"

"That's a great idea, Bryce. Why don't you guys go play in the den? That way you can spread your toys out."

I was glad that when I set up the game, Sophia decided she didn't care about Superman anymore. She was too young for the other games, but I figured, how hard can it be to hold a pole out for snapping fish? She watched while I showed her what to do, and then played along. Pretty soon she started squealing because she was having so much fun, and I saw her sister's blonde hair before her head disappeared around the corner of the doorway.

"Sophia, do you like M&M's?" I asked, pulling out a fun-size bag. "I sure do. I guess we'll just have to share them between the two of us."

That did the trick. Elliot slowly walked into the room, but I didn't look at her straight on until she sat down across from me. She was a lot smaller than me, probably a kindergartener I'd guess, with blonde hair and eyes that matched the sky. She was real shy, like the deer that were always crossing through our yard.

"You're Elliot, right? I'm Bryce. Want some M&M's?" I held out a couple toward her, and she nodded, but didn't say anything. "I've also got Starbursts, but maybe we should save those for after dinner." She shrugged, and I wondered if she knew how to talk. "You know…Uno's my favorite game. Have you ever played?" She shook her head. "Want me to teach you?" Another nod.

I explained the rules, but frowned when I got to what to do with a wild card. "How about you point to the color you want?" Nod. "Hmm. You're supposed to say, 'Uno' when you only have one card left, but you can just hold it up," I said. I showed her by shaking my hand around in the air, then I put my whole body into it, wiggling like a worm.

Elliot started laughing, and I knew I must've looked crazy. But it made her happy, and that was what I wanted.

After a few minutes, I was down to two cards. Elliot played a yellow four, and I threw down my blue four and quickly called out, "Uno!" before she had a chance to see I only had one card. I almost felt bad for beating her, but I hated to lose more than anything.

She slowly put her next card down, and the second it landed, she smiled and yelled, "UNO!"

I jumped at the sound, then looked down and confirmed she only had one card left. And—worse—she played a draw four wild card. I groaned and drew the cards.

"Yellow," she said.

I played my only yellow card.

She dropped her last card on top of mine, and immediately broke into a big smile before copying the silly dance I'd done. "I win!"

I still hated losing, but maybe…just this once, it wasn't so bad.

∾

BRYCE - 11, ELLIOT - 8

"I WIN!" I yelled, touching our home-base tree a good two seconds before Elliot caught up to me. She almost took me out when she did catch up, though; that's how fast she was barreling down on the tree and me. We'd run from her grandparents' house all the way across their property to reach this tree. It separated their property from the vineyard my parents owned.

"Ugh!" she whined. "You cheated, Bryce. I want a rematch!"

I just laughed. It was what we always said whenever we lost. Elliot was probably the only person on earth who hated to lose as much as I did, which meant we were always finding new ways to compete against each other. I was bigger and (usually) faster than her, but she never used that as an excuse for losing. Instead, she usually just found something else for us to do—swimming, board games, video games, tic-tac-toe, foot races, bike races, who could clean their room faster…there was always some competition we'd come up with.

"You wish I'd cheated. I'm just faster," I said, catching my breath and shaking my head before holding my hand out. "Hand over the candy, Uno. A deal's a deal."

We both sank down to the ground, putting our backs against the tree as we caught our breath, and Elliot pulled out the Starburst packet from her pocket. She handed it to me, and I ripped it open, separating out the candies by color. We both liked the pink ones the best, so that's what we were racing for—winner take all. I handed her the oranges (her second favorite) and kept the reds (my second favorite), and neither of us made a move for the yellows.

She glared at the pink Starbursts like it was their fault she lost, and I sighed, handing her one of the four. We both loved winning, but we weren't mean about it.

"You staying over for dinner?" I asked eventually.

She nodded and stood up, turning back to offer me her hand. "Yep. I love your mom's enchiladas." Before I reached her hand, she yanked it back and took off. "Last one there has to set the table!"

"Now who's the cheater?!" I shouted before scrambling up and racing after her.

BRYCE - 17, ELLIOT - 14

"BRYCE, HI. HOW ARE YOU?" Mrs. Kincaid asked, pulling the door open and ushering me in.

"I'm good, Mrs. Kincaid. Is El here?"

"She's in the game room."

"Thanks," I said, heading toward the stairs.

The closer I got to the game room the louder the sound of a

ball rolling across a table became. I stopped at the doorway and held in a laugh when I saw Elliot playing foosball by herself.

My friends thought it was weird that I still hung out with Elliot outside of the occasional get-togethers my parents and her grandparents had. I understood why they thought that, but they didn't know the whole story about my friendship with her, that I was basically the first person she ever spoke to after she came to live with her grandparents.

"Doesn't matter how much you practice, Uno. You'll never beat me at foosball."

She didn't even miss a beat, just kept playing without looking up. "Am I supposed to be intimidated because you finally got a car? You wish."

"Nah. I think my winning record speaks for itself." I was bull-shitting; we never kept track of our victories, but I definitely won more than she did.

"Whatever, loser. You here to talk or play?" she asked, finally looking up. When her eyes landed on my bag of Starbursts, she released her grip on the table handles.

"Both. Let's talk first. There's something I gotta tell you."

"Okay."

We sat on the couch, and I dumped the Starbursts on the cushion between us. We both reached for the pink ones. There was comfort in the routine, in the familiarity of hanging out with Elliot.

Too bad that was about to change.

"Listen, there's no way to make this suck less, so I'm just gonna say it. My parents are assholes, and they're sending me to some prep school in Washington. I leave in a few weeks."

She was quiet for so long I worried she'd choked on a Star-burst or something.

"El?"

No response.

Without a word, she bolted off the couch and stormed down the stairs and out the door.

I let her go, knowing where I'd find her. By the time I got to our tree, she'd lost the battle against tears. I hadn't seen her cry in years, and the sight made me uncomfortable.

"It's not the end of the world."

"Yes it is. You're going to leave and forget all about me. Just like…" She stopped herself from finishing that thought, but we both knew what she'd meant to say.

Just like her mom did.

"No. That will never happen, Elliot. I'll come back for breaks." I turned and nudged her with my shoulder, giving her a handful of Starbursts. "And think of it this way, now you won't have to share the pink ones."

That earned me a small smile, and it reminded me of the day we met.

"Promise?"

"Promise. This isn't forever, Uno. I'll be back, dominating you in foosball and Mario Kart before you know it."

CHAPTER 1
BRYCE

THEN
BRYCE - 22, ELLIOT - 19

I don't even know why I thought coming home was a good idea.

I trekked through the vineyard, wandering aimlessly, and watched the sun flirt with the horizon, painting the sky with a display of vibrant purples and oranges. If I'd been in a better mood, I could've appreciated the beauty.

I had four weeks left until graduation and about four years' worth of shit to get done before then. But when my mom called and begged me to fly home for the weekend to attend the winery's anniversary party, I caved. *"It's important for you to start learning the ropes around here. You'll be taking over before you know it."*

It wasn't the assumption that I was taking over that pissed me off. I was used to that. It was the fact that she and my dad just assumed my life could be put on hold, that it wasn't asking much for me to drop everything and come running just because they asked.

If I was being honest, what pissed me off even more was that, as much as my parents said they loved and supported me, I knew that was only half true. If they really supported me, talking to them about what *I wanted* for my future wouldn't feel like torture. They'd never expressed interest in seeing my designs. It was like they thought if they just pretended my love of architecture didn't exist, it would eventually go away. They treated it as a fad, like I'd lose interest in it the same way I had lost interest in my Tamagotchi and my pet rock.

Architecture was my passion. Winemaking was my obligation.

My parents would never understand. The fact that I was about to graduate with a double major in architecture and business—an accomplishment I was immensely proud of and that most would find admirable—was another point of contention between us. As a compromise, I'd taken classes in viticulture during the summers, while also working my ass off to secure an internship at the top architectural firm in Seattle.

And it paid off; my boss, Mr. Martin, offered me a full-time job after I graduated. The salary was outrageous, the benefits were unbeatable, and the job was everything I'd ever wanted. It was basically a dream come true.

But accepting the job would mean destroying my already strained relationship with my parents.

Turning it down would be like throwing away my one chance to be truly happy.

Taking one last look at the sun before it disappeared for the night, I lifted my half-empty bottle of sauvignon blanc and drank straight from it. I hadn't even realized I was walking toward it until I looked over and saw the '*B + E*' tree in the distance. As in *Bryce + Elliot*. This tree was our designated meeting place as kids.

Elliot Kincaid.

After I moved away, we texted some, but eventually the days between responses dragged out until we just fell out of touch completely. It didn't help that I never came home.

I paused, immediately overcome with the desire to call her. To see her. It had been years since we'd seen each other, but I had a feeling if anyone could break me out of this shitty mood, it was El.

The closer I got to the tree, the more apparent it became that calling her wouldn't be necessary.

She was there. Sitting against the trunk.

I practically sprinted toward her, only slowing down when I got close enough to take in her entire frame. Long blonde hair draped over her shoulders. Toned, tanned legs for days. Same slender build she'd always had. Except...this Elliot was all grown up.

"By now you should know I'll always beat you here, Bryce," she said, looking up from her phone with a smile tugging at her lips.

One sentence. That's all it took for Elliot to brighten my mood.

My lips split into a smile that matched hers. "Can it really be considered a win if the other person doesn't know you're racing? Plus, we both know you always cheated your way to victory."

"You wish. But I guess I can understand your need to justify losing all the time." She sat a little straighter and tugged down the hem of her blue and white dress, eyeing me slowly. After dragging her eyes over the length of my body, she settled back on my face. "I've never seen you in a tux before. You look...different," she finally offered.

I arched a brow and ran a hand along my jaw, fighting a smile. "Different?"

Her eyes swept over me again before meeting my gaze. "I mean...good different. But yeah, different."

I couldn't be sure if it was the dim evening light playing tricks on my eyes or if she really did have a light blush staining her cheeks.

"You're awfully dressed up to be wandering around the woods by yourself though."

I shrugged and loosened the tie around my neck. "The party sucked. Your grandparents were the only people there that I knew. I kinda thought you'd be there."

"I was planning to go, but..." She trailed off and started picking at an invisible thread on her dress.

I zeroed in on her hands and felt my smile falter. Messing with her clothes was El's tell that something was bothering her; it had been that way since we were kids. I was about to ask what was wrong when she jerked her hand back and looked up, her smile back in place. Only this time it looked less genuine, more forced.

"But something came up. So, uh, I see we had the same idea," she said, holding up her own bottle of wine.

I knew why *I* was wandering around in the woods with a bottle of wine, but why was Elliot apparently drowning her own demons with booze?

I tossed my jacket onto the ground, rolled up my sleeves, and settled into a spot next to her against the trunk of the tree. "I guess great minds think alike."

For a few minutes, we just sat there, neither of us making an effort to engage in conversation. It wasn't awkward or weird. Despite the fact that El was definitely no longer a kid, she still felt like the same girl I'd had to coax out of her shell with candy and card games.

I downed the last of my wine and set the bottle aside.

"You know, I still have the scar from the first time you ejected me from the go-kart," I said, lifting my arm to show her the thick white line. It wasn't big, just a couple inches along the outside of my forearm, but I used to make up crazy stories about how I'd gotten it.

She just laughed and rolled her eyes. "And I'm sure you've got some elaborate fake story about it that you use to give yourself street cred or to pick up chicks."

"Nah. I mostly just tell people this wild lunatic I used to run around with was trying to take me out so she wouldn't keep losing to me in foosball and Uno."

She let out another laugh, a little louder this time, and I couldn't stop myself from laughing along with her. El's laugh was the epitome of contagious. More often than not, her laughter would turn into us both cracking up like hyenas.

"Since we're swapping confessions," she said. "I should probably tell you that I threw you under the bus to Pops and Nana in high school when they asked about a purple stain on my bedroom carpet. My friend and I had snuck some of their wine into my room and I never knew it spilled. I panicked and the first thing I could come up with was that you knocked over a glass of grape juice several years back. Genius, I know."

I snorted a laugh and nodded toward the bottle next to her. "Should we come up with another brilliant explanation for why this bottle's missing?"

"Not necessary. My friend just turned twenty-one, so this was left over from the party last weekend."

"Ah, fair enough. Well, feel free to use me as a scapegoat for any other illicit situations you get into."

Our conversation flowed easily, and for a while we reminisced about old times and caught each other up on what we'd both been up to over the years.

I couldn't remember the last time I'd laughed so hard or the last time I'd enjoyed a conversation so much. For the past four years, my life had revolved exclusively around school, which meant I had zero time for friendships beyond ones of convenience. I'd almost forgotten what it felt like to confide in another person.

Leave it to Uno to bring out the sentimentalist in me.

"So what are you going to do after graduation?" she asked after I'd waxed on about the job offer and my internship for probably longer than she cared to listen.

"I don't know. If I stay in Seattle, my parents are likely to disown me."

"But is it worth sacrificing your own happiness just to meet their stupid, selfish expectations? I just listened to you talk about architecture with the same smile and love on your face that you had when you talked about it as a teenager. Bryce, you can't give up something that makes you that happy."

"It's not that simple, Elliot."

"Seems pretty simple to me. You haven't spent the last four

years working your ass off only to come back and be caged into a life of apathy. You deserve more than that. Pops has always told me that ignoring our life's calling is the biggest disservice a person can do to himself. He says *'that kind of acceptance snuffs out passion and binds you to a life devoid of purpose.'* I don't know what my purpose in life is, but I do know he's not wrong. And I think we both know winemaking isn't your purpose in life, Bryce."

"I wish my parents gave a shit about things like passion and purpose. Actually, I guess they do. Just not *my* passion or purpose." I grabbed the bottle between us, now close to empty, and brought it to my lips. "Okay, enough about my shitty drama. Time for a new subject. Tell me something about your life. Anything."

It was strange how easily we slipped back into a comfortable dynamic, despite the fact that we'd basically become strangers. But at the same time, it wasn't that strange at all.

El bit her lip and started twisting a blonde lock around a finger. Another one of her tells. Something was definitely weighing on her. "Helen wants to meet Sophia and me. Next week." She exhaled a long, heavy breath and turned toward me. "And as of now you're the only person I've told."

"Helen, as in…?"

"As in the woman who brought us to Nana and Pops almost fifteen years ago and vanished, never to be seen or heard from again. Until she left me a voicemail yesterday."

"Holy shit, Elliot. That's…"

"Insane? Random? Utterly terrifying?"

"Yeah. Wait, you haven't told Sophia or your grandparents? A friend?"

"You know what the word 'only' means, right?"

"Why haven't you told anyone else?"

"Honestly, I'm not even sure how to answer that. Talking about her just never feels right. With you though…I don't know, it's just always been…different. Easier."

For a second, we each let her words linger without saying anything else.

Elliot had always struggled with talking about her mother, but occasionally I'd gotten her to open up. I still didn't know much about her time before she came to live next door, but I knew it wasn't pretty.

I leaned over to bump her shoulder with mine. "I've missed this. Missed you, Uno."

She nudged my shoulder back. "I guess I've kinda missed you too. Or maybe I just missed beating you at everything."

"Big words for a girl who still owes me about fifty pounds of Starbursts," I said, a skeptical brow arched at her.

"What?! No way. Pretty sure your memory is failing you, Bryce."

I grabbed my phone and turned on the flashlight, bathing us both in a bright glow. "El. What are you going to do?"

She sighed and pulled her knees up into her chest, grabbing my jacket to drape over her legs before taking another sip of her wine. "I don't know. My instinct is to protect Sophia, to keep her out of the equation until I know Helen won't just vanish again. I just...Bryce, how can I not meet her? I've lived with the questions and the unknowns for so long. She could give me answers."

"But you don't...you don't know her, Elliot. You can't trust her. How did she even get your number?"

She shrugged, like she hadn't considered that. "Does it matter? She's my mother, Bryce."

"Who's had fourteen years to contact you but chose not to, which also makes her a stranger. I'm sorry, El, but I think it would be a mistake to trust her. I understand why you want to meet her, and I know you deserve answers, but DNA doesn't mean you owe her an ounce of trust. You don't know what kind of person she's become or what she's capable of. Trust is earned, not granted freely."

Her brows shot halfway up her forehead before she pinned me to the spot with narrowed eyes. "Do you, though? Understand?

Because I don't think you can possibly understand. I know you and your parents don't see eye-to-eye, but at least you *know* your parents, Bryce. I don't even know my father's identity."

Her gaze fell to the ground, but I couldn't look away from her. From the pain etched into her features. I wanted to absorb it all and have my smiling Uno back.

"I'll be forever grateful to Nana and Pops, don't get me wrong, but I just know this is my best chance—hell, maybe my *only* chance—to find out why my mom never came back for us. To find out why she did a lot of the things she did. Plus, it's not like I'm going to meet her in some creepy abandoned parking garage. We'll be in a public place, and if I'm not feeling it I can bolt."

When her blue eyes finally found their way back to mine, it felt like her pain had multiplied, and it killed me. As much as I wanted to protect her, I knew she was capable of making her own decisions. I didn't have to like it, and I might not even agree with her decision, but she deserved closure.

"You're right, El. I can't begin to understand what it's like for you to have these questions or to have the opportunity to finally get answers. It's your decision, and I'll respect whatever you decide. I want you to have the closure you deserve." I sighed and gently pounded my fist against her thigh. "Just promise me something?"

"Okay..."

"Don't go by yourself. I really think the best thing would be to tell George and Millie everything first. And Sophia deserves to know too. But if you're not going to tell them, at least take a friend with you to meet her."

She pressed her lips together and considered my request for a second. "Bryce...the last time I tried to have a conversation with my grandparents about her, they shut it down almost imme-diately."

"This is different, El. You know it is. Look..." I sighed, giving her hand a squeeze. "Bottom line is that you're not alone in this.

Just…let your grandparents and Sophia help you make this decision."

She hesitated long enough for doubt to creep into my gut and linger there.

But then she squeezed my hand back and nodded her head. "Okay."

The complete vulnerability in El's expression was enough to make me want to do something rash like offer to go with her myself. While I internally considered the logistics of that, she leaned over and grabbed something out of her bag, keeping the mystery item hidden as she turned back to me. "Close your eyes," she instructed, all traces of vulnerability gone, and a teasing smirk in its place.

I obliged, but cracked one eye open when I heard a plastic bag crinkle.

"Elliot Kincaid, you've been holding out on me," I exclaimed, tacking on an overly dramatic tsk.

She laughed and threw a handful of Starbursts at me. "And you peeked!"

I flashed her my most dazzling smile, but she just rolled her eyes and dropped the bag between us.

"Look, Bryce, a shooting star," she spluttered a minute later, gesturing behind me with a tilt of her chin.

I whipped my head around, but only saw the inky night sky and a handful of stars through the clouds. The second something pelted my shoulder I realized my mistake.

She bit her lip and grinned mischievously, and I couldn't help but notice how pretty she looked when she wore a genuine smile. For giving me *that* smile, she could hit me with every single Starburst in the bag. I opened my mouth to tell her that, but snapped it shut just as quick. *What the hell am I thinking? This is Elliot—my friend.*

Too much wine. That *had* to be the reason I was hyper-aware of every move El made and wondering if her hair felt as silky as it looked.

Instead of saying any of the borderline inappropriate thoughts filling my head, I just picked up an orange Starburst and pulled my arm back. "Oh, it's on, Uno. It's so on," I promised.

By the time we made our way to Kincaid Manor, our stomachs full of candy and wine, it was late enough that all the lights were out inside the house. We stood on the porch for what felt like minutes on end, neither of us willing to be the one to end the night.

Without warning, she pulled me into a crushing hug, both arms wrapped around my waist like I was her only lifeline.

"Thank you," she said, her cheek pressed against my chest. "For tonight. For making me laugh. For everything, Bryce."

I tightened my grip around her and rested my chin on top of her head. "You kidding? Thank *you*, El. Tonight was the most fun I've had in forever. Seeing you has been the only good part of this trip home."

I felt her cheek pull up with a smile. "I'm glad. Bryce," she said, pausing and tilting her neck back enough to meet my eyes but keeping her arms around me. I pulled a hand up to brush a chunk of her blonde bangs off her face. *Totally something friends do.* "I think you should stay in Seattle. You deserve to be happy."

Looking down and into El's eyes, brimming with sincerity and something else I couldn't name, the urge to kiss her coursed through me with unrelenting urgency. She pressed up on her toes and I lowered my head until our lips were past the point of return.

But at the last second, I redirected my mouth to press a kiss against her cheek. *I can't kiss her. Not when I'm leaving tomorrow and probably not coming back.*

Confusion was written plain as day on her face as she unwrapped her arms from my body and stepped back. She knew as well as I did that we were millimeters from crossing that invisible line *friends* don't cross.

"El, we've both had a lot to drink," I explained, trying not to wince as the words left my mouth. It was true, but I had a feeling I would've wanted to feel her lips on mine with or without the aid of alcohol.

She nodded, slipping on a mask of indifference. "You're right. Uh, I'm sorry, that was…I don't really know what that was," she babbled with an awkward laugh while she fumbled to unlock the front door.

"It's not that—"

"Bryce, it's fine. Really," she said with the kind of fake smile worn by the runner-up in a Miss USA contest. She dropped her voice and turned after walking into the house. "I should get to bed before Nana and Pops hear us. I meant what I said though; not many people can live their dreams, Bryce. This is your chance."

I swallowed the lump in my throat and gave her a smile. "Do me a favor? Call me to let me know what happens with Helen."

She hesitated, dropping her eyes from mine. "Okay. And, hey, let me know what you decide about staying." She looked up, a smile pulling one side of her mouth up. "Let's suck less at keeping in touch this time around."

"Deal."

I wish I'd known that we were both lying that night—to each other, to ourselves.

CHAPTER 2

ELLIOT

NOW

"Someone want to tell me why I smell like I took a vodka and champagne shower?" I asked, sitting up slowly and trying not to gag at the pungent stench of alcohol. I blinked my friends into focus and brought my left hand up to rake through my day-old curls.

Neither Milo nor Carleigh made an attempt to answer right away. Instead, they stood at the foot of my bed, trading looks of uncertainty.

Their hesitation gave me a second to take in my surroundings. A black and white polka dotted quilt draped over me. A poster of Yellowstone National Park on the wall to my right. A photo on the dresser across from the bed of Nana, Pops, Sophia, and me smiling.

My childhood bedroom.

Okay, so I obviously slept here last night after the party.

"Guys. What happened? And for the love of God, *why* did y'all apparently let me drink enough to lose chunks of my memory? I remember sending Pops and Nana off in the limo, then getting

Sophia to do shots with us after everyone else left. Things get a little fuzzy after that."

Last night was my grandparents' 'do-over' wedding in honor of their fiftieth anniversary.

I had poured my heart into planning it, and up until my memory went blank, everything had gone off perfectly. They adorably pledged to spend another fifty years together (I'd be dubious about them living to see the age of 119, but my grandparents were the type who never aged, so I wasn't taking that bet), everyone danced and partied at the elaborate backyard reception, and they'd given me crushing hugs of appreciation before jetting off for their mystery honeymoon destination.

Milo plopped down on the bed next to me. "First things first," he said, handing me two ibuprofen tablets with one hand and a glass of water with the other.

I swallowed the tablets and turned my full attention to my best friend, knowing he'd give it to me straight. Milo, Sophia, and I had lived together for a couple of years now, so he was no stranger to our sisterly spats.

"We were hoping you could tell us. After you finally got Soph to do a tequila shot you decided we should play stack cup. You also said we should 'make things interesting' by making the last cup a cocktail of vodka, tequila, rum, and a healthy dose of mimosa. One guess how that ended for you."

Well that explains a lot. Sort of. "Did I drink it or bathe in it?"

Carleigh cleared her throat. "Uh, well, after stack cup, Sophia pulled you aside. We didn't think anything of it, but then you both started shouting. She stormed back over, grabbed her phone, and walked into the house without looking back. You tried to go after her, but you tripped and dumped your whole drink all over yourself."

As kids, my sister and I had our fair share of sibling brawls, but these days we were mostly civil and rarely argued about anything other than things like why she raided my closet without permission, why there were fifteen episodes of *Millionaire Match-*

maker filling up the DVR, whose turn it was to do the dishes—superficial, everyday things of little consequence, for the most part. The only time things got remotely heated between us had occurred almost a decade ago—the last time we tried to have a conversation about our mother. Helen had always been the biggest point of contention between us.

Even now, thinking about her summoned a ball of dread deep in my stomach.

I frowned and pushed the quilt off, suddenly feeling hot. "And y'all have no clue what I said? I didn't mention anything after Sophia left?"

Milo shook his head, sending his shaggy brown locks cascading across his forehead. "Nope. One minute y'all were shouting and slinging insults in that delightful sisterly way y'all do, the next she was running off. All you would say is that you were just looking out for her, and she didn't need to take things so personally."

"Great. Why didn't one of you interfere?" I groaned.

Milo shrugged. "Because that would've been like trying to stop a train from derailing after it's already veering off the tracks."

"Fair enough. Is she...still here?"

"No, she went back to the apartment, and I'm pretty sure she's not coming back to help clean."

I sighed and slung my legs over the side of the bed.

Carleigh watched my sluggish movements and eyed me skeptically. "Are you going to be able to make it to the open house this afternoon? I could cancel my plans and go for you."

Carleigh and I had lost touch after she moved when we were in middle school, but reconnected via Facebook when she moved back to Austin last year. The timing couldn't have been better. We were catching up at happy hour when I realized she'd be the perfect one to take over my assistant position at Forget Me Knot Weddings. When Jade and Jasmine agreed and offered her the job, she accepted on the spot.

"No, don't do that. I'll be fine. Just need a shower and some food."

Truthfully, going to an open house for a new wedding venue sounded like torture. But a hangover wasn't going to prevent me from doing my job. I'd spent the last year working my butt off to prove to Jade and Jasmine they'd done the right thing by promoting me from being their assistant to handling my own weddings. Letting them down wasn't an option.

THE ROSE HOUSE, an old Victorian mansion in downtown Austin, was hosting an exclusive open house for event coordinators to showcase its recent renovations. One of the oldest homes in the city, its location in the heart of downtown and historic charm made it a perfect venue for weddings. Until recently, The Rose House had been a private residence and wasn't available to the public. Which made it all the more puzzling that, as I stood on the curb waiting for Jade, I was positive I'd been here before.

I pulled my phone from my pocket and used the front camera to quickly scan my face. Satisfied my makeup semi-cloaked my exhaustion, I flipped the camera and focused on the house in front of me. After snapping a couple of pictures, I caught sight of Jade speed-walking toward me from across the street.

"I'm so sorry I'm late! I completely lost track of time at the office."

"Don't worry about it, Jade. I only just got here a couple minutes ago. Hey," I said, turning toward her. "Why were you at the office? I thought you only had the Capps wedding on Friday, then you and Emmett were going to have some time off together."

"We were, but there was some kind of work emergency that he had to deal with. He spent the night at the office last night, and I got restless at home without him, so I figured work would be a good distraction."

I came to an abrupt stop on the path leading to the steps of the entrance. "Jade…"

"It's fine. *I'm fine.* I swear. I mean, it sucks that Emmett and I have basically been ships passing in the night lately, but I knew he was a workaholic when I married him. And, really, I'm being dramatic. We're together all the time, usually, and he's been good about keeping his work hours under control. We've both just been stressed out, I guess."

She didn't have to elaborate. They'd been trying to get pregnant for a while now. The fact that it hadn't happened was slowly driving her crazy.

I gave her hand a squeeze and offered a sympathetic smile. "Isn't your anniversary coming up? Maybe you could plan a surprise mini-vacation. Get out of town for a few days."

"Yeah, I've been thinking about planning something. Surprising Emmett is impossible, though. The man knows exactly how to get me to sing like a canary. It's incredibly frustrating," she huffed.

Her words said one thing, but the smile on her lips said another.

"Oh, sure. Must be *so* frustrating to have such a loving, devoted husband who bends over backward for you."

She laughed and started up the steps leading to the porch, pausing to take a brochure from a table by the door. "Whatever. You know what I mean. Enough about me. How was yesterday? The pictures looked incredible."

"Fantastic. The garden was the perfect setting for the ceremony, and the reception went off without a hitch. Nana was so beautiful, and seeing Pops brought to tears by watching his bride walk down the aisle was the sweetest thing ever. I'm so happy they finally got their fairytale wedding."

Jade smiled. "After fifty years of marriage, they certainly deserve it."

I mumbled an agreement, but my attention quickly shifted to the 'before' photos in the brochure I was holding. That déjà vu feeling was back and impossible to ignore. I peeled my eyes from the photos to look up and take in our surroundings as we crossed the threshold into the house.

The front door led straight into an open living area with a view all the way to the French doors leading to the back yard on the opposite side of the room. There was a narrow hallway to the right with three doors off of it, spaced about eight feet apart. A staircase to the left of the hall had a sign on the wall next to it listing the upstairs features—a bridal suite dressing room, bathroom, and access to a balcony overlooking the back yard.

We wandered deeper into the living area, taking in the details and features of the space. Although not an expert on design or architecture, even I could appreciate the time and dedication someone had put in to the place. A wall had been removed to open up the downstairs area, while maintaining the twentieth-century charm that made the house special. The hardwood floors looked original, like they'd been sitting underneath a layer of carpet all along. Crown molding had been added, its dark shade almost matching that of the hardwood, providing a striking contrast against the white walls and highlighting the high, coffered ceiling.

Jade and I both ambled through the house separately and met back up in the veranda off the living room.

"Wow," she mumbled. "This place is gorgeous. They'll be completely booked for next year in no time. C'mon, let's go check out the back yard."

Even the outdoor space had been given a facelift. Large pavers covered the ground beneath a dozen tables set up in a manner perfect for a wedding reception. Although the lots in this part of Austin tended to be small, the space available was used to its best effect by added shrubs and vines along the back fence, making the area feel cozy instead of cramped.

"I'm going to get a drink. Want one?" Jade asked.

Visions of Millie-mosas sprang to mind, and I silently swore off of ever drinking orange juice again.

"Not even a little. I, uh, got a little carried away last night. Alcohol and I aren't on good terms right now."

"Ah, gotcha. Okay, I'll be right back."

"I'll grab a table."

I settled into a chair and began scrolling through the photos I'd taken inside. Within seconds, a familiar figure dropped into a chair across the table from me.

"Damn. Why do you look like the one of us who was up till dawn?" Jasmine asked, tilting her aviator sunglasses down to scan my face. "You look like hell, but I love your top."

I was convinced Jas had never in her life even *attempted* to develop a filter when it came to being blunt.

"Is that why you're late? Why were *you* up all night?" I deflected.

A brow lifted as her lips curled into a sly grin. "Why do you think?"

"You were binge watching *Parks and Rec* again?"

"Jesus, El. You really need to get out more. Celibacy is turning your brain innocent. I don't even want to know how long it's been since you got laid."

I rolled my eyes in lieu of an answer.

"And yes, that's why I'm late. Dean's flight didn't get in until almost midnight, and we had a lot of catching up to do. And by catching up, I mean the sweaty, naked kind that involves—"

"Ew. Ew. Ew," Jade groaned as she sat down and realized what kind of conversation she'd walked into. "Do not finish that sentence. This is crossing a line I do not ever need to cross when it comes to my brother. You know the rules about bringing up the details of your sex life around me."

Jas huffed out a sigh. "Yeah, yeah. You want a clear warning and copious amounts of alcohol in your system."

"Seeing as how I'm not at all intoxicated and this is technically a work function, maybe we just *try* to keep it professional for once?" Jade asked, lifting a brow and moving her gaze from Jas to me.

My hands shot up. "Hey, don't look at me. According to Jas, my brain is innocent now anyway. I'm totally fine with redirecting this into a work conversation."

"You're only saying that because you're still deflecting, El," Jas insisted. "Answer the question, then we can switch to work mode. What happened last night—or should I say, *who* happened last night?"

I sighed and resigned myself to spilling the beans. Jasmine was annoyingly persistent, and I knew she'd get me to fess up eventually.

"Sophia and I got into a big argument last night after Nana and Pops left." I hesitated and darted my eyes across the yard to the food truck parked in the corner serving Korean barbecue appetizers before redirecting my attention back to Jade and Jasmine. "I'm a little fuzzy on the details because I lost a game of stack cup and had to drink my own idiotic concoction of vodka, rum, and tequila mixed with a mimosa. In addition to the tequila shots we did before the game."

Both of their faces twisted in disgust.

"Damn, no wonder you're looking a little rough today," Jas exclaimed.

"Gee, thanks. Okay, now that y'all are up to speed on the disastrous turn my night took, can we switch into work mode? Wasn't that the deal for answering Jasmine's question?"

Jas shrugged. "Fair enough. I was thinking we should compile a list of all clients whose tentative dates align with The Rose House's first few months of availability, and get them out here ASAP because this place will pique more interest than Milo's head shots on Tinder."

She shot me a wink and pulled out her phone, already looking at her calendar.

We spent the next twenty minutes comparing calendars and schedules and making a list of clients to bring here for a tour.

"So," Jas said eventually. "I overheard some ladies talking

about the architect who did the renovations. Judging by the way they were talking, he's hot and he's single."

I offered a hum and kept my eyes on my phone, ignoring the implication in her tone.

"Oh, come on, El. Aren't you a little curious?"

"No. Is it so hard for you to believe, for the first time in a long time, I'm happy being single? I swear, marriage has turned you into a hopeless romantic, Jas."

She balked. "Jesus, relax. Never. I'm not saying you have to marry the guy. Anyway, apparently he's some young hotshot from Seattle. He's Rose's nephew—as in *the* Rose who owns this place."

My head snapped up.

Young hotshot architect.

From Seattle.

Whose aunt was named Rose.

No way.

I would've heard if he had moved back. Nana and Pops would've mentioned it. *Wouldn't they?*

"Did they say what his name is?" I asked casually.

"Brian? Brad? No, not Brad. Some hot guy name that starts with a B, though. Why? Thought you weren't interested?"

I was too busy scanning the area to answer her question. Too busy searching for a face I hadn't seen in over five years.

"I, uh, I'll be right back," I said, pushing up from my chair and ignoring Jade's questions about my sudden urgency and weirdness.

My eyes swept across the back yard, seeking the mop of dirty blonde hair he'd always had as a kid. Of course, five years ago it was cut short and stripped him of that boyish charm I'd taken for granted when we were growing up.

Maybe he's not here.

Maybe Jas misheard.

Maybe it's not him.

Bryce McKnight had been an integral part of my childhood.

My earliest memories of the summer I came to live with Nana and Pops all included Bryce. He was the first person I spoke more than a few words to after my mother dumped me with grandparents I'd never met. He brought me out of my shell and showed me how to be a regular kid.

Bryce was my first friend. My lifeline.

But those days were long gone.

He was a stranger now.

At the exact moment I decided to give up my search and go back to the table, I turned and ran right into a waiter carrying a tray full of food. Honey-glazed chicken and fries smothered in caramelized kimchi rained down on me and stuck to my hair and my shirt as the tray clattered to the ground, garnering the attention of everyone around us.

"Oh my gosh! I am so sorry, miss," the waiter stammered, instantly helping me back to my feet and pulling a chunk of chicken out of my hair.

"It's okay. Totally my fault," I assured him, brushing off the remaining fries from my shirt.

Between the two of us, we cleaned the mess quickly, and I carried my small pile of ruined fries toward the trash can on the veranda. Everyone gawked and gave me a wide berth, as if they were afraid I'd plow into them next.

Good Lord, there are some catty people in this industry.

Further proof of that fact came when I made it to the trash can and heard the murmurs and snickers of a group of women nearby. I fought the urge to call them out. If Jas had been with me, she wouldn't have hesitated to put them in their place. But my big mouth had already gotten me on Sophia's shit list in the last twenty-four hours, so I swallowed that urge and combed my fingers through my hair to shake out any rogue bits of cabbage.

Bright side? I was pretty sure, between waking up with the hangover from hell and bathing in kimchi, things couldn't get worse for me today.

But then the mean girl wannabes stopped trying to be subtle.

"That was painful to watch."

"I don't know why she's even bothering with her hair. It's a lost cause."

"I bet she takes out the cocktail table next."

So much for thinking things couldn't get worse. I groaned under my breath and turned around to call them out. But someone else beat me to it from the other side of the veranda.

"That *was* painful to watch, but not nearly as painful as hearing you three make snide, bitchy comments."

I knew that voice.

CHAPTER 3
ELLIOT

THAT SMOOTHER-THAN-HONEY VOICE WAS BOTH ACHINGLY FAMILIAR and completely foreign. It belonged to a man who meant business, not the college kid he'd been last time we spoke.

Oh, god. Last time we spoke I made a complete idiot of myself.

I bolted off the veranda and hurried around the corner of the house without letting myself look in his direction.

When I heard his voice again somewhere nearby, accepting praise for his work, I took off again, this time headed for a tree with a swing hanging from its branches.

The irony of the situation was not lost on me. Bryce and I used to play hide-and-seek as kids, and now, here I was playing the adult version.

In my head, running and hiding was justified because I looked like a walking disaster, and I didn't want him to see me as the kid he used to know who constantly had dirt on her face and twigs in her hair from playing outside all day long.

"By now you should know I'll always catch you," he called from behind me.

Before I could turn to him, a pair of designer shoes stepped into my line of sight. I forced my eyes to travel up the length of his body, allowing myself a little longer than necessary to admire the way his gray slacks sat on his narrow hips. Taking in the V shape of his torso in reverse made it even more prominent, and I had to remind myself to breathe by the time my eyes landed on his face.

His voice might've taken on an unfamiliar authoritarian tone, but those eyes were the same blue-green hue I'd recognize anywhere, though now there were faint lines at the corners—the kind that came with the stress of a busy life. His dark dirty blonde locks were gelled and styled into place; a total contradiction to the wild mop that used to fall across his forehead when we were kids. His jawline was razor-sharp, only softening slightly when his lips parted into a broad smile as he gave my appearance the same perusal I had given his.

Bryce looked like he'd just walked out of a cover shoot for Forbes or Business Insider.

The look suited him. *Really* suited him.

I blinked him back into focus before my staring turned creepy.

"Hey," he said, "those women back there were—"

"Catty bitches who also happened to be right about my hair being a lost cause?" I finished for him, pulling at a clump of my hair that had morphed from blonde to sriracha-red.

We both laughed, and I breathed a sigh of relief that we'd managed to seamlessly break the ice.

"So, this was all you?" I asked, gesturing at the house and yard.

He nodded and shifted his weight uncomfortably. "Yep. Aunt Rose asked, and I couldn't say no."

That déjà vu feeling made total sense now; I'd come over here with Bryce a couple of times when we were young.

"Of course. Well, it's incredible. You're really talented."

"Thanks. I'm really proud of how it turned out. Can you believe Rose wanted me to get rid of the swing? I told her it'd be a good feature to keep kids occupied during receptions."

"Until the next little Bryce McKnight comes along and tries to be the king of the swing again. Better make clients sign a waiver saying The Rose House isn't liable for injury resulting from this thing."

His eyebrows shot up. "Hey, you're the one who asked me to push you higher."

"Is *that* how you remember it? I seem to recall you saying you wanted to push me high enough to touch the branches, right before I fell out and almost broke my arm."

"You should probably go see a doctor if you're having memory issues, Elliot. That seems like a real red flag," he said, the corner of his mouth tilting into a smirk.

Whoa. When did his smirk get sexy?

I rolled my eyes in an attempt to play it cool. "Always the comedian. Maybe don't quit your day job."

He laughed and pulled his hand out of his pocket to run his fingers over his jaw. "Always busting my chops. So how's life? How are your grandparents? Sophia?"

"Nana and Pops are great. They had what Nana likes to call a 'do-over' wedding last night, and are currently on their way to the honeymoon they never had the first time around. I'm really happy for them. Sophia's graduating in December, then going to Europe for a while with the family she works for. I kind of hate her for that."

"And you?"

"Oh, I'm good. Work keeps me really busy, but I love it. People think every female getting married is a bridezilla, but that hasn't been my experience. Plus, if I do my job well they shouldn't have a reason to turn into a bridezilla."

"You're a wedding planner now?"

I nodded. "That surprises you? Why?"

"I don't know. I guess you just never seemed interested in that kind of thing."

"Things change a lot in five years, Bryce." Realizing I'd made things awkward, I quickly moved on before he had a chance to address my comment. "So, you're back in Austin now? Permanently?"

"I am. Moved back about a year ago."

A year?

I tried to hide it, but Bryce caught the flicker of hurt that flitted across my face. So many questions came to mind, but I couldn't bring myself to ask a single one. "That's...good. Let me guess, you missed the insanely hot summers?"

A low chuckle rumbled from his chest as he stepped forward and closed the gap between us, grabbing the swing and boxing me in. I kept my eyes glued to the ground. "Elliot," he drawled, pulling my attention back to him. "Look, I owe you an ap—"

"You don't owe me anything, Bryce," I insisted, shaking my head.

An indecipherable look flashed across his face—confusion, if I had to guess—but vanished in an instant.

"We both know that's not true. I should've called. We said we'd be better at keeping in touch, and after I—"

I shrugged, cutting him off before he could finish. "Life happens. Plus, it seems like staying in Seattle worked out well for you. According to the rumor mill, you were a hotshot architect there. And after seeing this place I'm thinking that's true."

He gave a half-nod-half-shrug, but he was modest enough not to call himself a hotshot. "I did pretty well at my firm, yeah. Did the whole 'all work and no play' thing. But I want you to know I *am* sorry, El. If it wasn't for our conversation that night, I don't know that I would've let myself stay in Seattle. I should've made more of an effort to keep in touch."

"Bryce, it's okay. Phones work both ways; I should've called or texted you. I knew the kind of pressure you were under. We both had a lot of stuff going on back then. Friendships slip through the cracks all the time; it's a part of life."

"Still, I'm sorry," he repeated, reaching for my hand. I let him have it and tilted my head to meet his eyes. They were more blue than green at the moment and swimming with regret. His gaze fell to my mouth for a beat. "For, you know..."

Oh god. My eyes widened. *He's about to bring up that horrible, awkward-as-hell almost-kiss.*

"Let's just…not go there. Water under the bridge, okay?"

He nodded, relief washing over his face.

"So…what really brought you back to Texas?"

Bryce exhaled and stepped back, studying my face like he was seeking his own answer in the depths of my eyes.

But before he could answer, something caught his attention from behind me. I whipped my head around to follow his gaze. Jade and Jasmine were several feet away, whisper-yelling at each other, seemingly debating if they should come over or not.

I cleared my throat so they'd look up.

"Oh, uh, hey. Sorry, we didn't mean to interrupt," Jade said.

Jas shook her head and walked the rest of the way toward us, holding her hand out toward Bryce. "She's lying, we definitely did come over here to interrupt. I'm Jasmine."

"Bryce," he said, returning her handshake.

He stepped toward Jade and repeated the introduction, and Jas leaned toward me and mouthed *'hot guy name was right'* with a wink.

Ignoring her, I quickly connected the dots for them. "Jade and Jas started Forget Me Knot Weddings, so they're technically my bosses. And, uh, guys, Bryce…was my neighbor when we were kids."

I stopped short of elaborating on our friendship because, what exactly would I say? *'He was my best friend back then, until he moved away to go to boarding school, and this is only the second time we've spoken in the last decade?*

Yeah, no.

Jade mercifully bypassed any further questioning about our history, asking him about the house instead. They talked about that for a few minutes while I just listened and tried to wrap my head around the fact that Bryce freaking McKnight—a stranger for all intents and purposes at this point in my life—was standing in front of me. Looking good enough to give me some very R-rated thoughts.

Jas had just said something about me having clients interested in the history of the house when I realized what she was doing.

"Well, my aunt really knows more of the history. Why don't I set something up with her, and you guys can bring your interested clients over for a private tour sometime this week? Would that work?" Bryce asked.

"Perfect!" Jas squealed, looking all too pleased with herself.

After that painfully transparent attempt to ensure Bryce and I had to see each other again, she quickly diverted her attention back toward the house.

"Oh, hey, I think that's Martha Clark over there. Let's go say hi, JP." She waved, probably at a total stranger, and laced her arm through Jade's. "We'll catch up with you later, El. It was nice to meet you, Bryce," she threw over her shoulder as they left, ignoring my glare.

"Sorry about that. Jas is a wildcard; there's really no telling what's going to come out of her mouth sometimes."

"Don't be sorry. But yeah, if you hadn't told me she was your boss, I would've just assumed she was your wing woman."

I laughed, because he had a point. "Yeah, about that. You don't have to set up a personal tour for us."

"Don't you actually have clients that would want to book The Rose House?"

"Well, yeah, but—"

"Then it's settled. I'll get with Rose and make sure she's free sometime later this week to give you the private tour. Do you still have my number?"

"Um, I think so." I pulled my phone out and nodded when I found him in the Bs.

We both turned when we heard someone in the distance calling his name.

He held up a hand, gesturing he'd be there in a minute before turning his attention back to me. "I should probably go. Text me tomorrow about the tour?"

"Yeah, definitely. And thank you for doing that. I really appreciate it."

He hit me with another smile, and just like his voice, it was both comfortably familiar and totally different. The Bryce I knew was still in there, but it was clear we were completely different people now than we were the last time we'd spoken. Before I could stop it, curiosity about the Bryce in front of me tugged at my thoughts, making me wish we weren't both in the middle of a work function.

"Of course, El. I'm happy to help."

The woman called him again, and he instinctively took a step back toward the house. I looked behind him and fidgeted with the hem of my shirt, unsure if I should follow him or hang back.

"El?" he called, retracing his steps to come back and pull my hand into his.

"Yeah?"

"I'm so glad you came today. I'll see you soon."

I smiled, but before I could reply, he dropped my hand and jogged off toward the house.

I watched Bryce until he disappeared, trying to ignore the heat from his grip that was still tingling through my fingers.

This has definitely been the weirdest twenty-four hours of my life.

CHAPTER 4
ELLIOT

After a week of nothing but a cold shoulder from my sister, sitting down to a family dinner was the last thing I wanted to do. But Pops and Nana had returned from their honeymoon and wanted to catch up with us.

So, here I was, pulling into the parking lot of Pops's favorite restaurant. I should've been trying to come up with a last-minute plan for how to smooth things over with Sophia before facing our grandparents. But since Sunday's blast from the past with Bryce, focusing had become next to impossible. I stumbled my way through client meetings, zoned out during a wedding ceremony yesterday, and spent all of last night wondering how to handle seeing Bryce at the private tour he had arranged with Rose.

Except he wasn't at The Rose House today. When we scheduled the meeting, I assumed he'd be there too. I asked about Bryce with as much nonchalance as I could manage, and Rose told me he was so sorry to miss the tour, but something had come up last minute. She didn't offer more information. So far, I had successfully resisted the urge to text him.

That didn't mean I hadn't typed out various texts and deleted them, though.

I was scrolling through our brief text conversation when

Sophia knocked on my window. I jumped in my seat and fumbled my phone before it slipped through my fingers and fell to the floorboard. I groaned and stepped out of my car to fish it out. "Hey. Didn't even see you there."

"No shit," she replied dryly.

"Look, Soph, I'm sorry for last weekend. You're still pissed, I'm guessing, but I feel like we should just forget about the whole thing. How much longer until bygones can be bygones?"

She stopped walking and turned to me on a sigh. "You don't even know *why* I'm pissed. If you were in my shoes, you'd still be pissed too."

"So, tell me. What could I possibly have said that was so bad you had to storm off then ignore me for a week?"

Her jaw clenched, and she narrowed her brown eyes at me. "Now's not the time. Let's just push pause, play nice for Nana and Pops, then resume this conversation later. Okay?"

"Fine."

Before I could say anything else, Sophia flipped her dark locks over her shoulder and sped toward the restaurant's entrance.

Nana and Pops were already there and immediately waved us over to their table. All thoughts of the Sophia debacle vanished as soon as I saw my grandparents' smiles. "Y'all should bum around on the beach more often. You're like different people!" I told them.

"That French Polynesian sun really must have worked wonders. And we mean that in the nicest way possible," Sophia added quickly.

She was right; they looked great. Happy. George and Millie Kincaid were pushing seventy, but you'd never know by looking. They both prided themselves on staying in shape, swam laps in their pool every morning, and went for after-dinner walks every evening.

But I'd never seen them look so…relaxed.

Nana let out a chuckle and swatted at the air. "Oh, you girls."

"So, tell us all about paradise," I urged.

Once our food was served, Pops launched into storytelling

mode, painting vivid pictures of their adventures snorkeling, jet skiing, parasailing, and hiking. I knew they wouldn't be able to sit around doing nothing for long. Even our family vacations each summer were packed full of sightseeing activities and adventures. I blamed them for my perpetual need to plan.

"You two went *parasailing*?" I questioned, bewildered as Nana flipped through photos on her phone after our plates were cleared.

"Forget parasailing. Nana, you...*napped*?" Sophia asked, nearly choking on the word as images of Nana asleep in a hammock or on a lounge chair by the water flickered across the screen of my mind.

"Seriously, who *are* you two, and what have you done with our grandparents?" I asked.

Nana and Pops exchanged a quizzical look. Pops sighed and reached for Nana's hand. "I think it's time we tell them, sweetheart."

"Tell us what?" I asked, mirroring Sophia's furrowed-brow what-the-hell look.

"Girls, we've thought a lot about how we've been living our life, and how we *want* to live our life, and your grandfather and I have decided to retire. We're not spring chickens anymore," Nana explained, pulling my hand into hers. "We want to travel more and do the other things we've always talked about doing but never had the time for. You girls are grown now and don't need us like you once did. We're going to sell Serenity. That meeting we had before the rehearsal was with potential buyers."

Serenity Hotel was the massively popular and successful chain of boutique hotels they'd spent the last thirty years building and running.

If anyone had earned the right to retire and enjoy life, it was Nana and Pops. They'd married young, suffered two miscarriages before having their first child, worked tirelessly to build two successful businesses, and lost their only child when she ran away from home at fifteen. Then, at the age of fifty, they became parents all over again when my mother reappeared just long enough to dump Sophia and me on them.

Of course I wanted them to be happy. They were the ones who raised me, who had spent the last nineteen years helping me forget the life I had before they were in it. But so many of my happiest memories were from the cross-country adventures we had in our quest to stay at a Serenity Hotel in each of the thirty-three states that had one.

For some reason, I'd never realized their retirement would mean selling that piece of my childhood.

Now they were selling Serenity *and* leaving to see the world?

"So you're just going to sell it and what? Globetrot?" I asked. "Just like that? Couldn't you just step down and find someone else to run it, but not sell?" I realized my questions sounded more like accusations, but I let them linger anyway.

Pops shook his head. "Nothing is official yet, Elliebelly. We've got a few interested parties, but we're only going to sell to the right buyer. Look, girls, we love you, but this is not up for discussion. We have spent our lives making Serenity what it is, and it's past time we let ourselves enjoy the kind of life we've earned." Pops paused, registering the matching frowns Sophia and I wore. "This is a good thing, girls. Promise."

"I'm happy for you guys," I said quickly. "Really. It just feels like we'll be losing a chunk of our childhood." *And you two, if you decide to spend your golden days traveling the globe.*

Pops squeezed my hand. "Those memories are always going to be yours to keep, Elliot. Selling Serenity doesn't erase the wonderful times we had there. And I'm sure we could add a clause to the contract that we and you girls can stay at any one of the hotels free of charge during our lifetimes," he added with a wink.

That got a chuckle out of me, and I forced myself to let his words sink in.

"What about the inn?" Sophia asked quietly. While my disbelief had somewhat worn off, Sophia's frown was still there, and her dark brows were pulled down.

Let Love Inn was what started it all for Nana and Pops. They had worked tirelessly to make it a successful B&B before Serenity Hotel was even a blip on their entrepreneurial radar. It was their business baby. Even though they'd closed the doors on Let Love Inn once Serenity required their full attention, I couldn't imagine them letting go of the place completely.

"The inn is completely separate," Nana supplied quickly.

The sighs of relief Sophia and I both heaved were short-lived.

"The inn will be going to you both. It's yours, if you want it," Pops said casually, as if he were referring to giving us the last dinner roll instead of a business.

"*Wh-what*?" I sputtered.

"George! I thought we were going to wait to discuss the inn," Nana scolded before turning to us and sighing. "Girls, you both know how much that place means to us. We don't want to sell it to a stranger. In fact, we won't sell it to a stranger. Our dream was always to see it re-opened one day."

Pops nodded and bit into a piece of bread. "We've discussed it at length, and it would be passed down to you girls eventually, anyway. This is simply our way of giving you the option to see that day sooner rather than later. Now, you don't have to decide what to do with it right away, but we're going to have a consultation for potential renovations. We've been setting aside money for years with the intention of updating the inn, so that money will cover whatever changes you girls would want to make."

Our jaws dropped in unison.

Nana leaned across the table. "Please don't feel like you've got to make a decision tomorrow or even in the next month. The inn isn't going anywhere, and neither are we. Take some time to think about it, that's all we ask."

We both nodded but made no attempt to speak.

In no way, shape, or form were we qualified to own and operate an inn. Growing up around it, even spending countless hours in their office, hardly qualified as experience. Not to mention, I already had a job I really loved. And Sophia was still months away from graduating.

"Uh," I said eventually, still searching for the right words amidst all the questions swimming in my mind. "If—and that's a *huge* if—we were to take over the inn, we couldn't ask you guys to foot the renovation bill. It would be our responsibility. You've already set up the trust funds for us. We, or at least I, couldn't accept this from you too. It's too much, Nana."

I fidgeted with the napkin in my lap, fighting the familiar discomfort this topic always evoked in me. The trusts they'd set up for us were funded with the money they'd originally set aside for our mother. Most people would be elated to have zeros added to their bank accounts on their twenty-fifth birthday, but I was dreading it. Until coming to live with Nana and Pops, I'd never known what it was like to eat three well-balanced meals in one day, much less what it was like to live a life where money wasn't a concern.

"El, honey, we'd never give you the inn in its current shape and expect you to fix it up. Those trust funds are our way of ensuring you girls are taken care of. That money is for you, for your future. We've talked about this," she finished, patting my hand and giving me the same gentle smile she'd given me every day since the day we met.

I sighed, knowing this was a losing battle. Sophia offered me a sympathetic shrug that told me we were on the same page, but that she also knew arguing was futile.

"I just have to know; did you two get tricked into smoking some grade-A pot in Bora Bora?" Sophia asked, eyeing our grandparents as if they'd turned into strangers before her eyes.

I laughed at her comment, but it didn't seem that farfetched considering the abrupt changes in our grandparents.

Retirement. Selling Serenity. Giving us Let Love Inn.

All in one fell swoop.

And to think, just a week ago the craziest thing about my life was the drama caused by the revolving door of Milo's model friends traipsing in and out of our apartment.

Nana laughed and tucked a chunk of her light blonde hair behind her ear. "Girls, we realize this is a lot for y'all to take in at once. Like I said, you don't have to make a decision right away. There's no rush. We just want you to know the option is available to you."

A lot to take in.

Biggest understatement ever.

Also, the freaking theme of my life these days.

I ate dinner without paying much attention to any of the food going into my mouth. Or the words coming out of it. Somehow, Nana had managed to shift the conversation to safer topics, like Sophia's classes and my upcoming weddings.

It wasn't until the bill was paid and Pops was ushering us out of the restaurant that he dropped the final bomb of the night.

"Oh, there's one more thing, girls," he said, slinging an arm around Nana's shoulders. "The consultation for the renovations is the day after tomorrow. It would be great if you both could make it."

"Whoa. You've already *hired* someone? Who?" Sophia asked.

I knew who. I held my breath, waiting for my suspicion to be confirmed.

When it was, I realized how wrong I'd been to assume my life couldn't get any crazier.

ON THE DRIVE back to my apartment, I decided to table the whole Nana and Pops retiring situation and focus my efforts on fixing things with Sophia. She had an equal say about the decision with the inn, and figuring out what to do with the place wasn't going to happen until I was firmly back in her good graces.

One thing at a time.

After promising Milo that he had no reason to worry about

leaving the two of us alone when he left for work, I pulled out a bottle of rosé and poured generous servings into two stemless wine glasses.

"Knock knock," I called, tapping my foot against Sophia's door. "Can we talk? About last weekend?"

The door slowly opened, and Sophia's annoyance eased up once she saw my peace offering. "Okay. But you should probably go get the bottle if we're having this conversation."

I arched a brow, but wasn't going to question her. A few seconds later, I reentered her bedroom with the bottle and took a seat on the opposite side of the bed from her.

I waited until Sophia had downed half of her glass before summoning the nerve to broach the subject. "So...the only thing I remember about our conversation is that it was Helen-related."

When it came to our mother, we'd never found a way to have productive conversations. Mostly because I preferred to avoid the topic altogether. I was one day shy of turning five when Helen brought us to live with Nana and Pops—old enough that some memories of our life with her had stuck with me. Haunted me. Sometimes I selfishly wished Sophia shared my memories just so I'd have someone who understood. But most days I was grateful she was too young to remember seeing all the random men coming and going from our dingy, dilapidated apartment. When I, at the innocent age of four, had finally found the courage to ask Helen why she always went to the bedroom when they came over, she told me it was her 'grownup time,' and to go make Sophia stop crying so her 'special friend' didn't get upset. *"You remember what happens when Mommy's friends get upset, don't you?"*

"I'm sorry things got so heated," Sophia said, breaking me out of the memory from hell. "It's just...I'm tired of you treating me like a kid when it comes to Helen. I know you don't like to talk about her, and I respect that. But you, of all people, should understand why I wanted to find her. Then the opportunity to do so practically landed in my lap when I found someone who looked like her named 'Helen K Bates' on Facebook. I told you that I sent her a friend request and wanted to maybe give her my number eventually if it really was her. You freaked out and told me that was a terrible idea, and not to expect you to protect me from her anymore. You also said that I was an idiot if I believed she wouldn't stand me up too. That's when I started yelling. But, El, what did you mean by that—stand me up too? And protecting me?"

I tipped my wine glass back against my lips, purposefully taking my time while I debated how to handle my sister's questions and everything else she'd just thrown at me. Like the fact that I now knew Helen's last name.

She was right, of course; I couldn't blame her for being curious.

But she didn't know the entire truth about our mother.

"Sophia, I'm sorry I called you an idiot. But I just think you're setting yourself up for failure by going down this path. I don't want you to get your hopes up only to have them crushed when history repeats itself. If she decides you're not worth her time again."

She eyed me curiously over the rim of her glass before setting it down and hugging her knees to her chest. "Don't you have questions? Aren't you curious about what she's like or what she's been doing all these years?"

"Sure, I have questions. But, honestly? It's not worth my time. Or yours. As far as knowing what kind of person she is…she's the kind of person who neglected then abandoned her children. That's all I need to know."

"She's also the kind of person who gave us up in order to give us a better life."

I shook my head. "No, Soph, she gave us up in order to give *herself* a better life."

"Can't it be both? And doesn't it count that she gave us to her parents instead of social services?"

"I'm supposed to give her a pass for everything else just because she eventually did what she should've done right after you were born? That's not how it works, Sophia. And that's also my point—she gave us to Pops and Nana. The people who raised us and gave us everything. Wondering about her seems…"

"Like you're betraying them?" Sophia supplied.

I nodded.

"They wouldn't fault us for having questions about her, El. Don't you think they have questions too?"

"I think Nana and Pops wrote her off a long time ago. She burned them. Twice." I sighed, reaching out to put my hand on her leg to get her attention. "But I understand why you're tempted to seek answers. So, I'm not going to try and talk you out of going through with this, but I can't guarantee that I'll ever be willing to meet with her."

She lifted her head enough to meet my eyes. "You're okay with me seeing where things go if she accepts my friend request?"

"I know you think I still treat you like a little kid. And I guess I probably do sometimes; I can't help it. I'll always look out for you, Soph. Comes with the big sister territory. But I know you're perfectly capable of making your own decisions. And if you decide you need answers from our mother, I'm not going to stand in your way. Part of growing up is learning from and living with the choices we make…a lesson I'm still learning."

"You think I'm making a mistake?"

I hesitated, debating my response. "I didn't say mistake, I said choice. There's a difference."

"Fair enough. El, thank you. For hearing me out and telling me you don't think I'm an idiot. Even if part of you does."

I poured us both refills before turning back to her and clinking my glass against hers. "I don't think you're an idiot. And you're welcome. I'm glad we did this."

She smiled, and I knew she understood my meaning.

I didn't have all the answers, but I meant what I'd said—I was genuinely relieved Sophia and I had found a way to have a productive conversation about Helen.

I just hoped to God history wasn't about to repeat itself.

CHAPTER 5
BRYCE

It felt strange driving through the Kincaid property after so many years away. In fact, because their property directly backed up to my parents' land, I'd never actually driven up the driveway before; I'd always just cut through the Crush vineyard and walked along the fence line to get to the manor.

Kincaid Manor was situated at the north end of their property, and Let Love Inn was located in the southwest corner. All together the Kincaids owned about twenty acres, which allowed them privacy without being too far from the inn.

The sound of gravel crunching beneath my tires took me on a bittersweet stroll down memory lane as I turned onto the driveway leading toward the inn.

Flashes of bike rides, blonde hair blowing in the wind, and the most contagious laugh I'd ever heard washed over me. I surrendered to the memories, letting images of a young Elliot permeate my mind until I came to a stop and those images of the Elliot I knew were replaced by the sight of present day, grown-up Elliot.

The Elliot I no longer knew.

Seeing her at the open house had caught me completely off guard.

Actually, it wasn't just *seeing her* that caught me off guard. It was being reminded how gorgeous she'd grown up to be that I wasn't prepared for. Even globs of kimchi and sriracha couldn't detract from El's beauty, with her lithe little body and those big blue eyes, not to mention her breath-stealing smile.

When we were kids, I used to tease her about her mouth being larger than average.

If only I had known then that I'd grow up and fantasize about all the things that mouth could do.

Elliot was nineteen the last time I'd seen her, and by then our three-year age gap wasn't an issue, so I'd allowed myself to appreciate her girl-next-door good looks. *Hell, I almost fucking kissed her.* But at the time, I was in no position to even allow myself to think of her as anything but a friend.

Now?

In a completely different way, my life was still full of unknowns.

But one thing I knew with absolute certainty was that I wanted the opportunity to make things right with her. Somehow. The look on her face when she found out I'd been here for a year had haunted me all week, and I hated myself for not calling her any of the times I picked up my phone to do so over the last year.

I parked and realized El was the only other person here when I saw her sitting on the stairs leading to the inn's porch, twirling a thick blonde lock around her fingers. Even with a furrowed brow and scowl weighing her features down, she was beautiful.

But I was lying to myself if I thought her looks were the only thing responsible for this foreign warmth filling me up. It was *her* —all of her. For once, someone other than Peyton brought the organ resting inside my chest to life, disrupting its steady autopilot rhythm. It had been over two years since a woman evoked any kind of emotion in me, and I wasn't sure what to make of the feeling.

"Did you know?" she asked, crossing her arms and narrowing her baby blues at me.

Know what? Immediately, my thoughts turned to that night five years ago. To its aftermath.

Elliot didn't look angry, exactly, but she did look hurt. Again. Which made me feel like an asshole, but also told me she was probably referring to something else.

I took a tentative step in her direction. "About the renovations?"

"No. About Nana and Pops selling Serenity. Retiring. The whole shebang."

"George told me about it when he called about the inn a couple weeks ago, but I swear, El, I had no idea you didn't know about Serenity. I'm sorry."

The harsh lines between Elliot's brows softened, and her expression morphed into one of understanding. "I guess it's good they waited until after their honeymoon to tell us. It just seems like it's all happening so fast." She paused and picked at a frayed part of her ripped jeans, drawing my attention to the smooth skin hiding beneath. "Did they tell you they want to give the inn to Sophia and me? As in, we'd be the owners and have final say over all of the renovations."

"They mentioned that they hadn't decided exactly what to do with the place. I figured they meant whether they'd keep it or sell it, though."

"I don't know what we're going to do. I mean, can you imagine? It's not like I haven't thought about what it'd be like to reopen the inn, but I have a job that I love, and Sophia is jetting off to Europe as soon as she graduates. Plus, we're way too young to run the place ourselves. Right?"

"I don't know. Weren't Millie and George fresh out of college when they got the loan to build this place?" I asked, remembering that detail from the dozens of times George had told the story to us growing up.

Elliot sighed. "Yeah. But Nana and Pops are basically superhuman, so that doesn't count. At the same time, though, that's kinda my point." She paused, looking up from the ground to meet my gaze. "Nana and Pops worked so incredibly hard to make this place a success. What if Sophia and I fail? I can't disappoint them, Bryce. I can't be like *her*."

I took a step forward, instinctively wanting to close the gap and grab her hands. When we were young, on the rare occasion Elliot spoke about her mother, I'd developed the habit of squeezing her hands in mine. I never knew what made me do it the first time, but somehow it seemed to help. To reassure her. To calm her. To make her feel safe. So I kept doing it.

"You're not like her, El," I said, giving her hands that familiar squeeze. It was strange how natural the gesture felt all these years later. "And you won't disappoint them. Not possible."

"You can't know that."

It killed me to see how much El's deadbeat mother still affected her, that she still plagued this bright, brilliant girl with fears of inadequacy. We might've lost touch, but that didn't change the fact that I knew El was nothing like Helen, and she never would be.

The need to make her see her worth hit me all at once.

"I *do* know that, Uno."

"You don't get it, Bryce. I thought I was going to finally prove that to myself five years ago, when she was supposed to meet me. You remember?" She paused, waiting for a response, but all I could manage was a tiny nod thanks to the mass of dread knotting my stomach. "Well, she never showed. My train wreck of a mother couldn't be bothered to show her face after *she* was the one who reached out to me. I just don't get *why*. Why reach out to me—dangle a little sliver of hope after fourteen fucking years—only to blow me off?"

Fuck.

Seeing the anguish on El's face gutted me. That dread crawled up into my chest and squeezed the life out of my heart. *This is my fault. I should've done more to talk her out of the whole thing. I should've called her after I got back to Washington to see what happened.*

I thought I'd done the right thing back then.

"El, that's just it, though. That proves how different—"

The sound of a car door slamming stole Elliot's attention, and she quickly pulled out of my grip as George, Millie, and Sophia piled out of a Jeep and walked over to meet us.

After a couple minutes of slightly awkward small talk, we made our way across the threshold.

Elliot gave the immediate vicinity a quick scan before turning toward me. "Where do we start, Bryce?"

I knew she was referring to the inn, but a part of me wished she meant where do *we* start. The difference was, as far as the inn was concerned, I had a solid answer. The other? Good fucking question. *How do you turn back the clock to erase the days that became months, and months that evolved into years, turning us into strangers?*

Except, we're not strangers. There wouldn't be an underlying level of comfort between us if that was the case.

"For now, we just go room by room, and I'll take notes and photos. You guys can do the same or just make mental notes. I've already got a couple of preliminary ideas, but I'd like to get our bearings first, then compare notes after I've had a chance to firm up my plans. That work?" I asked, looking between the four of them.

They all gave me similar 'whatever you say' looks and offered varying forms of agreement.

I hung back, letting them take in the space first. The architect in me immediately started envisioning the potential changes and improvements that would need to happen first. Having those visions was second nature to me by now, and I could practically sketch ideas in my sleep.

I watched Elliot and tried to decipher what her expressions meant as she trekked through the rooms. I could tell she was overwhelmed, but she was more like her grandparents than she realized. The excitement that crept into her voice as she discussed ideas with Sophia was proof that she shared her grandparents' passion for the inn.

Eventually, after taking notes based on what I'd overheard

from all of them, I snapped my notebook closed and pocketed my camera, satisfied I had enough for a solid initial proposal.

"I think I have everything I need for now. Give me a few days to get the ball rolling, then we can sit down and brainstorm about where to go from there. Sound good?"

Millie and George agreed right away, but Sophia and Elliot became quiet and exchanged looks of uncertainty.

"Nothing's going to be written in stone. You guys still have time to decide what you're going to do."

Elliot nodded and gave me an appreciative smile.

"That sounds wonderful. Will you be ready by Sunday evening, Bryce?" Millie asked.

"Sunday works for me." *Considering my only other Sunday night plans are sitting around, staring at my phone in case something comes up with Peyton.*

We finalized plans and made idle chitchat until Elliot received a text and said she had to go. Sophia went with her, leaving me alone with George and Millie.

"She's single, you know," Millie offered, drawing my attention.

"Uh…" I started, unsure of how to respond. *Thanks? Good to know?*

Nothing felt quite right. Did it even matter? *Could* it even matter?

I wish I knew.

George sighed and muttered something under his breath.

"What?" Millie asked, holding her hands up innocently. "She is. Just letting the young man know. It's called conversation, George."

He snorted. "It's called meddling, hon. You're going to scare the poor kid off."

Millie scoffed. "Bryce, dear, tell George I did not scare you off."

"I'm not…we're just…" I stopped myself from forming an

actual response, turning to face Millie with an eyebrow arched in question.

She smiled sweetly and patted my arm. "Trust me, a man doesn't look at a woman the way you've been looking at Elliot without having such questions. And just between us, I think you're exactly what she needs right now."

I wanted to ask her to elaborate on what she meant by that, but she just winked at me and linked her arm through George's before strolling toward their Jeep.

Huh.

Driving home, I thought back to the last conversation Elliot and I had before I decided to stay in Seattle.

That night, Elliot convinced me not to resign myself to a life of shackles and apathy. *That kind of acceptance snuffs out passion and binds you to a life devoid of purpose,* she said.

I stayed in Seattle to avoid being weighed down by a future full of unhappiness, and in an ironic twist of fate, that's exactly what I found there.

Following Elliot's advice was the best and worst decision of my life.

I MUST'VE BEEN delusional to think meeting my cousin on a Saturday morning was a good idea. The dude spent every Friday night in recent memory holed up with a random flavor of the hour. Twenty minutes after we were supposed to meet, my phone pinged with a text from him, apologizing for being late and saying he'd explain when he got to the coffee shop in an hour.

I actually didn't mind the delay because it gave me more time to go over my sketches. It also gave me more time to let my thoughts drift from the plans for the inn to plans of a whole different kind.

I was flipping through my notes and sipping on my second

cup of coffee when Elliot's voice interrupted my thoughts. *Speak of the blue-eyed devil…*

"You know, some people might call this stalking. We don't see each other once over the past year, now I feel like I see you everywhere," she said.

I looked up and felt something churn in my gut when I took in El's appearance. In more ways than one, being this affected by the sight of Elliot Kincaid was completely unexpected.

A knee-length navy blue dress hugged and highlighted the subtle curves of her body, making my fingers itch to explore. A quick glance at her feet confirmed my suspicion about heels being responsible for showing off her toned calves, and I had to force my brain not to think about what it'd feel like to have those legs wrapped around me. I brought my eyes up in an effort to pull my thoughts out of the gutter, but I should've known better. Her soft blonde locks were trapped in a tight bun atop her head, and the sudden desire to tug it loose and see her hair fall wild and free was enough to make me suck in a breath and dig my fingers into my thighs.

Elliot was subtly, effortlessly sexy, and I was pretty sure she had no idea the kind of impression her appearance made.

Which only made her that much more appealing.

"Oh, you're stalking me now?" I teased, closing my sketch pad and picking up my coffee cup to keep my hands busy. "I mean, I was here first, so how could I possibly be stalking you?"

Elliot's sky-blue eyes narrowed as she crossed her arms, but her lips tugged into a smile. "Okay, I'll give you that. But then again, that's probably the exact logic a stalker would use."

"It is. I actually took that straight from my Stalking for Dummies book."

We both started laughing, and I realized her laugh was still as contagious as it had been when we were kids.

Her eyes fell to my sketch pad. "Are those for the inn?" She stepped closer when I nodded. "Can I get a preview?"

I was about to tell her yes, but only if she joined me, when a barista behind the counter called Elliot's name and pushed two four-drink cartons across the bar.

"That's my cue. I'm gonna have an angry bridal party if I don't get them caffeinated ASAP."

"Of course. Here, let me help you get that out to your car," I offered, stepping up beside her and taking one of the cartons before she could protest.

"Thanks. There's a pretty good chance I would've dropped one of them."

I turned left in the parking lot and came to a stop at her red sedan.

"Tell me again how you're *not* stalking me."

"Hey, you're the one who showed up at the coffee shop I go to almost every weekend."

She lifted a brow. "Every weekend, huh? You're like a stalker's dream target with that kind of predictability, Bryce."

"You know this from personal experience?"

"Yep. I've been stalking you for a year, just waiting until I had food stains all over my clothes and hair to make my presence known to you. You know, had to make a memorable first impression. Er, second first impression?"

I laughed, but her comment made me realize I still needed to explain myself. I wanted to tell her I'd come close to calling her so often, but stopped each time reality crashed into me. I wanted to tell her everything—why I came back, why I never called her, but I needed more than half a minute to explain all that. So, instead of opening up to her like I needed to, I stepped back and stuffed my hands in my pockets, forcing my eyes to meet hers.

"El, about that...I want you to know I thought about calling you a thousand times. It's just...there are complications in my life. I know that sounds like a cop-out, but I hope you'll give me a chance to explain why it's not. Let me bring dinner tomorrow so we can talk after going over plans."

"Bryce, you don't have—"

I shook my head. "I know I don't have to, Elliot. But I want to. Say yes."

She hesitated, but slowly nodded her head. "Okay."

I smiled and gently closed her door. "I'll see you tomorrow."

As soon as Elliot's car disappeared from view, a hand clamped down on my shoulder. "I'd apologize, but that grin on your face tells me you should be thanking me for being late. Who was that? And does she have a sister?"

I turned and shook Xander's outstretched hand, finally peeling my eyes from the direction Elliot's car had gone to look at him. With rumpled clothes and an uncharacteristic five o'clock shadow lining his jaw, I'd have bet serious money he was fighting a hellacious hangover. "Jesus, did you even go to sleep last night?" I asked, knowing the answer by the smirk he flashed. "That was Elliot Kincaid. Also, potentially my new client."

"Why does that name sound familiar?" he asked as we walked back through the coffee shop's doors.

"Elliot and I were friends when we were kids. Her grandparents' property backs up to my parents', and we played all the time. You probably heard me talk about her a lot back then. We lost touch when I moved, but now there's a good chance I'll be seeing her a lot."

Xander nodded and pulled his wayfarer sunglasses off. "*That was Elliot? Damn. I guess I forgot Elliot was a chick. No wonder you were smiling. What about now? Please tell me you're not still in the friend zone.*"

I didn't answer Xander's question right away because I wasn't sure *how* to answer it. Each time I laid eyes on Elliot, my thoughts went way beyond friendly territory, but the same reality that had kept me from calling her before was never far from my thoughts.

Plus, I'd soon be working for her, and any kind of complication in our relationship was a recipe for trouble.

Then again...some of the best things in life are the most complicated.

"I don't know, man," I finally answered with a shrug. "Things are different now, for sure. But you know my life isn't exactly normal. I have responsibilities. It wouldn't be fair."

Xander shook his head, displeased with my reasoning. "What's 'normal' these days, anyway? And fair to whom?"

I cut my eyes to him so he could see them roll. *This from a guy who barely grasps the concept of responsibility.* "Don't give me that, Xander."

"I'm just saying you should think about yourself and what you want too, Bryce."

"So you're saying I should be a selfish womanizer like you? Bounce from bed to bed, always on the lookout for my next conquest? No thanks." I sighed, realizing how harsh my reaction was. "Sorry, no offense. You know what I mean."

He waved off my apology, unaffected by my rude words. Probably because he knew they were mostly true. "None taken. Look, I get it; you don't want romantic advice from a guy who doesn't know the first thing about relationships that extend beyond the bedroom. Well, that's not necessarily true. I don't discriminate when it comes to a location for fucking."

I held up a hand to stop him, simultaneously shaking my head. "TMI, Xander. Jesus. Can we just change the subject? Weren't you going to explain why you're late?"

Xander threw his arm around my shoulders as I gestured for us to get in line to order. "I met a girl last night. I think I'm in love."

"Bullshit. Alexander Black doesn't *do* love. I believe those are your exact words every time anyone asks about your relationship status."

"You've got it all wrong. Well, not *all*. I'd never call myself Alexander. That name's reserved for the ladies, and only in the bedroom. You know…Alexander the Great."

I stopped and gave him a death glare. "Thanks for that. Now I'm never going to be able to hear your name without making that association. Why do I even bother hanging out with you?"

"Because you have no other friends, and I'm your cousin, so you're kind of stuck with me."

"Doesn't your mom call you Alexander sometimes?"

His smile fell completely as his face twisted into a grimace. "Why the fuck would you say that right now?"

I pointed at him. "Just to have the pleasure of that reaction. Priceless."

"You're an asshole, Bryce. The real question is why do *I* even bother hanging out with *you?*"

I shrugged and flashed him a grin. "Because I'm your cousin and you have no other friends, either. Tell me about this girl you love."

"Well, her name is Leah and she's a gymnast…"

CHAPTER 6

ELLIOT

Two weeks ago, I thought I knew exactly what I wanted in life. I loved my job and had zero regrets about giving up my social life to focus solely on my career for the past year. It was a sacrifice I'd gladly make again.

Now?

I must've lost my mind.

How else do you explain the fact that I keep letting Bryce seep into my thoughts while I'm on the clock?

Or the fact that I'm actually considering Nana and Pops's offer?

"I'm sorry?" A man's voice called from the table next to mine. I'd just wrapped up my last appointment for the day and was mindlessly organizing my notes and folders while I waited for my latte.

I whipped my head up, realizing the man was talking to me.

"Oh, uh, nothing. I guess I was thinking out loud. Sorry to interrupt your...work," I finished, eyeing the notes and iPad he had propped up with an attached keyboard. A split-second glance was enough to notice the Serenity Hotel website on his screen. *Huh. What are the odds?*

"Not a problem," he replied with a dismissive flick of his wrist. "Just doing a little research anyway."

I nodded, a little curious, but not enough to be nosy. "Enjoy your smoothie."

He offered me a smile before directing his attention back to his screen.

I let my eyes wander over the stranger's frame, trying to ebb my curiosity about his 'research.' He was what I would call 'classically handsome' if I had to label the look. His slim build was cloaked by a navy suit that fit too well to be anything but designer-made, and creases along his forehead plus a handful of grays sprinkled throughout his otherwise inky black hair told me he was somewhere around forty. A bulky Bulgari watch and monogramed silver cufflinks further piqued my curiosity, but my name was called to get my latte before I could act on it.

"Excuse me," that same voice called a few minutes later. I looked up and confirmed he was speaking to me. "This is going to sound strange, but are you familiar with the area?"

"I am. Lived here all my life."

He angled his iPad toward me. "Do you happen to know anything about this hotel?"

I hesitated, a little taken aback by his abrupt question. Misinterpreting my silence when I dropped my gaze, he flashed me a suave smile that I had a feeling usually got him whatever he wanted. "Don't worry, if I was hitting on you, I'd come up with a better pick-up line."

I couldn't help but smile. The possibility hadn't occurred to me because he was a good decade and a half older than me and way out of my league, but his reassurance did strangely put me at ease. "That's not what I was thinking, but good to know. And yes, I'm actually pretty familiar with the Serenity. Are you staying there?"

He shifted in his seat, pursing his lips together in contemplation. "Something like that."

I lifted a brow and inspected his appearance again. Everything from his shoes to his haircut was a walking advertisement of his wealth. "You're interested in buying it, aren't you?"

"What makes you say that?"

"Call it a hunch."

Now he was the one looking me over with a raised brow. "Clever girl. But I'm not in the habit of discussing my business with random strangers, regardless of how...insightful they might be."

"Well, this 'insightful, clever girl' will be sure to let her grand-parents know that Mr. Two-hundred-dollar-haircut was sketchily asking strangers about Serenity, so they probably don't want to sell to him."

His eyes widened momentarily, and satisfaction replaced my annoyance.

"You're the Kincaids's granddaughter?"

"Look who's being insightful now," I tossed back before standing to leave.

"My apologies, Ms. Kincaid. I feel like I gave you the wrong impression."

I failed to suppress a snort. "Oh no, I think you gave me the right impression, Mister...?"

"Adams. Greg Adams."

"Right. Well, have a nice day, Mr. Adams. Good luck with your research."

"Wait," he called, standing before I could walk away. "Please." He paused, and the clench of his jaw told me that word wasn't usually part of his vocabulary. Eyes that matched his gray tie locked onto mine. "I truly would love to hear about Serenity, and I feel like running into *you*, of all people, is fate. A sign."

"Do you actually believe that?" I asked, skepticism flooding my tone.

He nodded.

"Why should I believe you? Better yet, why should I tell you about Serenity? You've found the website, you've clearly met with my grandparents, and you've probably got underlings to do grunt work for you."

A practiced look of indifference washed over his features, bringing him back to calm and collected businessman status. "You should tell me about Serenity because I'm the right buyer. I'm the only one interested in maintaining the history and qualities unique only to Serenity. Brant Douglas is notorious for gutting practically every business he takes over, and I overheard Lorraine LaMarque discussing her 'rebranding' ideas. Despite whatever bullshit they're selling your grandparents, the second the ink dries with either of them, the Serenity you know and love will be gone, and you'll regret this moment. Unless you help me. I want to show your grandparents my commitment to Serenity, and this seems like a win-win."

My mouth fell open. I was not expecting that answer. At all. As skeptical as I had been moments ago, his plea and interest in Serenity felt genuine. Plus, it's not like he wanted trade secrets.

"All right," I said, sitting back down. "I've got a few minutes to spare before my next appointment. What would you like to know?"

SINCE THE TECHNICAL status of Bryce bringing dinner was unclear, I refused to label our meeting a date. Plus, *technically,* I was maybe going to be his boss now.

I switched gears and forced myself to focus on the task at hand —Let Love Inn and its future.

In the end, it was Nana and Pops that convinced me to seriously consider their offer. *"We're retiring, Elliebelly, not catching the next flight to Mars."* Pops. *"Of course we'd help get it up and running. We'll be here to help you every step of the way."* Nana.

They weren't catching a flight to Mars, but they'd neglected to mention that they *were* catching the next flight to Vegas. Seriously. They'd sent us a group text this morning apologizing for the date mix-up and promising that they'd catch up on what was discussed as soon as they got back. *We're old geezers now. Our memories aren't what they used to be. Good thing we're going to Vegas while we still remember how to play blackjack, right?*

Yeah, right.

I wasn't buying it.

"What do you think their angle is?" I'd asked Sophia.

She gave me a 'wow, you're hopelessly dense' look, and said she'd bet money that it had to do with trying to get a certain granddaughter of theirs to cozy up to a certain architect.

I told her I thought she and Bryce would probably live a long, happy life together.

She rolled her eyes and called me an idiot.

Aren't sisters the best?

I pulled up to the inn, turned my car off, and looked up to find Sophia perched on the steps of the front porch with a book in her hand and a guilty look on her face.

I hopped out and joined her on the top step. "What's up, Soph?"

She closed the book and gave me a 'don't kill me' smile. "You remember how I told the Millers I'd keep the kids on my off day so they could go to that children's literacy fundraiser?"

"Vaguely."

"You also remember how it was a couple of weeks ago that I mentioned that?"

"Yeah..."

When I just stared at her dumbly, she picked at a lock of my hair. "Sometimes I forget you're blonde. Thank god there are moments like these to remind me."

"Hey!" I objected. "Ohhhh. The fundraiser is tonight?"

"Ding ding ding! I have to be at their house in an hour."

"But what about Bryce?"

She shrugged. "If he gets here soon, we can do a quick run through before I have to go."

I folded my arms over my chest and narrowed my eyes at her. "Did Nana put you up to this?"

"Yes, months ago the planning committee called Nana, and

she suggested they schedule the fundraiser for tonight knowing I'd have to bail early on the meeting we scheduled five days ago. We all conspired to make sure you and Bryce would have some alone time."

"You're lucky I find your sarcasm endearing," I shot back, using the book she'd set down to playfully hit her on the arm.

We both laughed as we walked through the door.

"Seriously, though, El, sorry I have to bail. I know you're stressed and have a lot going on right now. When Nana and Pops get back, we can sit down and figure this whole thing out. Deal?"

"Deal." I looked down at the book for the first time as I held it out to Sophia. A ridiculously buff, half-naked male torso graced the cover. *Ripped & Ready for Love.*

She quickly grabbed the paperback and stuffed it into her oversized purse. "Oh, please. Like you walk around carrying the New Testament as your light reading material."

I laughed and held up my hands. "No judgment here. I'm sure Mr. Eight Pack is a surprisingly deep character."

"Mr. Who?" Bryce asked, simultaneously rapping against the open front door as he stepped across the threshold.

We both whirled around to face him.

Holy mother of hotness.

I'd forgotten that Bryce wore glasses.

They were black and square-framed, and I suddenly lost all desire to do anything other than stare at his face. *It shouldn't be possible to look this hot in glasses.*

"No one. Nothing," Sophia sputtered quickly. "So, uh, what'd you bring?"

Only then did I look down and notice his hands were full.

He had a notebook in one hand and a bag in the other. I lifted my gaze from the bag back to his face and caught his broad smile. It was genuine and warm, but more than that, it was full of an all-encompassing happiness. That feeling you get on the first day of a vacation, when your troubles and worries seem distant and irrelevant…*that* was the feeling Bryce's smile effortlessly emanated.

"Tía Maria's. Is it still your favorite? And these are my preliminary sketches," he added, shaking his other hand.

"I can't believe you remembered that."

He grinned.

Sophia cleared her throat. "Uh, as much as I'd love to stand around and be the awkward third wheel indefinitely, I can't stay long, so we're going to have to speed this along."

He set the bag down and flipped open his sketch pad. "Works for me."

I scanned the room while Bryce and Sophia jumped right into conversation about his ideas. After seeing what Bryce had done with The Rose House, I knew whatever he'd come up with for the inn would be just as magical, but I couldn't stifle the apprehension I felt about altering the place Nana and Pops worked so hard to build. This was where Sophia and I differed; she felt pure excitement at the prospect of restoring and revamping the inn, and I was terrified we'd tarnish our grandparents' legacy.

"El, what do you think?" Sophia called. They were both looking at me expectantly, and I realized I'd been totally spaced out for the past several minutes while they talked and swapped ideas.

My eyes zeroed in on the page Bryce had open, which was a fireplace framed by neutral-colored stones of various sizes with a simple wooden mantel. Living in central Texas meant a fireplace was rarely necessary, but it was the focal point of the living area, and it had been one of the first parts of the house I'd thought about updating. Apparently, Bryce either heard me say that or we were on the same wave-length. I nodded toward his notebook. "I love that."

"Yeah?" Bryce beamed. "Since I wasn't sure exactly what y'all would want yet, I kept it broad. I want to take out that wall," he pointed behind us before continuing, "to open up the kitchen a little, but put in a bar to keep the kitchen removed from the dining area and to keep it from being totally open. Kind of the best of both worlds."

The sketch showed exactly what he was describing, and though it wasn't detailed, I could see what he was going for. It was everything Sophia and I had discussed last week. He wasn't kidding about hearing what we said and knowing where to go from there.

Bryce stood from the couch and walked through the kitchen, tilting his head to signal us to follow.

"I'm thinking that corner would be perfect for a big booth, then the rest of the seating can be tables of different sizes.

"Oooh, I've always wanted a booth," Sophia exclaimed.

I liked that idea too, but my eyes stayed glued on Bryce. He was completely in his element, and I understood now that his decision to take a job at the firm in Seattle was the right one. Bryce working at Crush would've been like Ellen Degeneres designing shoes instead of pursuing comedy.

He was born to share his talent with the world.

"I've got some ideas for the upstairs, but for the sake of time, we can go over those later on," Bryce called, walking toward the door to the back. "As far as the exterior goes, it seems to be in pretty good shape structurally, so I'm thinking a fresh coat of paint would do the trick. I've also got some ideas for the back."

He walked over to some old, sad lawn chairs and spaced them out, then used a few sticks to outline a circular area. I watched, equally mesmerized by his ideas and the way his muscles contracted with his movements. "I'd put in a fire pit here. Nothing too fancy, but a nice area with some chairs and a bench, where guests could roast s'mores or hot dogs or whatever." He nodded his head across the yard. "Over there would be perfect for a little pergola with seating underneath, or even a hot tub if you're okay with the upkeep for those things. Just a couple of options to consider."

I stared at Bryce for a few seconds, unable to respond thanks to the images his ideas summoned in my mind. One of those images—Bryce in a hot tub—short-circuited my brain and robbed me of the ability to form words.

Bryce registered my reaction and frowned, his eyes drifting to Sophia. "Yes? No?"

"I love it," Sophia answered, bumping my shoulder. "Elliot just needs a minute to let it all sink in."

Bryce eyed me with curiosity, uncertainty lingering in his features.

I blinked reality back into focus and nodded. "Soph's right. I, uh, just needed a second. But I do love those ideas."

"Yeah? I'm glad," he replied with an excited grin.

Sophia cleared her throat and drew our attention. "On that note, I've gotta get going. You know, mac n' cheese to cook, kids to entertain. Nanny duty calls."

She skipped off toward the house, tossing a *"later, B-lice"* over her shoulder.

Bryce grinned at her use of the nickname she'd given him as a little kid. "I think she's warming up to me."

I shrugged, watching her go. "Guess so."

When I looked back, Bryce was right where Sophia had been standing, less than a foot away. If I reached out, I could touch him.

"What about you, Uno? Are you warming up to me too?"

CHAPTER 7
ELLIOT

I LOOKED UP TO MEET BRYCE'S GAZE AND TRIED TO PROCESS HIS question. *Am I warming up to him?* If the heat burning through my veins was any indication, I was probably more along the lines of melting than just warming up.

"Um, that depends," I answered.

"On what?"

"On what you brought for dinner." I slowly stepped back toward the house, waiting for him to follow.

He flashed me another one of his way-too-sexy smiles and trailed behind me.

I picked up the bag holding our food and looked around the bare room. "I was thinking, unless you're a fan of eating in stifling heat, we could eat out back. Not that it's much better outside, but at least we'd have a breeze." I stepped around Bryce and eyed the back yard. The grass was wild and overgrown, and I wouldn't let a garden gnome use the rusted chairs. "Though I don't know where we'll sit."

"I've got some towels in my car. I'll go grab a couple, and you can scout the best spot for us."

"Perfect."

After Bryce returned with the towels, we found the least-over-grown spot and quickly set up a picnic.

"So...do you always drive around with spare beach towels in your car?" I asked.

He shrugged and leaned over to unfold the far corner of his towel, and I ogled his oh-so-bitable backside. I would've felt guilty about it, but he was the one who put it on display by leaning over that way. I wasn't about to look a gift horse in the mouth.

"Get caught in enough downpours without an umbrella or raincoat and you'll learn to keep enough towels to cover every inch of upholstery in the car at all times."

His response snapped my concentration, and I pulled my eyes away from his butt faster than a tween busted watching porn. "Exactly how many downpours did it take for you to learn that lesson? Isn't rain kinda the norm in Washington?"

"Let's just say a few."

I shook my head with a playful *tsk-tsk* sound. "Typical guy. Never learning your lesson."

A laugh rippled through him as he pulled out the aluminum container holding our food. "Didn't Millie ever teach you not to tease the guy who brings you dinner?" He peeled back the lid and waved the container around so I could get a whiff of the mouth-watering goodness inside. "Beef fajitas, to be exact."

I edged my way closer to the food, crawling across the towel on my hands and knees. "Didn't your mom ever teach you not to tease a girl about food? Nobody comes between me and my faji-tas, Bryce."

He leaned back, supporting his weight with his free hand. My intention was to steal the container, but from this angle I could make out the ridges of every vein in Bryce's forearm. The sight was distractingly sexy. *As in, what-even-are-fajitas sexy.*

"I forgot how deep your Tex-Mex love goes," he said, drawing my attention away from his arms.

"It doesn't go *that* deep. But really, just try and think of something else that would taste as orgasmic as these fajitas or that queso."

"Oh, I can think of a couple things."

Bryce's brow and the corner of his mouth lifted, and as soon as I registered his reaction, I froze and felt my eyes widen in horror over what I'd said. I pushed off my hands and sank back onto my knees. "Walked right into that one, didn't I?"

"Yep, sure did." He nodded and diverted his attention to the food, pulling out another container and setting it between us. I was still trying to figure out a way to gracefully recover when he looked up, hitting me with a full smirk. "And, just so we're clear, your Tex-Mex love isn't the only thing that goes deep."

Sweet Jesus, I think Bryce McKnight is flirting with me. FLIRTING.

All I could do in response was stare at him.

Just in case I wasn't sure of his insinuation, he gave me a wink that confirmed we were no longer talking about food.

I forced my jaw not to fall open (because letting out all the drool would be the only thing more embarrassing than my initial comment), and instead bit down on my lip while my eyes missed the memo not to stray south.

"I bet," I said, quickly lifting my gaze. "I'm, uh, I mean, let's eat!"

I twisted around to dig into the bag, focusing entirely on pulling out the food and utensils and ignoring Bryce's quiet laughter.

I bet? Seriously, Elliot? Just do yourself a favor and swallow your freaking tongue. Right now.

I piled a couple strips of beef onto my tortilla, followed by onions and peppers, and topped it all off with a dollop of queso. "So, were your parents glad you moved back?"

He hesitated, wiping at the corner of his mouth with a napkin before answering, "Yes and no. We, uh, didn't talk for a long time after I graduated. I kept justifying the radio silence by telling myself I was too busy for a family reunion. I figured it didn't matter if they knew about my accomplishments. So you can imagine their shock when I showed up unannounced at their doorstep four years later."

Holy crap.

So much more to Bryce's story was hidden in his tone and woven into his words. Curiosity commandeered control of my thoughts. *Why didn't Bryce tell his parents about his success? Why didn't they reach out to him? What changed?* But the biggest question of all, the one I wanted the answer to most, was one I also had a feeling I needed to wait for him to share voluntarily—*why, after all of his success in his career, did he leave Seattle?*

"Wow. Bryce, I'm sorry. I guess I kinda thought your parents would come around and support you."

He shrugged, trying to brush off my concern. "Our relationship is a lot better now, but it didn't happen overnight."

I nodded. "I'm really glad things are improving."

"So am I. You know...I didn't go back to Seattle planning to cut all contact with them, but my life after college was chaotic from the start. At first, it was a chaos of my own doing; I stayed for work, so working was all I did, all I cared about. But then..." Bryce paused, and I could tell he was debating how much more to say. "Things changed. So, I know it doesn't make it right, but at least now you know you weren't the only one I lost touch with."

I wasn't sure what to say, so I just nodded and we spent the next few minutes eating in silence. Evening approached, and vivid shades of orange and purple mingled across the darkening sky. The view was part of what made this place so special; between the sprawling hills to the east and the towering oak trees framing the bottom of the sunset to the west, nothing else compared.

At the moment though, the view wasn't holding my attention.

Every so often, my eyes gravitated to Bryce and lingered on the slant of his jawline as he chewed, or the furrow of his brow. Each time, he seemed to feel my gaze, and I'd quickly look away. *What am I, twelve?*

When our shared cup of queso dwindled down to lick-the-sides status, Bryce reached into the bag and pulled another one out, handing it to me without speaking. This is what I never realized I missed most about Bryce and our friendship—the easy comfort that I always felt in his presence. The way drawn-out silences didn't feel awkward. Despite practically spending the last decade as strangers, it seemed we still had the foundation of our friendship to fall back on.

But you never wondered what Bryce looked like shirtless when you were friends. Shirtless? Ha. Good one. Let's be honest, my imagination went way beyond shirtless the second I saw his ass in dress pants.

While I didn't want to pry, there was so much I didn't know about Bryce that I was dying to learn. Swallowing my nerves, I looked up at him and broke the silence. "You said that, at first, all you did in Seattle was work. What about after that; did you make friends, find anyone special?"

Bryce hesitated, and the pained, conflicted expression that fell across his handsome face made me want to wrap my arms around him. I was ready to rescind the question when he slowly nodded, his focus somewhere over the distant treetops.

"Eventually, I made time for socializing and met someone. She wasn't at all the sort of girl I was used to dating. I think that's what drew me to her. It's the whole 'opposites attract' scenario; she was wild and carefree and had a way of reminding me what being young and in your twenties should be like. She broke me out of my shell and helped me live a little." He stopped abruptly and turned toward me, searching my face for answers to unspoken questions. "Do you think it's crazy to believe in fate? I'm not talking just soulmates or love at first sight, necessarily. I mean, do you think it's possible certain people come into our lives at a specific time for a reason?"

The question caught me off guard. I uncrossed my legs and leaned back onto my palms, mimicking his position while I contemplated my answer. Meeting Jade and Jas when I did certainly felt a little serendipitous, but not in the 'meant to be' kind of way I could tell Bryce was talking about. I'd never really taken the time to consider the concept of fate or destiny.

"I don't know. Honestly? I think fate is something a person can only truly believe in after they experience it. Like, if life presents you with a person that you just know was meant to find you at that exact moment. That kind of occurrence is rare, though—one of those 'when you know, you know' things." The need to downplay my response hit me as soon as I looked up and found his blue eyes studying me with renewed curiosity. "At least that's what I think. Then again, one could also argue that it's all just luck and timing. It's a matter of perspective, I suppose."

He lifted a brow. "Spoken like a true pessimist."

"I prefer the term 'realist', thank you very much."

"Oh, is that so? All right, Ms. Realist, what about you?"

"What about me? What do you mean?"

He smirked and rolled his eyes, undeterred by my faux-confusion. "You know what I mean, El. Anyone special in your life?"

I was about to lamely explain how I'd also adopted his no-time-for-fun work ethic when I realized that, while he used the past tense to talk about the girl who broke him out of his shell, he hadn't actually spelled out their status. I still knew next to nothing about Bryce's life aside from his professional capabilities. I needed answers.

"Bryce. What happened? You and the girl you met...are y'all still together?"

"Do you always answer questions with a question?"

"I could ask you the same thing," I pointed out. "And no, to answer your previous question."

His hesitation sent my imagination into overdrive, but before it could go too far, he brought his eyes back to mine. The sun was lost somewhere beyond the horizon, shadowing his features and making his expression difficult to read. "No, we're not still together. She's the kind of girl who's always down for a good time, always making life one big party. So when things got too real for her, she chose the path of least resistance and moved to California. I haven't seen her in two years."

Bryce's words were laced with the kind of pain that engrains itself into your being and leaves scars on every cell of your body. He didn't say it, but he didn't have to; *she* was the reason he left Seattle behind.

"Well, she sounds like an idiot." I jumped up and stuck my hand out for him to take. "C'mon, there's something I wanna show you."

"Oh…kay," he agreed with a mixture of intrigue and skepticism. I gripped his hand and pulled him to his feet.

We walked in silence as I used my phone's flashlight feature to light our way down the footpath toward the woods beyond the yard. Bryce and I had played in those same woods after dusk so often as kids that we probably didn't need a light to find our way, but that was a long time ago, and there was no telling what kind of creepy-crawlies called this place home now.

I stopped when my light found the tree I was looking for—the one Bryce and I dubbed the tallest in all the land. My fingers traced over the letters we'd carved into the bark a lifetime ago. "Do you remember this?"

"Of course. We'll *B + E* friends forever," he recited.

I smiled. "Man, we thought we were geniuses for coming up with that."

He laughed. "We were also so sure Millie and George would appreciate our woodwork that it never occurred to us they wouldn't approve of stealing George's knife to carve up the tree. I don't think I've ever seen them as pissed as they were that day."

"I'm pretty sure they still hide the knives when I come home. I guess they had a point, though." I shook my head when Bryce gave me another 'did you just say that' look. "Oh, come on. No pun intended." I laughed.

"Your puns always were a little dull." He grinned.

"Wow, Bryce. That one was way worse than any of mine."

We spent the next hour and a half reminiscing about our childhood adventures, comfortably trading jokes and more terrible puns. I reminded him of all the times I'd won our races. He insisted he'd only *let* me win because I wouldn't have continued the competitions if he beat me every time. I asked if he also 'let' me win every time I had dominated in Mario Kart.

"I don't remember you *dominating* me so much as you cheating your way to victory."

I crossed my arms and narrowed my eyes in the dim moonlight. "Oh, really? Well I happen to have a Nintendo, and I'd be more than happy to prove you wrong."

A lopsided grin split his lips, and he crossed his arms too, feigning seriousness. "Bring it on. Any day, any time."

"Are you free tomorrow? I'm off Mondays."

He nodded. "I can make tomorrow work. What time?"

"Three?"

"Three it is." He narrowed his eyes. "I get the feeling you're about to go home and start practicing. Scared?"

"Please." I laughed. "I could beat you in my sleep."

"So cocky, Kincaid. Hope you can back it up."

"I believe the word you mean is 'confident,' McKnight."

"Okay, that's fair. Your *confidence* is adorable. I'm almost going to be sad when it morphs into silence after I beat you. Almost."

"Keep telling yourself that."

On the walk to our cars, he told me he hoped my driving skills had evolved since the days of recklessly ejecting him from the go-kart.

I scoffed. "Hey, it's not my fault they used to make go-karts without seat belts. Why'd you keep riding with me if you knew there was a chance you'd get thrown out?"

Bryce's head tilted to the left and his eyebrows pulled together. I could've sworn his eyes were telling me my question was silly. "Back then, I would've done just about anything to make you smile or laugh, El. Your laugh was my favorite sound, and I loved being the one who brought that joy and happiness to you."

I sucked in a sharp breath. *I wonder if he knows that the day we met was the day I found my smile.* "So that's why you were always telling lame jokes and doing stupid stunts for me."

"Seems those lame jokes and stupid stunts worked out all right for me." He paused, cupping his chin and stroking his thumb and forefinger along his jaw. "I forget; what was that last name you gave yourself because of one of my 'lame jokes'?"

My eyes went wide, and I coughed to cloak my reaction. "Uh. I can't remember. Hmm. Maybe you had a point about my memory issues after all. I should probably consult with a doctor."

"Yeah, okay. Whatever you say, McPickles."

I groaned. "Oh my god, Bryce. I was seven! I thought you were serious when you said people got to choose their own last names when they turned ten. You were obsessed with knights; in my mind that name made perfect sense."

"So you would've chosen to be named after the most disgusting food known to man," he said with a laugh. "Which also sounds like a rejected McDonald's meal."

"I just really liked pickles. Still do."

"I've always liked salads, but that doesn't mean I would've named myself Caesar."

I felt the corner of my mouth twitch into a smile and waggled my eyebrows playfully. "Too late. I think you just gave yourself a nickname."

"What? No. I'm way too old for a nickname."

"Says who? No such thing. Plus, you're still calling me Uno."

"That's different, Elliot." His eyes found mine, and even in the dim light, I felt the weight of his gaze. "Do you not like when I call you that?"

"No, I do," I said quickly. "It reminds me of…all the fun we had as kids. I'll make you a deal—never call me McPickles again, and I won't make Caesar a thing."

"Done."

"Besides, Caesar wasn't even my best work. I'm sure I can come up with something better. Give me some time."

Bryce sighed. "This sounds like it's going to be about as fun as a root canal."

I turned up the volume of my music and pretended not to notice his sarcasm.

"Hey, care to make things interesting tomorrow?" he asked.

"Like a bet? I'm in. What'd you have in mind? Five pounds of Starbursts?"

His smirk made my pulse spike. "Starbursts? C'mon, El. That's child's play. Loser plans a follow-up date."

I couldn't stop my eyebrows from lifting. "A date-date? Or a friend date?"

He bit his lip and shrugged. "Why do we have to label it one or the other? We could just call it an outing?"

"Sounds suspiciously like a devious plan to ensure there's a second *outing*."

"Maybe it is."

"All right, Caesar," I called. He groaned at the name and slid into the driver's seat of his SUV. "You know, the more I think about it, the more that name suits you. Salads, mastermind like Julius. It works."

Bryce smiled, and the warmth it radiated slid over me like honey. "Goodnight, McPickles."

And just like that, Bryce McKnight managed to make me forget about the looming decision I had to make about the inn.

CHAPTER 8
BRYCE

"Bryce, tell me you did not bring that bitch up in conversation with Elliot," Xander demanded, pinching the bridge of his nose aggressively from across the bar.

Usually Xander was so self-involved he never bothered to ask about my love life or social life, or lack thereof. I shouldn't have been surprised though; El wasn't easily forgotten, no matter how brief his view of her had been.

"First of all, don't call her that." *Even if it is accurate.* I cut my eyes to my cousin and took a drawn-out sip of my beer. "And secondly, I didn't *bring her up*. Elliot asked if I'd met anyone in Seattle, and I answered."

"What exactly did you tell her?"

I hesitated, debating whether the free drinks I got by coming to the bar where he worked, Sipology, were worth having this discussion with him. *I've got beer at home. Sure, I prefer it on tap, but I also prefer it without a side of conversation.*

"I told her the truth."

"The *whole* truth?"

I gritted my teeth. "I didn't lie, if that's what you're getting at. I just haven't had the right opportunity to explain everything."

It was such a horribly lame excuse, even to my own ears. It's just…explaining *everything* wasn't something I was ready for yet.

Xander groaned and threw a cocktail napkin at me. "Whatever, man. Your life, your decision." He didn't bother looking back at me before picking up a crate of glasses and taking it across the bar, leaving me alone with my laptop and thoughts.

Solitude suited me perfectly, though I knew I didn't have long before the bar opened. I gathered my laptop, sketchpad, notes, and portfolio and headed to a booth in the corner to claim my usual spot. My house was only a few blocks away, but changing scenery usually kickstarted my brain's creative side.

The truth—the one I'd never utter to Xander—was that I knew I should've told Elliot everything that night at the inn. Or even the next day at her apartment. But the timing was never right, and I still wasn't entirely sure what exactly to say.

After she won the fifth straight Mario Kart race (yeah, she might've had a reason to be cocky after all), I bowed down and admitted defeat to avoid further humiliation. We had segued into conversation easily when I asked how she became so good at Mario Kart…

"Turns out living with a guy isn't all that terrible," Elliot said. "Milo got the Nintendo last year, and I realized playing video games is like riding a bike, only without the calorie burn."

"So, you and Milo…?"

"What?! God, no," she exclaimed immediately.

"So y'all have never hooked up or anything?"

Her face twisted in disgust. "Definitely not. I love Milo, but like a brother. Plus, I'm not even sure Milo is familiar with the term 'relationship,' much less willing to stay in one for any length of time."

"I know the type," I muttered. "What about you? Do you ever think about marriage, kids, the whole nine yards?"

"Kinda hard not to think about marriage in my line of work. But I'm not in a rush to walk down the aisle. I've always been what Milo calls a 'serial monogamist,' but I've learned there's really no 'fake it till you make it' when it comes to love. And that's what I used to do with every guy I dated. Somewhere along the way, thankfully, I realized love isn't one-size-fits-all. It's gotta happen organically, and if it doesn't then you're with the wrong person. You know?"

I nodded.

"As for kids…I don't know. If—and that's a big if—kids are in my future, it's way down the line. I'm incapable of eating the recommended daily servings of fruits and vegetables myself, so there's no way I'd be qualified to make sure another human being does."

I HAD CONSIDERED TELLING her the whole truth right then, but didn't want to risk losing what little trust I'd built with her. Opening up to Elliot was never a problem when we were kids, but that's because childhood's the golden age of honesty, when the biggest concerns in life revolve around video games and trading Lunchables.

But things were different now. I was reminded of that fact every time my stomach knotted as my phone rang, and again each time I caught Elliot looking at me with a smile on her lips and a promise in her eyes. The same promise I'd seen when we were kids, and again five years ago when I hadn't known I needed it.

I just wasn't sure she'd still give me that promise after she knew the truth about everything.

Instead of letting hypotheticals run wild in my thoughts, I forced myself to focus solely on work—on the plans for the inn. I'd spent the last week and a half at my desk, or here at Sipology, hunched over my computer. I had a vision for the inn, and, if our last meeting was any indication, I was pretty sure Elliot and Sophia would love it.

Xander stopped in front of my booth and tapped on the wood, drawing my attention. "Dude, not trying to be a dick, but you're kinda killing the vibe. People usually come here to get away from work and their problems, not to be reminded of them."

My head snapped up. "Huh?"

"You've been sitting here for three hours, alternating between slaving away at your laptop," he shouted over the music, picking up a handful of stray blueprints, "and staring at your phone like you've lost your damn puppy."

I pulled my phone out and sure enough, he was right. I looked around and realized the bar had filled up with a typical Friday night crowd. Customers lined the bar and were scattered throughout the room, laughing and basking in that anything-is-possible, early-weekend happiness that only comes on Friday nights. Xander might've had a point; it was one thing for me to lose myself in work here while it was empty, but nobody wants to be the depressing loner in the corner.

"Sorry, guess I lost track of time. It's just easier to work here. Can I use your office?"

"Yeah, sure. We're about to get slammed, so I'll probably be at the bar until closing."

Xander hadn't always been a model citizen, but after he got expelled from Duke and was one more idiotic decision away from hitting rock bottom, Sipology's owner took a chance and gave him a job bartending. This bar and his job had somehow provided Xander with the kind of stability he so desperately needed. Seven years later, Xander was still a far cry from normal, if you asked me, but I had to give him credit for how far he'd come. His personal life was still a damn circus, but I mostly thought that was for the best. The day Xander looked at a woman and cared more about her heart than her bra size was a day I'd pay to see.

My phone pinged with a text, and seeing El's name was

enough to make me jump up and haphazardly stuff my things into my bag.

"Hello? Bryce, did you hear anything I said?" Xander asked after a few seconds.

"What? Uh, yeah. Sorry. I won't be needing your office after all. I have to go."

Xander crossed his arms and arched a brow. "Guess you found the puppy."

THANKS to the sudden threat of a rainstorm, Elliot had been forced to throw together a last-minute plan B for her client's upcoming outdoor wedding. When the forecast changed during the rehearsal dinner to include overnight thunderstorms, Elliot told her clients she'd take care of the logistics to get everything moved indoors. By herself.

Her offer didn't surprise me; she'd always been selfless beyond belief. Once she started, though, she quickly realized she'd need reinforcements.

"Thanks for letting me cash in on the bet so last minute. I don't know what I would've done without your help." Elliot's smile spread as she picked up a couple of folding chairs to take inside, and in that moment she could've asked me to fry an egg underwater and I would've tried to find a way to make it happen.

I picked up the remaining chairs and followed her into the renovated barn, the alternate reception location. "You're welcome, but I would've come regardless of the bet. This doesn't count."

"Really? Why? This more than makes up for you losing to me in Mario Kart."

"Nah, this isn't even close. This is just...helping a friend in need. Tomorrow night's still good for you, right?"

She paused, chewing her lip in contemplation before waving her hand dismissively. "You really don't have to do anything else, Bryce. You're practically a lifesaver already."

I dropped the chairs in place at the table and stopped. When Elliot realized I was no longer following her, she stopped and turned back. "What is it, Uno?" I said, now that I had her full attention. "Are you having second thoughts about the date thing, because we can—"

"No," she said quickly, cutting me off. "I mean, I don't know. I, uh..." She paused, groaning and dropping her head back. "God, this is going to sound so lame."

"I used to let you talk me into participating in your Barbie weddings. Think you've got my number on lame, El. Talk to me."

Her shoulders dropped as a smile appeared, and I gave her one in return.

"True. Okay, so...a while back I decided my dating habits needed an overhaul. I had this tendency of trying to mold every boyfriend into 'the one.' I went into relationships with the intention of meeting my future husband. Which was absurd, of course, because I was way too young for that. But I craved a healthy, stable, long-term relationship. It doesn't take a shrink to figure out why..." She trailed off, shifting her attention to the centerpiece before continuing. "But then I realized I needed some time to be single and independent. And I swore to myself that I wouldn't put any pressure on my next relationship. But with you...it's complicated because we have history. I'm just not sure how to navigate whatever it is we're doing. Or not doing. Or will be doing eventually. I mean, this is exactly what I said I wouldn't do —pressure. We haven't even been out yet, and I'm already over-thinking things. Do you see—"

"Elliot," I interrupted, coming up to her and putting my hands gently on her shoulders. "Breathe. Look, I know you've got a lot going on in your life right now. My life is crazy too. The last thing I want to do is stress you out any more than you already are. There's no way to know where this will go between us, so let's just take it as it comes and see what happens, yeah? We can go slow. No pressure."

Relief flooded her features, and knew I'd said the right thing.

"Okay. If you're sure. But if you're having second thoughts or don't want to—"

"Is that your default response for everyone, or is it reserved just for me?"

"What do you mean?" she asked.

"You keep making excuses for me or trying to downplay things, almost like you're waiting for me to bail. Like you expect it."

Elliot slowly set down the wine glasses she carried and shifted her attention back to me. "Bryce, I'm not waiting for you to bail. It's just…" She dropped her gaze to her feet. "It's easier this way. You know, setting realistic expectations based on…"

Based on my history of bailing.

But that history had nothing to do with her.

I knew telling her that would sound like just another excuse, and I had no intention of giving her any more reason to question my presence in her life. I'd just have to shift her expectations until they didn't include a question mark about how long I'd stick around.

"I can't erase the past, El. But the beauty of the future is that it hasn't been written yet. That's what the present is for. Give me a chance to rewrite myself into your life and future. In whatever capacity."

"Okay," she murmured. "I'd like that."

"Yeah? So tomorrow? Six o'clock?"

"It's an early wedding, so six works for me. You never said where we're going."

I smirked, grateful that things were back on track. "Guess. You can ask me three yes or no questions and then try to figure out what it is."

Her eyes lit up, and I could already see the wheels turning in her head as she considered her first question. "Is it the kind of thing that requires tennis shoes and shovels or high heels and champagne?"

I balked, too caught off guard to correct her non-yes-or-no

question. "Shovels? What the fuck kind of surprises are you used to?"

She laughed off my shock and shrugged. "Hey, who am I to judge if the mystery date includes getting rid of a body?"

"I usually save surprises that involve committing felonies for the third date. Don't wanna scare 'em off too soon."

"Good thinking. Wouldn't wanna alert anyone to your stalker-like tendencies too early on," she quipped with a wink.

"Pretty sure you're the one stalking me."

"Agree to disagree."

"Whatever helps you sleep at night." I laughed, shaking my head at her. "Tennis shoes, by the way. It's definitely a tennis shoes kinda thing. Shovels optional, but not necessary. Next question. And no more cheating. Yes or no, Uno."

She hummed in contemplation while we carried the last of the tables into the barn. "Will we be eating dinner there?"

"It's an option, though we could do dinner somewhere else afterward."

"Okay...tennis shoes and the option to eat dinner. Third question." She paused, arching a brow as her lips curled into a sly smile. "Will one of us be embarrassed before the date is over?"

Damn, she's good.

She was referring to the way she jokingly apologized for embarrassing me the other night in Mario Kart. Our lives were vastly different now, but when it came to competing against each other, some things never changed.

I rubbed the back of my neck and tried to keep my face neutral. "It's possible."

She laughed. "That means yes. Which also means it's probably going to be you. I know where we're going," she exclaimed triumphantly.

"What? Where?"

"Has to be some kind of real life go-kart place. You said the other day you only lost because you're rusty from not playing video games anymore. Still not sure that I believe that."

"Wow. Either that was some sorcery mind reading shit or you missed your calling as a detective."

She scoffed and waved her hand in the air. "Hardly. Adult Bryce McKnight might be a virtual stranger, but I still remember a lot about ten-year-old Bryce McKnight. And that Bryce hated losing. It doesn't take a detective to figure out you'd want revenge. Bring it, Yoshi."

She wiggled her eyebrows playfully and hit me with a smirk. *God, she's adorable.* I laughed, but the sting of the truth in her words was a tough pill to swallow.

I hate that she's right. I hate that there's so much we don't know about each other. But at the same time…maybe being semi-strangers now will work in my favor. Maybe I can redesign the boundaries of our relationship.

In that moment, I chose to believe the friendship we once shared was simply the foundation for something deeper.

It had to be.

We spent the next hour moving the rest of the decorations and tables into the barn-turned-reception hall behind the venue's ceremony location. Elliot thanked me again before we finished, but I refused to take any credit for the magic act she'd performed by transforming the space into what surely would be this bride's dream reception. Sure, I'd strung twinkle lights and moved tables where she told me to, but Elliot was the one who took the time to painstakingly rearrange centerpieces until each one was perfect.

Watching Elliot work, seeing the way she problem-solved when she wasn't happy with the space between tables or with the location of a certain decoration, felt like I was watching a live performance of art in motion. Which was cheesy as hell, but that's the only way to describe it. Where some people, myself included before this experience, might've just seen a typical wedding reception with a few decorations and mementos scattered throughout the space, she had transformed it into a time capsule of Jeremy and Hannah Stone's lives. I'd never met either of them, but through personal touches such as childhood photos and fun facts about each of them on chalkboards along the buffet line, Elliot made the space theirs.

Elliot did a double take and froze when she caught me with my phone up, snapping a shot of her humming along to the music playing through the speakers as she worked. "What's that for?"

I shrugged. "Maybe I just want you to see what I'm seeing." I pulled up the photo and walked toward her, holding my phone out for her to look at. She was focused, wearing an effortless smile that made me wish I could read her thoughts. "At the risk of sounding like a crazy stalker, I could watch you work for hours. Your passion is obvious, and it's really inspiring to see, El. I don't know that I've ever witnessed so much consideration and thought put into every detail of an event."

Her face contorted into an almost-grimace. "You make me sound OCD."

I quickly shook my head and snatched my phone back before she could try to delete the photo. "Nah. It's more like you turn your job into an art. It's a compliment. Trust me."

Elliot tilted her head back, and the lights above us reflected like tiny little sparklers in her eyes. "You know, it's funny, I actually had the same thought when I was watching you at the inn." She paused and stepped close enough for me to notice the way her icy irises had melted, darkening into the last shade of blue in the sky before sunset. "Your talent is rare, Bryce, and denying the world of your gift would've been a crime. I'm really glad you followed your heart and stayed in Seattle after college. But self-ishly, I'm also glad you came back."

"Seattle gave me more than I could've ever imagined or expected, and I'll never regret my time there. But I realized how much I missed living here. I used to trick my brain into believing home was a state of mind, that if I could build a life around my professional success, Washington would feel like home. Turns out that's not the case. At least not for me."

"I guess that makes sense. Though I didn't really peg you as the 'home is where the heart is' type."

"I, uh, wasn't until about a year and a half ago." I hesitated and pressed my fingers into the back of my neck again, this time to relieve the tension. After a beat, I cleared my throat, finally summoning the courage to tell her about Peyton. "There's actually something I need to tell you…" I trailed off when I realized a sudden downpour of rain had hijacked Elliot's attention.

"Wow, it's really coming down out there. Okay, sorry, what were you going to say?"

I shifted on my feet, summoning the courage that had disappeared with the rain's arrival. "Early last year, I got a phone call and found out—"

CRACK! The rest of my sentence was drowned out by the roar of lightening somewhere outside.

"What?" she asked. Before I could answer, her eyes grew round, and she shoved past me, moving toward the door. "Shit! My windows are down!"

I chased after her, muttering a string of curses under my breath. Not because I was worried about getting my clothes wet. Or even the possibility of being struck by a billion volts of electricity.

Because I just told her about my daughter, and she couldn't fucking hear me.

CHAPTER 9
ELLIOT

"SOPHIA! WHAT DID YOU DO WITH MY LEOPARD PRINT TOMS?" I shouted into the apartment after hastily dropping my bags on the dining room table.

No answer.

I don't have time for this.

The wedding ran longer than I'd expected, so I only had about twenty minutes until Bryce was supposed to come pick me up.

I kicked off my heels and trotted over to bang on Sophia's door. "Soph, I need my shoes!"

Milo's door opened, and he poked his head out. "She's at the library, but I saw her go into your room before she left."

"Was she wearing my leopard print Toms?"

He shrugged. "What do I look like, the fashion police? I don't notice that shit."

I groaned and walked toward my closet.

Milo followed behind and leaned against my door frame. "Don't you have, like, forty pairs of shoes?"

I groaned again, annoyed at his inability to understand female logic. "It's times like these that make me wish you were gay. And not just any gay—the kind that would understand and help with fashion dilemmas."

"Uh, sorry I'm not into dudes? But I don't need to be gay to solve a nonexistent fashion dilemma."

"What? You know what other shoes would pair perfectly with this outfit?" I asked, turning and holding up the pair of white cutoff shorts and a black tank top.

"Yeah. These." He held up the very shoes I'd been searching for. I went to take them, but Milo pulled them back. "Wait. Where are you going? You never go out after a wedding."

"How do you know? You're usually at work or out when I get home. Maybe I'm a wild party animal when you're not around."

Milo had the audacity to laugh. "We both know you're not. Mild party animal, at best. Plus, you always come to the bar when I'm working if you go anywhere. What's up?"

"I'm going out."

"With Bryce?"

"Fine, yes. Hey, you're a guy," I said, narrowing my eyes in contemplation. *He might be able to help me settle something.*

"Last time I checked," he replied, pulling on the waistband of his shorts to look at his junk. "Yep, Excalibur's still there."

"You named your—never mind. This. This is why you're single, Milo."

"Nah. I'm single because Excalibur is very friendly, and monogamy is not the way to make new friends. But I doubt that's why you pointed out my gender. What's up, El?"

"Should I be concerned that Bryce practically jumped at the chance to 'take things slow' with me?" I asked, using air quotes. "I kind of brought it upon myself, but what if that means he isn't attracted to me?"

Milo crossed his arms over his chest and eyed me skeptically. "I'm not an expert on dating, by any means, but I can tell you that he wouldn't be taking you out if he wasn't interested. And he's an idiot if he's not attracted to you."

"How can you be sure? What if he's just trying to be friends again?"

He held a hand up to shush me. "Did he call this an actual date?"

"I'm not sure. He said something about our next date though."

"Then he definitely wants in your pants. Don't worry about it. This trepidation and wavering self-confidence isn't like you, El. What gives?"

Damn it. He was right.

"I don't know, Mi. I think it's Bryce. I usually have a fresh slate when it comes to dating. I think our past history is throwing me off. Everything with him is…different now."

"Good different?"

"I think so, yeah."

Milo's head jerked to the left, sending his overgrown locks out of his eyes. He pushed off the door frame and lightly rapped his fist against it. "Then just go with it. Have fun."

"You're right. Okay, I need to change, so you gotta go," I said, shooing him out of my room.

He gave me a mini-salute and ducked out.

I stood in the middle of my room digesting Milo's words for a solid minute before realizing precious seconds were ticking by. I hurriedly changed clothes, made a few adjustments to my makeup, and attempted to curl my hair before giving up and letting it do its own weird half-wave thing.

I was in the middle of giving Demi Lovato a run for her money as I sang along to "Sorry Not Sorry" when I heard a knock. I turned the music off and forced myself not to run out of my room, in an attempt to play it cool, which turned out to be a mistake when I came a half-step short of beating Milo to the front door.

He pulled it open with a triumphant smile that only widened as he spoke. "Hey, you must be Bryce. I've heard shockingly little about you, which means she likes you. I'm Milo," he said, sticking his hand out to Bryce.

I not-so-subtly elbowed Milo in the ribs and tried unsuccessfully to shove him out of the doorway.

Bryce dropped his eyes from Milo to me before shaking Milo's traitorous hand and plastering on a smirk. "I've heard little about you too. Nice to put a face to the name."

"Likewise. So, where are—"

"Oh, good, introductions are over," I spat quickly, grabbing my purse off the hook. "We should go. Preferably before Milo opens his mouth again."

I stepped in front of Milo in an attempt to block him from Bryce's view, even though I barely came up to Milo's shoulders without the aid of heels.

Bryce and Milo both let out clipped laughs before exchanging an odd, indecipherable look. The longer the three of us hovered around the doorway, the greater the likelihood Milo would either try to give Bryce more ammunition for questions later or pull some kind of over-protective best friend intimidation act.

I didn't plan to stick around long enough to see which route he chose. Stepping forward, I grabbed the doorknob and glanced back at Milo, silently willing him to be cool. "Later, Mi. Don't wait up."

"Have fun, and don't forget to use protection!" Milo called as the door clicked closed between us.

I'm going to kill him.

"Sorry, he's got the social skills of a homeschooled preteen. I'd say he's not usually like that, but I'd be lying."

Bryce laughed behind me. "It's fine, I get it."

Once we were in the elevator, I faced Bryce, finally letting my eyes roam freely over him. He'd worked his hair just enough for it to look like the longest ends flopped to the right naturally. His tanned forearms were on display thanks to the cuff of his sleeves, and I tracked the veins along his muscles until they disappeared beneath his shirt. When my eyes finally made the trek back to his face, they landed on the curve of his lips before lifting to meet his warm gaze. He'd opted for contacts tonight, which was probably for the best considering how many times he had popped into my dreams lately because of those damn glasses.

I fidgeted with my keys and smiled at him. "Hi."

Bryce gave me the same perusal I'd given him, and I tried to ignore the goose bumps his eyes burned into my skin. "Hi. You look beautiful, El."

"Um, thanks. So do you. I mean handsome," I replied with a laugh, tilting my head up to offer him another smile before looking down at my feet. "I hope you were serious about the shoes."

"I was. Can't have you wearing heels to bury the body in my trunk."

"Thought you saved the felonies for the third date?" I narrowed my eyes to glare at him, but at the same time my grin exposed my amusement. "Not sure if I'm flattered because that makes me special, or disturbed that you're already trying to make me an accomplice."

"Be flattered. You're definitely special, Elliot," he said, the heat in his eyes conveying the sincerity of his words. "Hey, how'd the wedding go?"

"It was great, minus a few bumps. Is it weird that I kind of thrive in the stressful moments? It's a special kind of chaos, but I love getting to problem-solve, and I love that no two weddings are the same. First the caterers got lost, then the band was late, and right before the ceremony the groomsman with the rings thought he left them at the hotel. Then at the reception..." I paused, turning to him as he led me toward his SUV. "I'm sorry, you probably don't want to hear about my work drama."

He paused mid-reach for the passenger door of his Range Rover. "Of course I wanna hear about it. I told you yesterday, your passion for your work is inspiring."

I was still smiling by the time Bryce rounded the hood to get in the driver's seat, and I quickly eyed the interior. Everything from the leather seats to the shiny surface of the dashboard was black. I searched for signs of personal touches, but found nothing. I didn't see a single speck of dust or even a gum wrapper littering the floorboards. Bryce clearly took pride in keeping things in order.

"Not what you were expecting?"

"I guess I didn't peg you as the type to keep everything so…impersonal."

"Oh, believe me, it's usually not nearly this clean." He paused and flickered his gaze to the second-row seats before turning back toward me. "Never, actually. Told you, you're special, Uno," he said with a wink that was way too sexy to be considered just a friendly act.

Knowing Bryce took the time to thoroughly clean his car before taking me out meant more than I expected it to. I tried to remember if any of my previous boyfriends had put in that kind of effort before any of our dates, but stopped myself when Milo's voice popped into my thoughts. *Just go with it.*

Right. No comparing this to past experiences. And definitely no comparing Bryce to previous boyfriends.

"So, you were saying the wedding went well? With the exception of all the fires you put out?" Bryce prompted, bringing me back to earth.

I nodded before launching into a summary of today's events. I told him about tracking down the caterers myself when their phones cut out and lost signal. He laughed when I explained how the mystery of the rings was solved by another groomsman who had gotten the rings stuck on his fingers (*thank god for coconut oil*). He shook his head and wore an awed expression when I finished describing the system I'd perfected when it came to cleaning up after weddings.

"I don't know how you do it. I'm betting you've been up since before the crack of dawn, then spent hours upon hours running around to give these people the best day possible, and now you're here telling me about it and still have the energy to be genuinely happy when you talk about what went on."

"I know. It's not always like this, trust me. Some days I want to rip the bride's veil off and hang myself with it," I admitted with a chuckle. "But overall, I just really love being the one to make people that happy. To know I've played a small role in giving them something special they'll always share and remember. That kind of satisfaction gives me a weird work-high...which I'm now realizing sounds lame when I try to describe it out loud."

"Nah, I get it. Seeing my designs brought to life gives me that same feeling. Maybe not exactly, but I know how rewarding it is for your hard work to manifest into something great. To know you're doing something you're passionate about."

Then why did he leave Seattle?

I knew his ex must've played a role in his decision to move back here, but the need to know the whole answer was burning under my skin. Something told me it wasn't that cut and dry.

We rode in a comfortable silence for a few minutes, and I looked out the window and watched the downtown buildings grow smaller as Bryce drove us toward north Austin.

"El?" he asked eventually, drawing my attention back to him.

"Hm?"

"Have you thought any more about what you want to do with the inn? I know George mentioned there's no rush on a final decision, but I can't imagine you and Sophia enjoy having this looming over your heads."

"Actually, I have." I turned in my seat and sucked in a deep breath, seeking his smile for the encouragement to tell him what I hadn't even discussed with Sophia yet. "I have an idea. I haven't told anyone, so I need you to promise you'll be honest if I'm completely crazy. Okay?"

He nodded and lifted one hand from the wheel to draw an imaginary cross over his heart. "Of course. Lay it on me."

When I hesitated, he reached across the center console and squeezed my hand. The familiar gesture instantly cloaked me with comfort. "My biggest struggle with this decision is weighing my love for the inn and everything it represents against my love for my job. I mean, I've loved the inn for as long as I can remember. At the same time, FMK and Jade and Jasmine have become family to me; I can't imagine walking away. But I think I've found a way to have my cake and eat it too." I paused, biting my lip and trying to rein in my excitement. Bryce smiled and gave me a nod in a 'keep going' kind of way. "What if I turn Let Love Inn into a wedding venue? I mean, not get rid of the inn part, but add another part that would be used for weddings. We could even make it FMK-exclusive. Or I'd find another way to keep my job and make this possible. I've given it a lot of thought, Bryce. You know that clearing near our 'B+E' tree? I really think it would work for a ceremony location. And then we could turn the old barn into a reception hall, or even build one from scratch, if not. I'm not entirely sure how much that would cost. I know it's way more than the renovations Nana and Pops had in mind, but I could get a loan. And I don't know what Sophia's thoughts will be, but I think she'd want this for me." I finally stopped talking and took a breath before bringing my eyes back to Bryce to see his reaction. "That was a lot. Sorry. But, um, what do you think?"

"I think…" He lifted a hand to rub his jaw, and I felt myself stop breathing again in anticipation of his next words. "El, I think it's perfect. Honestly. So perfect for you."

"Yeah? Really?!" I practically leapt across the console and onto him, throwing my arms around his neck. Thankfully, my impulsive excitement didn't make us crash. He just laughed and brought his left hand up to squeeze my arm.

"I mean, I know it's going to be crazy and a ton of work, and I have no clue if Jade and Jas will even go for it, but I have to at least try. You know?"

"If there's one thing I know for sure, it's that you, Elliot Kincaid, are not the type to back down from something just because it's going to be a difficult journey. You're way too tough for that. And I'm sure they'll all love this idea. It's kind of impossible not to after seeing your enthusiasm."

He wove his fingers through mine and held them there the rest of the car ride.

By the time we pulled up to the go-kart place, I'd been so consumed by excitement over my plans for the inn that I forgot what we were about to do. I turned to Bryce after unbuckling my seatbelt and smirked. "You're going down, Diddy Kong."

His lips curled at my attempted new nickname. "You gonna cycle through all the Mario Kart characters, or what?"

I shrugged. "Maybe. At least all the sucky ones. One's bound to stick."

"Don't hold your breath."

"Whatever. You're still going down, *Bryce*."

"So you keep saying." He paused, dropping his eyes down my body and bringing them back up at a blatantly slow pace. "You really can't wait for me to *go down*, can you? I gotta say...as much as I still hate losing, the idea of *going down* to you makes the fall incredibly fucking appealing."

His voice held both a threat and a promise, and I wasn't sure which one was responsible for the tremor that raked through my body, but I itched to find out.

"Bryce—"

"Patience, El. Right now I'm gonna kick your ass on the race track."

Heat fully flooded my neck and cheeks by the time Bryce made it over to my door. He pulled it open and held out a hand.

I lifted my chin and eyed him curiously once my feet touched down. "Bryce McKnight...boy-next-door gentleman one minute, and smooth-but-dirty talker the next. Aren't you just full of surprises?"

He arched a brow, and at the same time a corner of his mouth lifted up into a wicked grin that made me want to forgo our date and pull him into the back seat of his Range Rover. "You have no idea, Elliot. No fucking idea."

"Enlighten me," I challenged, planting my feet instead of following when he moved to walk toward the building.

He turned back, but not before quickly surveying our surroundings. I licked my lips and kept my head tilted up, too shocked to look away. *Pretty sure he just set a record for how turned on one simple exchange can make a person.*

I blinked and he was there, casing me in against his car with his body. My chest brushed his torso, adding fuel to the sparks flying underneath my skin. Everything about this moment drew me in and made me crave more of him. I gripped his shirt at his waist and held him close, unwilling to let him move without finishing what he had started.

He brought one hand up to cup the side of my face and the other to lightly caress my opposite cheek. "Careful what you wish for, El. Enlightening you completely right now would involve saying and doing a lot of things to you in the back seat of my car that are definitely not family-friendly. And it *definitely* wouldn't be taking things slow to put my mouth between your legs before our first date ends. But I don't think I can go another minute without doing what I should've done five years ago," he said roughly, dropping his mouth down to brush against the outer shell of my ear.

A moan erupted from my throat, and that's all it took for his mouth to crash into mine. I pressed up on my toes and met his kiss with matching desperation.

Where his touch had been gentle two seconds ago, it was anything but now. He pressed into me, and I was vaguely aware of another moan escaping into his mouth when I realized just how hard and toned Bryce's body was. His hands held my head in place and mine dug into his sides, holding on for stability.

Leading up to this moment, I would've expected my first kiss with Bryce to be sweet or reserved on both of our parts. Ours was an unusual situation, and I never would've expected things to explode this way with him.

But they did. In the best way imaginable.

Fireworks—that's what I felt with Bryce's mouth on mine and our tongues dancing and exploring like we'd been deprived of each other for decades.

I was seconds from sending us both tumbling to the ground when he pulled back.

"That was..." I trailed off, breathing hard and at a loss for words.

"I know," he agreed.

I was on the verge of suggesting that he *should* completely enlighten me when he took a step back and quickly ran a hand over my hair to smooth out the mess he'd made.

"Uhh, ye—uh huh," I sputtered. *Great, now full sentences aren't a part of my verbal skillset?*

Bryce smirked, and I would've been annoyed at how unaffected he looked after our kiss if not for the way he turned to adjust things below the belt.

He reached around me and closed the car door while I continued to do nothing but stare at him, still not trusting my brain to send messages to my mouth.

"C'mon." He motioned toward the go-kart park. "You might've beaten me at Mario Kart, but we both know who's going to be on top by the end of tonight. Though, in this case, I might be willing to make an exception about you coming out on top."

My mouth fell open, but before I could say a word, he grabbed my hand and tugged me forward.

Who freaking knew. Underneath the high-end clothes and the charming, unassuming boy-next-door demeanor, Bryce McKnight is a dirty-talking Romeo.

And I was pretty sure the taste he'd just given me barely scratched the surface of what he was capable of doing.

CHAPTER 10
ELLIOT

I REGAINED MY COMPOSURE BY THE TIME WE WALKED THROUGH THE door, driven back to reality by my desire to beat Bryce. Our impending competition was the only reason I didn't drag him back to his SUV to finish what he'd started. Knowing that *I* would have the satisfaction of being the (metaphorical) one on top by the end of our competition was a great motivator.

Truthfully, it was probably for the best that Bryce put the brakes on when he did. Without the sensation of his lips possessing mine, of his hand sliding to the small of my back, of his hard chest pressed into me, I could think straight again.

Well, straight enough to know the whole 'taking it slow' thing would've gone right out the window if my lady parts had gotten their way.

Over the course of the last year, I'd casually dated a handful of times and had a few hook-ups. But I'd gone into those flings knowing they were all temporary and being totally on board with that. With Bryce, 'temporary' sounded too...brief. Too unmemorable.

With his deep blue-green eyes, his perfect, dark dirty-blondish hair, and that same Bryce charm he'd always possessed, nothing about Bryce belonged under the 'unmemorable' umbrella.

Taking things slow—savoring that getting-to-know-each-other phase—had to stay my priority.

The building was massive, and in addition to the race track, featured oversized love seats in the waiting area, a cafe, and a variety of arcade games. When we walked in, Bryce found the nearest employee and asked if they gave trophies to the winner of each race. Much to his disappointment, the sweet elderly lady at the front desk told us they did, but only for group events. For the rest of us, they only handed out certificates.

Bryce and I scoped out the different games we wanted to play after our race, then sat through a mandatory ten-minute safety and instruction spiel about how to operate the karts and what each flag meant. Afterward, Bryce and I stood in line to get our helmets with the other competitors. I looked up and caught him smiling down at me.

"What?" I asked.

"Just trying to decide what kind of frame I should get for my certificate and where to hang it."

"So cocky, McKnight. I wouldn't go picking out colors or styles just yet, Mr. Hope-you-can-back-it-up," I teased, reminding him of the words he'd said to me after I'd told him I would beat him at Mario Kart. The difference was that I'd actually backed up my claim.

"Oh, I can back it up." He stepped toward me and nudged my shoulder with his, leaning close enough that his breath tickled my cheek. "I always follow through with my promises, El."

My back snapped a little straighter, and I resisted the urge to look at him, knowing my cheeks were probably flushed. Fortunately, I was saved from having to answer because it was our turn to step up and pick our helmets. We grabbed matching ones, along with some kind of weird head-sock, and I said a quick prayer to the hair gods that a) the thing wouldn't give me lice, and b) it wouldn't totally ruin my hair when I took it off later.

The rest of our group selected their helmets as well, and we all made our way over to the track when an announcement came over the speakers telling us to find the karts we'd been assigned. Somehow, I'd ended up in one of the karts at the very front of the pack with Bryce directly behind me.

Bryce set his helmet down and held out his hand for my head-sock. "Here, let me help you with that." I could've managed on my own, but I liked having his hands near me. My nose wrinkled when he slipped the fabric over my head and into place. "What? Afraid it'll mess up your hair?"

"No. Just lamenting the fact that there's no way to make this look remotely sexy."

"Gonna have to disagree with you there, Uno," he countered, easing the helmet on and fluffing my hair over my shoulders. "I can promise you that this look right here is the picture of a hot race car driver fantasy I never knew I had."

Huh. Hot race car driver. Definitely not something I ever imagined myself embodying, but I didn't hate it.

We all settled into our karts as the instructor went through another run-down of the rules. The race was three laps around, and the track was long and narrow, featuring a series of sharp turns with stretches of long and short straightaways separating them. It was only a matter of time before someone went sailing into the red and white-striped barrier walls, despite the instructor's warnings about not bumping other racers into the wall.

I knew I'd be the first if Bryce had his way. On normal first dates, some hesitation would probably exist on both sides about being ruthless in a competition, with each person feeling the other out and not wanting to show up their date.

But this was far from a normal date. We'd resorted back to the days when raced each other on bikes around my grandparents' land or his parents' winery, desperately trying to back up the shit-talking we did to each other on a regular basis. Back then, our competitiveness was real but innocent; we never wagered anything serious. Hearts and feelings were never part of the equation, never put on the line. Now, whether either of us was willing to admit it, that—hearts becoming vulnerable and feelings taking root and growing—was exactly where this was headed if things between us stayed on track.

With the blare of the horn, we were off.

An adrenaline-fueled surge of excitement struck me like lightning as I rounded the first turn. I focused on the next two quick turns and forced myself not to risk a glance to my left, knowing Bryce was probably in the process of overtaking my lead. When I came to a straightaway at about the halfway point, a kart pulled up next to me, and I knew it was Bryce without looking. A grin spread under my helmet until the kart edged forward and he flew by, somehow gunning it around a corner and leaving me in his dust.

Another kart pulled up next to me, and we were neck-and-neck until I maneuvered my way around a sharp turn, preventing it from passing. Dealing with the other kart slowed me down and allowed Bryce to pull even further ahead. I glanced above the barrier walls and saw him closing in on the last straightaway of his first lap.

Taking the last turn without slowing brought me closer to Bryce, but not close enough. He used the second lap to stretch his lead, and by the time he rounded the last corner, he was far enough ahead that he had a shot at breaking the record.

I spent the entire third lap distracted and cursed into my stupid head sock when a kart passed me at the last second, putting me in third place.

I slowed to a stop next to Bryce's kart and focused all my efforts on being indignant about his victory. But the second he tugged the head sock off, my lips parted and a breath caught in my throat. Nobody should be able to pull off a helmet and head sock and somehow maintain such a level of sexiness. Instead of having wild, windblown zombie hair like the rest of us, Bryce had an early morning bedhead look, and it was the epitome of sexy. Only the hair on each side of his head had moved, and thanks to static electricity, it extended in all directions, but somehow only highlighted his hotness.

Bryce looked up at the leaderboard, and when he realized he'd surpassed the previous record, a victory smile spread across his face, making him all the more appealing. He swiveled his hips in a hilarious, yet adorable, victory dance.

"Well, well, well. Looks like I was right to start thinking about frames after all," he said. "But I guess you've already had a whole lap to realize that." His rich, smooth tone dripped with a playful arrogance only he could pull off. That, combined with his victorious smirk, nearly made me drop my helmet so I could fan myself.

"I can't decide which quality is more attractive right now— your undying humility or your terrible dance moves," I retorted, peeling the head sock off and attempting to smooth out my hair.

Bryce laughed and set our helmets on a table. "You forgot my charming personality and dashing good looks."

"It's definitely not your humility."

"Knew it was the good looks."

"I didn't say they were attractive to *me*."

Bryce's mouth gaped, but only for a second before he snapped it shut and rubbed his hand along his jawline. "Ouch. You wound me," he jested, grabbing at his heart.

My eyes rolled of their own accord, but I caught my smile before it could twist my lips. "Oh, whatever." I patted the top of his head. "Your ego's up here, and we both know that's the only part of you that's wounded." I tilted my head toward a group of elderly ladies sitting at a table across from us, all of them eyeing Bryce with appreciation. "But I bet your fan club over there would be willing to build your ego back up."

Bryce followed the tilt of my head, and the women giggled and waved. I couldn't blame them for staring; now *he* was the one who brought the whole 'sexy race car driver fantasy' vibe to life.

"Nah, I'm good. Nothing like a shot to the pride to keep a guy grounded. Plus, something tells me you're bluffing."

I crossed my arms. "Why's that?"

Bryce leaned across the table, bracing himself at an angle

that showcased his toned forearms. I tried not to stare, even though he was close enough that I could easily reach out and run my fingers along the ridged veins. *When did forearms become sexy?*

His five o'clock shadow gently tickled my cheek as he whispered, "Let's see...it's either because of the ten different ways you eye-fucked me just now when I pulled off my helmet or the sounds you were giving me back in the parking lot. Take your pick."

I couldn't exactly deny either of those allegations, but I realized I wanted to give Bryce a taste of his own medicine. Turn the tables on him. After all, Milo was right—I wasn't some timid, self-conscious girl who lacked confidence. At least I wasn't before Bryce came into the picture and made me tongue-tied. I straightened my shoulders, sucked in a breath, and pushed back from the table. "Let's not pretend I was the only one affected by that kiss." I dropped my gaze down his body, letting it linger just long enough for him to notice before looking back up at his face. "But the moment's passed, Caesar. C'mon, let's go play Skee-ball. Losing to you doesn't sit well with me."

He grinned. "Better buckle up, then, Blondie; I have no intention of losing to you."

We spent the next hour trading victories. I beat him at Skee-ball. He dominated me at air hockey. I narrowly won the NASCAR game. He smoked me at the basketball game. When we were tied at two victories apiece, Bryce suggested pool as a tie-breaker. Technically, Bryce was one victory up on me because of the race, so winning pool was my only chance to actually even the score.

I rolled up my metaphorical sleeves, twisted my fingers together, stretched them out with a few satisfying cracks, and got to work.

Bryce was halfway decent, but I was better.

"Oh, did I neglect to mention that Nana and Pops got a pool table for the game room when I was sixteen?" I asked, batting my eyelashes before bending over the table to sink the last ball. "Oops."

Bryce's head dropped down, and he groaned in defeat. "I'd like the record to reflect this was not a clean victory," he said, meeting my gaze with a disbelieving smile.

"Thought you liked it dirty? Thought you said you didn't mind going down?" I asked, biting my lip and stepping closer. "I gotta say...not many things feel better than being on top. Wouldn't you agree?" I tilted my head back and traced my fingers along the scoop of my tank top. He froze, eyes widening in shock. "What's the matter, Bryce? Afraid I'll beat you at your own game?"

I had to admit, this seductive sex-kitten act felt really good. Natural, almost. Which was strange, considering how much my attraction to Bryce had thrown me off initially. But, if there was one way to snap me out of my uncertainty over the way grownup-Bryce made me feel, it was competition. Competing against each other eliminated the potential for awkwardness from being on a first date and reshaped the parameters of our relationship.

Bryce leaned forward, boxing me in, then reached around my body to put his pool stick away. He braced his hands against the wall on either side of me. "Afraid you'll out dirty-talk me? Please. I'd fucking love to see you try, El. But I told you we'd take it slow, and *that* particular competition is a slippery slope into the danger zone. Plus, I think I wanna drag this out and enjoy this side of you a little more." He brushed two fingertips along the same path my hand had just traveled, then leaned back, his blue eyes conveying all the dirty thoughts his mouth left unsaid.

I swallowed hard and blinked slowly. "Drinks! We need drinks. I'll go. Be right back." I ducked out from under him and hightailed it toward the cafe without looking back.

Holy crap. In what world did I think I'd ever be able to talk sexier or dirtier than Bryce? Just hearing the word *fucking* coming out of his mouth had me squeezing my thighs together.

After hurriedly buying two beers, I walked back toward the table, gripping the plastic cups as if the condensation would seep into my skin and cool off more than my hands. Fortunately, between the relaxed smile Bryce wore and the refreshing taste of the summer shandy, we successfully avoided veering into conversations with more than a PG-13 rating.

"Oh!" I exclaimed after Bryce mentioned something about renting a house a few blocks from Sipology, the bar his cousin managed. "I just realized you were going to tell me something yesterday when it started pouring, and then you never got to tell me. Something about your concept of home."

The conflicted expression that fell across his face confirmed I'd been right to bring it up again. He dropped his eyes to study the last of his beer, leaving me to wonder if he would reply, or if he'd try to brush off the topic.

"Bryce..." I started, but quickly trailed off when our eyes met.

His eyes darted away after a heartbeat, then, exhaling slowly, he looked back up at me. But as he opened his mouth to speak, my phone buzzed loudly against the table, lighting up with my sister's name.

"Crap! Sorry," I sputtered, scrambling to silence the device.

"I told you that I didn't call you after I moved back because there are complications in my life." He paused, then added, "That wasn't exactly a lie, but it's definitely not the explanation I should've given you. There's so much more to it. The truth is—"

My phone started vibrating again. *Sophia.* I silenced it again and flipped it over. It wasn't like her to double-call, but she'd have to wait.

I gave Bryce my undivided attention, urging him to continue.

"The truth is, about a year and a half ago I got a call from a hospital in California on behalf of my ex-girlfriend, asking me to please get to Monterey Park as soon as possible. They wouldn't tell me what was going on over the phone, but I assumed something had happened to Bridgette and that she still had me listed as her emergency contact. I caught the first flight I could and got to the hospital later that day. They immediately started asking me all kinds of questions. Did I know she had listed me as her baby's father? Did I know anything about her whereabouts? Did she try to get in touch with me? At the time, I was too stunned to put the pieces together; all I could say was that I hadn't seen or spoken to her since she moved to California six months prior. She'd never told me anything about being pregnant. They told me Bridgette had been thirty weeks along when she gave birth to a baby girl a week before, but had disappeared without a trace sometime during the previous night. None of it made any sense. Until they took me to the NICU and I laid eyes on the baby. *My baby.* She was tiny—just over three pounds. So much of her was hidden behind wires and tubes, but she was the most perfect thing I've ever seen. After I held her and let the magnitude of the situation sink in, they sat me down and explained the risk factors associated with her prematurity.

"It was...terrifying, to be honest. In an instant, without warning, I became a dad. To a baby with a laundry list of potential health complications. The next few months are a bit of a blur—I can probably count on one hand the number of times I left the hospital. Bridgette never came back; she fell completely off the grid. I called her parents, who were also my bosses, and they were as stunned as I was, but were absolute godsends, taking turns flying down until I was able to bring Peyton back to Seattle. Becoming Peyton's dad flipped everything about my life upside down, but I wouldn't trade that title for anything."

He paused, and I wanted to say something...anything...but words escaped me. I could barely process everything he'd just said.

Bryce has a baby.

He's a parent.

"Look, El," he said. "I know this is so far beyond anything you were expecting me to tell you, and I know it probably seems like I should've told you sooner, it's just...you have to understand how protective I am of Peyton. For almost two years, this little girl...," he stopped to pull up a picture on his phone and hand it to me. "She has been my life. My world. My only priority. So this—going out, letting myself have a life—is all a little new to me. Uncharted territory."

I took the phone on autopilot, replaying his words inside my head. An endless sea of questions flooded my mind with each piece of information he gave me. But as soon as I laid eyes on the tiny figure smiling at me through the phone's screen, my heart filled with an indescribable warmth that silenced all the questions.

I felt my lips pull into a smile.

"She's beautiful." I couldn't tell how old she was in the photo—maybe six months—but she was his spitting image with big blue-ish eyes and dark lashes and a smile that matched her dad's.

In that moment, I understood.

Why he moved back.

Why he jumped on board with taking things slowly.

Why he seemed to carry the weight of the world at times.

But what I didn't understand was his reluctance to tell me about her. It was the one question that refused to be silenced. And, ultimately, it was the one question I didn't want to ask, but needed answered.

"Bryce," I said, though it came out as a hoarse whisper. "She's so precious. Amazing. Perfect. I don't...I don't know what to say. This is just..."

"A lot, I know," he supplied for me with a nod. "I get it."

I was relieved. He seemed to understand my need for a few minutes to digest everything. I had no idea how long I stared at Bryce's phone—at Peyton—before I looked up at him again.

"You have a baby. You're a dad," I stated dumbly, feeling my eyes widen as the words left my mouth.

Bryce nodded slowly, keeping his gaze on me to gauge my reaction.

Despite my efforts to care for Sophia when we were still with Helen, I'd never been a 'baby person.' I didn't play with baby dolls as a kid. Never really felt any maternal instincts.

But seeing Peyton's picture...*I don't know.*

Maybe it was because I'd once considered her dad to be my best friend.

Maybe it was knowing that she'd been abandoned by her mom, like I had been.

Maybe it was knowing that Bryce must've felt so incredibly overwhelmed.

Maybe it was knowing that, despite everything I went through as a child, Peyton had already overcome so much more.

Something about this little girl in the photo made me want to protect her from the world.

It was a foreign feeling, and I had no idea what to make of it.

"Where...who's with her right now?"

"She's in Washington with her grandparents. When I moved us here, I promised them Peyton would come back for visits. It's the least I can do after everything they've done for me, for us."

I nodded, still struggling to wrap my head around everything. I picked up my drink and gulped the rest of it down, hoping it would calm my racing thoughts.

It didn't.

I can't believe he kept this from me.

"Bryce," I finally said, fingers absently picking at the frayed hem of my shorts. "I get that she's your priority, and she should be. One-hundred percent. And I get that you're protective of her. I do. But I don't get why you waited until now to tell me. It's not like I'm some random stranger you just met and asked out. You've had multiple opportunities to tell me before tonight."

He shook his head slowly and sighed, as if he'd anticipated this kind of reaction. "That's not fair. I did try. But then I got interrupted by Mother Nature."

"That's my point, Bryce!" I exclaimed, trying and failing to temper my frustration with the situation. "You tried *yesterday.* What about the other times you saw me before that? You had every opportunity to tell me!"

"What exactly should I have said? 'Hey, it's so great to see you again, El. By the way, I have a child.'"

The sarcasm in his voice pushed my frustration to new heights. "Yes! No. I don't know. I just…this is a lot. It's a big deal, Bryce." I shifted in my seat, my eyes bouncing around the room in an effort to avoid Bryce's gaze.

By the time I forced my attention back to the man across from me, his clenched jaw and crossed arms told me I wasn't the only one exasperated with this conversation. "This, Elliot." He uncrossed his arms to gesture the space between us. "*This* is why I didn't tell you sooner. Because I knew you would use her as an excuse to put some distance between us. To put the brakes on before anything even happened."

"What? No. That's…not true," I argued, but the words sounded hollow even to my own ears.

"No?" he asked, brows raised in disbelief. "Can you honestly say you'd be here right now if I had told you about Peyton earlier? That you'd let yourself see me as anything but a friend?"

"You don't get it, Bryce. I'm not…" I shook my head, swallowing the rest of my sentence.

He reached across the table and pulled my hands into his. "I *do* get it, El." Squeeze. I met his eyes and found nothing but sincerity in his gaze. "Look, I told you we'd take things slow. That hasn't changed. Day by day, yeah?"

I nodded, but before I could verbalize a response, my phone vibrated again. Through the entire conversation my phone had vibrated with incoming calls several more times, but each time I'd muted it to focus solely on Bryce. It was probably the seventh time Sophia or Milo had called, so I knew something was up.

"Something's not right. I need to take this," I said, pushing up from my seat. I didn't wait for Bryce's response before walking away and swiping to answer Milo's call. "Hey. What's up?"

"I know you're on a date, and I'm sorry to do this, but you need to get home. Soph is freaking out. I think…El, I think she found your mom."

The second Milo's words registered, my heart rate skyrocketed and my brain conjured the last memory I had of living with Helen.

"Shh, Sophia. You have to keep quiet," I whispered, patting my sister's back while she cried. "Or Mommy will get mad."

She cried harder.

I heard laughing from Mommy's room, so I didn't think they were asleep, but Mommy always got real mad when we made noise while she had friends over.

"Elliot! Shut her up," Mommy yelled from her room.

I felt around in the dark, trying to find Sophia's pacifier, but it must have fallen off the couch. I needed to find it before Mommy or her friend got up. We'd be in big trouble. I got up and looked around on the floor, but I wasn't fast enough.

Mommy's door opened, and I jumped up, turning to face her. Light from her room made it easy to see the pacifier right by her door.

"I'm sorry, Mommy! I couldn't find—"

"You can't even do one thing right! I should've known you'd be nothing but a screw-up." She grabbed the pacifier off the floor and shoved it into Sophia's mouth.

I froze, too scared to ask what that meant.

She looked at me and laughed. "That means you'll grow up and be just like me one day."

"Elliot? Did you hear me?" Milo's voice snapped me out of the memory and brought me back to the present.

"I'm on my way."

CHAPTER 11
BRYCE

They say sometimes dads who are expecting a baby don't feel like parents until their child is born. In my case, I'll never know if that would've held true or if I would've immediately felt connected to my baby when she was barely the size of a pea. In spite of the shock, the confusion, the thousands of questions I had about it all, the second I held Peyton in my arms I knew my life would never be the same. I knew I'd never find another love as pure as what I felt for her.

I was in no position to become a parent—after things ended with Bridgette, I reverted back to the workaholic I'd been before letting her disrupt my life. And I was fine with that. I dated casually, but was in the process of climbing the proverbial ladder at work, and I made that my priority. I lived in a one-bedroom high-rise condo, and loved being centrally-located. My co-workers were my only friends, and even those relationships were mostly superficial. Nothing about my life screamed, "I'm ready to be a dad!"

But, in a way, maybe that's for the best.

I didn't have time to panic or question my abilities like most expectant parents. I didn't have time to debate which brand of formula or diapers to use. I didn't have time to think about the ways I was sure to royally screw up this whole parenting thing.

I just had *her*.

And she had me.

She'll always have me.

I don't know what I expected would happen when I told Elliot about Peyton, but I certainly hadn't anticipated the way it would send our night spiraling into the gutter. After Elliot got off the phone, she looked a little sick and said something was going on with Sophia and she needed to go home immediately. When she didn't offer any further explanation, I decided not to press the issue. Our car ride back to her apartment was quiet and awkward; basically the opposite of what our car ride had been only hours before.

The real irony of the situation was, while Elliot was upset I hadn't told her about Peyton over the last couple of weeks, *I* was kicking myself for not calling Elliot over the last year.

Then again, as a single parent to an infant with health issues, socializing wasn't even on my radar.

I told Elliot the first couple months of Peyton's life were a blur, but it was probably more like the first year. Between the sleepless nights and countless doctor visits, I was in survival mode as a parent back then. When I wasn't desperately trying to get her to fall asleep or stop crying, I was worrying and doing my own research about colic and infant ear infections and retinopathy of prematurity.

I was a mess. *How could I have expected Elliot to understand any of that?*

There was a time that confiding in and trusting Elliot was the easiest thing in the world. In a lot of ways, it still was.

But trusting her was one thing.

Divulging everything about Peyton and the reality that came with being a parent was entirely different.

There were so many layers of complications between the two

of us that the risk-to-reward ratio of a potential relationship was staggering. Her life was hectic, and I knew that wasn't changing any time soon. Plus, she had baggage. I'd never call my daughter baggage, but El was right when she said Peyton was my priority —that would never change.

But when it came to Uno...all bets were off.

"DON'T you have Wi-Fi at your house?" Xander asked, forgoing a formal greeting as I walked into Sipology.

"Yeah, but it sucks and freezes every time I try to FaceTime. And I'm out of beer."

Xander nodded and slid a pint glass across the bar toward me. As much as he gave me grief for siphoning Wi-Fi and free beer from him, I knew he didn't really care. Especially when it gave him the chance to see Peyton.

"This is the only one I'm having though; I'm heading out to the Kincaid property in a while," I told him before picking the glass up and walking toward his office.

"Okay. I'll be back there in a bit to see my girl," he called.

A few minutes later, my toddler's smiling face greeted me through the computer screen. I smiled back and studied her features. She was born with a little mop of dark hair, but eventually it lightened into a bronzish-brown. I used to wonder what color her eyes would be, and I found myself thankful that they'd turned green instead of darkening into brown like her mom's. Only time would tell what all she'd inherit from Bridgette, but so far I saw a lot of myself in her. What I'd tell her when the day finally arrived that she asked about her mom...I had no idea. *Especially considering that I can hardly stand to utter Bridgette's name out loud.*

"Hi, baby," I cooed, waving at the screen like a lunatic. "How's it going? Are you having the best time with Lulu and Papa?"

Bridgette's parents—David and Louise—had chosen their own

grandparent names, insisting that 'grandma' and 'grandpa' sounded far too old and outdated for them.

Louise was a lifesaver, flying to Texas every other month to see Peyton. When I made the decision to move back home, I knew I owed it to David and Louise to allow them to continue being a huge part of Peyton's life. Which was why we'd agreed that she would spend a few weeks with them every summer. While I knew it was good for her to be away from me, it still killed me every day to think about how much she was growing and changing without me.

Peyton waved and babbled a handful of the mostly-gibberish phrases she knew, throwing in a 'Dada' every now and then.

Louise moved the computer so they'd all three fit in the screen before shifting Peyton to her other leg and giving me a reassuring smile. "Can you tell Daddy what we did today? What we saw?" Louise asked, leaning down to whisper in her ear.

"Duck!" Peyton squealed, clapping her hands together.

"You saw ducks? Lulu is spoiling you with all the adventures you're going on," I said, mostly teasing. I was seriously going to have to step up my parenting game when Peyton returned; the flexible work schedule David and I had worked out was designed so I could spend time having fun with her. I'd just been so occupied with The Rose House that I'd been accepting my mom's offers to keep her more and more.

Again, I knew it wasn't healthy for Peyton to rely on being with me 24/7, but I also knew I'd probably turn around and she'd be a teenager. I wanted to freeze time and keep her little for as long as I could.

Finding the perfect balance as a parent was fucking impossible sometimes. *Most times.*

Louise, David, and I continued talking about what they'd been up to over the last couple days, and I felt my worries melt away. I even let go of my questions about the colossal disaster my date with Elliot had turned into.

Xander barged into his office and wasted no time hijacking the computer from me a few minutes later. "Sweet P! How's my favorite girl doing?"

After meeting Peyton last year, Xander had immediately taken to her, despite the fact that he always swore up and down he'd never have kids. I pointed this out to him, and he insisted that it was different because he just got to be the fun uncle instead of the parent. He said it allowed him to spoil the hell out of her, then give her back to me when it came time to be an actual parent.

God help me when he actually keeps her by himself.

Peyton's smile when she saw my cousin was genuine; she was the one female Xander had ever had to work to impress, but once he did, it was game over. Peyton was totally infatuated with her Uncle Xander.

Louise coached her to give Xander the same information she gave me, so they went through the routine of talking about the ducks. Apparently, Peyton had ended up running around and scaring them off. Eventually, Xander blew her a kiss and left, mumbling curses about inventory and late shipments.

I checked my watch and sighed, realizing I'd be late if I didn't leave soon. I looked back at the screen, allowing myself a couple more seconds of Peyton time. David was pretending to pop off her toes and eat them, and she was squealing and trying to cover her toes for protection. He continued to eat 'po-Pey-*toes*' off of an invisible plate, much to Peyton's amusement. After a second, she shifted her attention back to me, and I felt the familiar one-two punch of gratitude that she was so happy, and guilt for being away from her.

"Did Papa eat all your toes?" I asked, feigning surprise. She shook her head, and a broad smile lit up her face, causing her eyes to squint into tiny slits. She was the picture of blissful happiness, and I almost drove to the airport then and there.

"Okay, baby girl, Daddy has to go," I said, knowing not to drag this part out.

By now, we'd come up with a strategy for saying goodbye

without the waterworks—distraction. "Oh! Peyton, I think it's time to feed Moe!" Louise exclaimed.

Moe was their seventy-pound pig. They'd given Peyton a stuffed pig right after I brought her home to Seattle, and she'd practically been attached to it ever since. Seeing their real pig for the first time cemented her swine obsession.

"Tell Daddy goodbye," Louise prompted, waving at me.

Peyton waved and offered me a sweet, "Buh-bye, Dada!"

I blew her a kiss and promised to call her tomorrow.

Fuck, I miss her.

After I hung up, I gave myself a minute to quiet the part of my brain that questioned if I could handle being away from her for much longer.

She'll be fine. I'll be fine. This will be good for us.

It was impossible to keep my mind from drifting back to Elliot as I drove out to the Kincaid property. My head was all over the place when it came to the situation with her. I knew she felt like I'd pulled the rug out from under her, but I refused to regret the timing of telling her about Peyton.

The panic and self-doubt in her eyes told me everything her words failed to convey. She didn't think she was worthy of any kind of parental role, whether temporary or permanent.

Fortunately, I knew better than to believe that for a second.

The fact that ghosts from El's past still haunted her killed me. It also made me desperate for answers about what happened with Helen five years ago.

The similarities between Elliot's mother and my daughter's mother weren't lost on me. Both were selfish and flighty at best, and self-destructive at worst. Both had absolutely no right to call themselves a parent. In my eyes, the day a parent walked out on a child, that's it. There's no coming back from that.

In the event that Bridgette wanted to see Peyton one day, I knew I'd move heaven and earth to shield my little girl from any pain that would cause. I'd do what I thought was best for her, whatever that turned out to be.

Just like I had when Elliot confided in me about Helen.

"BRYCE? What can we do for you?" George asked, taking a seat at the conference table across from me.

For the hundredth time, the nervous tapping of my foot made me question my decision to come today. Last night, after walking Elliot home, sleep eluded me. El's pain became my own; her tortured expression when she spoke of her mom haunted me, and I knew I had to do *something*. Even if it meant Elliot would hate me for it.

I swallowed the lump forming in my throat. "There's something I need to tell you both, and I don't think you're going to like it."

"What is it, honey?" Millie asked, concern lacing her tone.

I took one more breath and told them everything El had told me about the voicemail from Helen. "I told her to talk to you guys, that you should all go together, but she seemed to think y'all wouldn't want her to go through with it."

I studied their expressions and felt another sliver of doubt creep in. George's jaw was clenched tight, his eyes hard and brows pulled tight. I wasn't sure it was possible for a person's entire face to frown, but that's exactly what Millie's face was doing. I couldn't put my finger on what it all meant, but something told me this was not their first time dealing with their daughter in recent years.

Millie reached out and gripped George's hand in hers, directing her gaze to him with concern etched on her face.

Their silence spoke volumes.

"What aren't you guys telling me?" I asked.

"Helen has tried this sort of thing before," Millie explained.

Her hesitation gave my confusion roots. *What? How? When?* "Though this is the first time we know of that she's contacted one of the girls directly. Every few years when the girls were younger, Helen would show up here, at the office, begging us to let her see them. But each time, she was high or drunk, always making a huge scene. Last time she even said she would go to rehab if we let her see Elliot and Sophia. But then she stole George's wallet and disappeared. So, you can understand why we wouldn't be eager for the girls to see her."

Jesus. Shit. Fuck. That's a lot.

"I..." I shook my head, still trying to process it all. "I had no idea. And you never told Elliot or Sophia about seeing her?"

"No. Absolutely not," George boomed.

Millie patted his arm. "Bryce, it's not that we wanted to keep her from them. If she had been sober, things would be different. We know the girls have questions about her, but we've done what we thought was best for them."

"What if she's sober now?"

"She's not," George asserted immediately. "She's a junkie, a liar, and a thief, and those habits don't just disappear because you say you've changed." He turned to his wife and shook his head. "We've got to do something about this, Millie."

"With all due respect," I said, "you don't know she's not sober. Elliot is nineteen; she deserves answers, and this decision is hers to make. I came here so you could have the chance to go with her, to support her. Not so you could stop her."

"You're right, Bryce," Millie said. "She does deserve answers. We just want what's best for her. And for Sophia. Thank you for coming. We know this was probably difficult for you."

Difficult? Try fucking gut-wrenching.

Whether she decided to tell them on her own or George and Millie brought the subject up themselves, the second she realized her grandparents knew about the voicemail, she'd know I betrayed her trust.

In my mind, I was looking out for her, trying to help.

In my gut, I knew El wouldn't see it that way.

Between the way things ended last night and now going behind her back, I knew there was a chance I could lose her friendship permanently, regardless of the outcome with Helen.

"So you'll talk to El? Go with her?" I asked, locking eyes with Millie. Her expression looked conflicted, and I tried not to read into it too much. Desperate was not a feeling I experienced often, but that's exactly what I was—desperate to know my betrayal wasn't in vain.

George pushed back from the table to stand, and I took his cue and stood too. He stuck his hand out and met my eyes. "You've always been a good friend to our Elliebelly, Bryce. Thank you. We'll take care of it."

SWALLOWING the disappointment I felt when Elliot was nowhere in sight, I grabbed my laptop bag and stepped out of my car, heading toward the inn's porch.

"Bryce! So nice to see you, honey," Millie gushed, pulling me into a hug like she hadn't seen me in ages.

"You too, Millie. How was Vegas?"

"Let's just say I won't be giving those damn casinos any more money in this lifetime," George grumbled at the same time that Millie laughed.

I nodded along, but wasn't sure what to say, so I darted my eyes out to the driveway. "So are El and Sophia coming later, or…?"

Millie shook her head. "El texted earlier and said something came up with work, and Sophia had a paper to write. Kinda strange if you ask me; on Saturday they were both adamant about us all coming today. I thought Elliot was coming around to the idea of reopening the inn."

"No problem. We can just do a walk-through and I'll describe what the girls and I already discussed, then I'll show you guys the plans I've come up with."

They nodded, and we all made our way through the front door.

Half an hour later, we braved the sweltering, late-summer heat and sat in back of the inn with a pitcher of Millie's spiked lemonade. I showed them my designs, noting changes to make based on their comments.

Naturally, my mind drifted to Elliot. To the night she confided in me about her mother.

"Can I ask you guys something?" I asked abruptly.

"Of course, dear," Millie replied.

"It's about Helen."

George grumbled something under his breath before downing a healthy portion of his remaining lemonade. Millie reached over and placed her palm on his other arm, rubbing up and down in a soothing gesture.

I swallowed, searching for the right words to carefully navigate this minefield. "What happened five years ago? After I told you about that voicemail."

Until hearing El's comments, I had assumed she simply chose not to meet Helen. But something in her voice, in the pain and hurt that bled through her words when she spoke, told me otherwise.

Their silence amplified my doubt and replayed the events of that day on a hyper-speed loop in my mind.

"We took care of it, Bryce. That's all there is to it," George bit out.

The tic in his jaw warned me to proceed with caution. For a man on the cusp of his seventies, George Kincaid was still intimidating. The days of craning my neck to meet his eye were long gone, but that didn't make him any less physically imposing.

"George," Millie warned, giving him a stern look.

"What happened?" I repeated, refusing to pussyfoot around the topic.

"Soon after you left our office, Helen showed up. She begged us to hear her out, so we did. She swore she was sober, that she'd turned her life around. Even said she was married. We weren't... we didn't know what to believe."

I forced my jaw to unclench and took a breath. "What did you do?"

George's shoulders slumped, like this conversation was finally taking a toll on him. "Look, we're not proud of it, but you've got to remember that Helen had a horrible track record when it came to her attempts to see the girls. So, we put her intentions to the test. We wrote her a check for twenty grand, post-dated for a month later, and told her she could either go through with meeting Elliot or take the money and never come back."

"She never deposited the check, but she never came back either, and Elliot never mentioned anything about Helen contacting her to us. Her vanishing act was a pretty clear answer."

My mouth fell open. *No wonder Elliot hasn't mentioned anything about it. She has no idea what really happened.*

Still, I had to be sure. "Does El know?" I asked, praying the whispers and warnings in my head were wrong.

George shook his head. "We decided to keep the girls in the dark about our exchange with their mother. Why stir up unnecessary trouble?"

"Unnecessary trouble?" I repeated incredulously, turning to pace the yard as pieces fell into place in my mind. "I know it was an impossible situation, but she deserved to know. Keeping something like this from her feels...wrong. She still has questions, and I don't blame her. Do you realize the position this puts me in?"

"Do *you* realize Elliot suffered from nightmares into her teens?" George asked, his voice bordering between apologetic and frustrated. "You've seen the broad strokes of Elliot's scars from that time in her life. We saw the lasting damage it caused."

Those broad strokes I had seen growing up were enough for

me to have reservations about her meeting Helen, but everyone deserved closure, and that's exactly what Elliot wanted back then.

What she probably still wanted.

She'll hate me for taking that chance away from her.

I stood by my decision to tell them, but that didn't stop the tiny fissures of regret from slowly cracking my resolve.

CHAPTER 12
ELLIOT

Bright lights, followed by a loud thud, pulled me out of blissful slumber. Well, semi-blissful, considering it felt like I'd only just drifted off to sleep minutes ago. That was my new normal, though. With everything going on in my life right now, my brain refused to shut off for something as trivial as sleep.

By the time I got home Saturday night, Sophia had locked herself in her room and refused to come out, which was just as well; I still wasn't ready to talk to her about Helen three days later.

"El, what the hell?" Jasmine groaned, rubbing her knee after untangling her feet from the box she'd tripped over.

I lifted a hand to shield my eyes from the overhead lights of the conference room. I'd fallen asleep at the table while doing research and making a PowerPoint to present my idea for the inn to Jas and Jade.

"Crap. Sorry, Jas. Guess I made a bit of a mess. I'll get it cleaned up." I finger-combed my hair and rolled my neck back and forth, trying to expel the aching stiffness.

She frowned, taking in my appearance and the scattered papers that littered the table and floor around me. "It's fine. I'm not worried about the mess. Though we should definitely fix this before Jade comes in and her little neat-freak heart stops beating. I meant 'what the hell', as in, what is all of this?"

"I, uh, well...there's something I wanted to talk to you and Jade about."

Jas lifted her brows into matching arches. "Must be serious if you were willing to sacrifice sleep for it. Everything okay? You seem...out of sorts."

I bit my lip and considered her question.

I want to take on a potentially insane professional venture on top of the record-setting wedding season we're wrapping up. My personal life is full of more unknowns than a freaking crime show. And now I have the neck stiffness of an eighty-year-old because I fell asleep in the most awkward position possible. So...yeah, everything's just peachy.

"El?" she prompted, flipping a lock of my golden hair over my shoulder.

"Short answer? Everything's fine. Mostly. The long answer will have to wait until we can all go out for drinks." I sighed, realizing that answer probably stoked the flames of her curiosity. "Look, I promise I'll explain later, but for now can we just clean this up before Jade murders me? I think she's got a client coming in at nine. And I need to run home to shower before my first appointment."

Jas acquiesced, but only after I agreed to a girls' night tonight.

I WAS the last to arrive at Rae of Light, our usual after-work-bar that boasted a gorgeous view of Austin in the back garden area, as well as an array of great drinks at affordable happy hour prices.

Carleigh already had plans for the night, so it was just the three of us.

Jade smiled and slid a nearly-overflowing margarita glass toward me as soon as I sat down. "Mango, just for you."

"Mango margaritas *and* fried pickles? You guys must really be worried about me," I replied before taking a sip and reaching for a pickle slice.

"Not worried. More like...moderately concerned," Jade corrected.

"Those are synonyms, Jade."

"Semantics aside," Jasmine interjected. "What's going on, El? Start with whatever it was you were working on last night, then we'll get to the Bryce thing."

I choked on my drink, startled by her leap. "What Bryce thing?"

She rolled her eyes. "Please. We might both be blonde, but let's not pretend either of us is dumb, El. He's hot and obviously into you, and you've got history, so there's definitely a 'Bryce thing' to discuss."

"You and Dean had history, yet you spent years ignoring the other's existence," I deflected.

Jade's brows rose, and she buried her smile behind her water glass.

"Yeah, and look how that turned out," Jas countered, lifting her left hand and wiggling her ring finger at me. Her engagement ring and wedding band dazzled brilliantly, thanks to the low-hanging light above us. "Now we spend every night making up for lost time. Seriously. As a joke, I asked him how much sex he thinks we missed out on during those six years, and he totally flipped out when he did the math. He thinks it's only right that we try to make up for lost sex."

"Whew! I was starting to worry my brother's sex life *wouldn't* come up in conversation tonight," Jade mocked.

Jas leaned toward her BFF-slash-sister-in-law and bumped her shoulder. "That was tame, JP, and you know it. It's not like I went into detail about our *fuck-et* list..."

Jade turned to me. "El, change the subject, please, before I'm forced to pull a Van Gogh and cut my ear off with this butter knife."

"Actually, fun fact—he used a razor, not a knife," I rattled off.

"Can you imagine—"

"Cute attempt to stall, Kincaid," Jasmine inserted. "But we're not looking for an art history lesson. Now, what was it you needed to talk to us about?"

I took a deep breath and forced myself to stop fidgeting with my margarita glass. *Here goes nothing.* "Y'all know how much I love FMK and couldn't imagine not working with you guys." They both nodded in agreement. "Well...I haven't worked out every detail yet, but I want to add a wedding venue to the inn's property. There's a spot that would be perfect for ceremonies, and I've got a couple of ideas for reception options. With the inn itself being on-site, it's the total package. I really think it has the potential to be a massive success. And obviously it would be FMK-exclusive. I know this is a lot to consider, and I'm just kind of throwing it at you guys out of the blue, but what do y'all think?"

Jade was the first to snap out of her shock as a broad smile lit up her entire face. "I can't speak for Jas, but I love it. Seriously, El. I was a little worried when you told us about George and Millie's offer because I knew there was a chance we'd lose you, but I would've supported you in any decision. This is like you getting to have your cake and us eating it too."

Jasmine nodded enthusiastically. "Jade *can* speak for me because I couldn't have said it any better myself. Holy shit," she squealed, scooting around in the booth to my side and pulling me into a hug. I laughed at the unexpected gesture, but returned her embrace with equal fervor. "I'm so fucking proud of you, Elliot. I never doubted your abilities, but you've stepped up in a big way over the last year, and you've amazed me at every turn. I love everything about this idea, especially the fact that we'd get to keep you."

More often than not, Jas joked her way out of serious conversations. Or, at least the old Jasmine did. The old Jasmine was uncomfortable with deep conversations of any kind—letting her guard down came only on the rarest of occasions. But the new Jas was practically an emotional open book.

"Really?" I asked, looking between my bosses-turned-friends and fighting the wave of excitement surging through my limbs.

"No, we got all emotional and sincere just to screw with you."

Jade rolled her eyes and slapped Jasmine's arm. "You would ruin the moment with sarcasm." She turned to me, ignoring Jasmine's attempt at feigning offense. "Yes, we're interested, El. Okay, I'm going to get y'all refills, and we're going to talk details."

We spent the next hour drinking celebratory margaritas and brainstorming ideas, and I'd never been more excited to talk shop outside of working hours. The real progress and plans would come eventually, but for now, I was perfectly content to spend the evening laughing and jotting down notes on cocktail napkins.

It wasn't until we were in the parking lot that Jasmine realized I'd successfully avoided discussing Bryce—which wasn't exactly easy, considering how many times his name almost slipped past my lips when we talked about designs for a reception hall.

When it came to Bryce, my feelings were a jumbled mess. It still stung that he hadn't told me about Peyton sooner, but a part of me understood why he didn't. I had no idea where we stood. After talking to Milo, my only concern had been getting to Sophia. But now I worried Bryce probably thought I'd run from our date—from him—because of everything that happened between us.

Honestly, after getting that phone call, the truth bomb Bryce dropped on me slipped down the priority ladder in my mind. It wasn't that I didn't care; more like my brain's way of coping with all the chaos was to choose one facet to focus on.

The anxiety caused by whatever was or wasn't happening with Helen was paralyzing and left no room in my mind for anything else.

Now that the dust had settled, I could think clearly enough to make a few realizations about things with Bryce.

One—Bryce having a daughter definitely added another layer of complication to the situation.

Two—Bryce having a daughter definitely *didn't* change the fact that, until it came to a screeching halt, I'd had more fun with him than I'd ever had on a first date. Or any date, really.

Three—no matter which road we took, I owed Bryce an apology for ruining our night.

Jade honked and waved on her way out of the parking lot, pulling me out of my thoughts. We waved back, and I was about to turn toward my car when Jas cleared her throat, her golden brown eyes softening with sincerity.

"Did something happen with Bryce? Or was it something non-Bryce related? You were mumbling in your sleep this morning about…Helen. Something about being like her…"

My silence all but confirmed her suspicion that it was the latter.

The corners of her mouth pulled down, sympathy painting her features. "We're here for you, y'know. Take it from me, El—the deeper you bury whatever it is you're keeping inside, the more control you give up. Taking back control comes from within, but it helps when you let friends in. We've got shovels, too."

The underlying promise in her words almost made me open up on the spot. "Thanks, Jas. I'll keep that in mind."

"The offer has no expiration date, El. Whenever you're ready." She gave my hand one more quick squeeze before strolling toward her Mustang.

Jasmine's shovel comment sent my mind tumbling back to Bryce, and I tried to nail down exactly what I was feeling about us. Before I could summon the nerve to text him, my phone lit up with a text from Sophia.

SOPHIA: Can we talk about the Helen elephant (Helephant?) in the apartment? I'll grab the wine on my way home.

ELLIOT: Perfect. There' something else I want to talk about too…I've got an idea for the inn.

Sophia replied with a thumbs up and two wine glass emojis.

~

"JUST LIKE THAT? YOU'RE SURE?" I asked, staring at my sister while she calmly sipped her wine like I hadn't just asked her to take a Grand-Canyon-sized leap of faith.

For some reason, I hadn't actually expected her to immediately jump on board, much less express interest in running the inn or venue with me.

Her milk-chocolate-colored eyes met mine as she nodded. "Just like that. El, I trust you with my life. Of course I trust your judgment about the inn and its potential. You've done your research so far, and I know you'll do your due diligence to figure out the rest." She set her wine glass down on the coffee table and scooted closer to me on the couch, sighing. "I'll admit that, as much as I'd love to see the inn renovated and brought back to life, I've never actually imagined myself being the one to run it. But, El, if this is your dream, I'm happy to jump on board with you. I've loved working for the Millers, but being a nanny was always going to be short-term. I just haven't figured out what comes next."

"Soph, you're twenty-one. Plenty of college grads don't stroll off the stage with a perfect plan for anything beyond getting wasted that night."

"You did."

"I was lucky. Don't get me wrong, doing this with you would be a dream, but I also don't want you to feel obligated to say yes. Promise me you'll let me know the second you get the urge to spread your wings if you decide it's not what you want."

She shrugged. "I don't really know what I want. But I do know that I want this for you."

I smiled and squeezed her hand. "So...about the Helephant..."

"I want to meet her."

"Soph..." I trailed off, needing to organize my thoughts before replying. I pushed off the couch and stood to pace the living room. "I don't know if that's a good idea. How do you even know the woman you found is really her?"

Sophia grabbed her phone and pulled up a picture before turning it toward me. "This is how."

My eyes fell to the photo on her screen, and I nearly dropped my wine glass when I got closer.

In the photo was a smiling woman with dark, shoulder-length hair, milk chocolate eyes, a button nose, high cheekbones, and a tiny scar by her left temple. *I remember the day Helen got that scar.*

I forced myself to study the picture again, but another scan didn't change the fact that, though I shared her facial structure and shape, she looked exactly how I imagined Sophia would look fifteen or twenty years from now.

"Wow."

"Yeah," she agreed. "Crazy, right? I don't know how meeting her would work, but El, I have to see this through. And I know you said you wanted nothing to do with her, but I don't want this to be something you regret one day. Just promise me you'll think about it."

She had a point.

But I'd already been burned by Helen too many times.

"Deal. As long as you promise me you won't get your hopes up. Take things one step at a time with her. Sharing DNA with someone doesn't make them family. Nor does it merit placing blind faith in them. Trust is earned, not given, Soph. Please don't lose sight of that."

"I know, El. I know we don't know anything about her, but I can't stop thinking this is our chance to get answers. The other night, I was just overwhelmed and freaked out a little. But I can do this. I *need* to do this."

I sighed, knowing by the resolution in her voice that nothing I said would change her mind.

"Then we'll do it together."

I've been through this before. I can do it again.

Only, this time…it'll be on my terms.

CHAPTER 13
ELLIOT

I'd always been a firm believer in the philosophy that if you want someone in your life, you'll make time for them. Period. No matter what.

And I wanted Bryce in my life.

As a friend, if nothing else.

I shoved aside the concern and reservations I felt about mixing business with pleasure and vowed to fix things with him to get us back on the right track, whatever that might be.

Without giving myself the chance to chicken out, I shot him a quick text between meetings.

ELLIOT: Hey. I feel terrible about the other night. Can we talk? Tonight?

BRYCE: I'd like that. Dinner at my place?

ELLIOT: Perfect. I'll cook. Maybe you'll get lucky and I'll even bring a salad. ;)

BRYCE: It's not nice to tease a guy about getting lucky, El.

*ELLIOT: OMG! So not what I meant, you gutter-minded perv. *Face-palm**

BRYCE: Freudian slip, I'm sure. ;)

BRYCE: And just so you know, I always get lucky.

BRYCE: I mean, "I'm always lucky."

ELLIOT: Ugh. I rescind my salad offer. No more luck for you.

BRYCE: We'll see about that.

I loved that things came so naturally with him. That a few teasing words could convey so much.

I couldn't wipe the smile off my face the rest of the morning, and I felt it creep back into place by the time I bolted out of the office for the day.

With an extra pep in my step, I quickly ran into a grocery store to pick up the ingredients for my chicken parmigiana recipe. Other than getting Bryce's address and confirming he had eggs, flour, olive oil, and ground pepper, we hadn't texted since this morning, and I couldn't deny how excited I was to see him. I was committed to leaving work and other distractions behind and just spending time with Bryce. I owed him—*and myself*—that much.

Without even checking the address, I knew Bryce's house as soon as I turned down his street and saw the bright yellow door and a black Range Rover in the driveway. The front was cute, with gray siding and a garden in front of the small porch. A blue plastic swing hung from the yard's only tree, and I smiled at how simple, yet homey, it all felt.

Throwing my purse over one shoulder, I hooked a reusable freezer bag over each arm and walked up to the yellow door. It swung open before I could even lift a hand to knock.

"Sorry I'm a little…" Every word in the English language

evaded me when my eyes landed on Bryce's bare, chiseled torso before he quickly finished throwing a t-shirt over his head. The ridges of his abs, the tousled state of his hair, and the intoxicating scent of his shower gel hit me all at once.

Turned on. Hot and bothered. Tongue-tied.

Okay, so not *every* word evaded me.

How can my timing be both perfect and cruel at the same time?

"Early?" he asked, the corner of his mouth pulling into the slightest smirk.

I nodded and cleared my throat, trying to pretend I wasn't still picturing the smooth plane of muscle hiding underneath his plain black tee. *Good god. The man shouldn't be allowed to own clothes.* "Uh, yeah. Sorry. I thought there'd be more traffic."

He shook his head, dismissing my apology before reaching out to take the bags from my arms. "No worries, Uno. Come on in." He stepped back, and I followed, eager to see the place Bryce called home. "So...this is my place. Well, the less chaotic version. It usually looks like a tornado came through and left behind an entire toy store. Come by five minutes after Peyton gets home and you'll see what I mean."

I smiled at the thought. Somehow, picturing Bryce as a dad just felt right. Like the unknowns and questions I'd had about his life the past couple years now made sense.

"This is nice," I said, my eyes roaming across the open space.

The front door led right into the living room, which was small, but Bryce had utilized the space efficiently. A brown microfiber couch sat on one side of the room, angled toward the entertainment center, with a small table separating it from a matching recliner. On one side of the entertainment center sat a box overflowing with blocks and books and various toys, and on the other side was a ride-on plastic car and a plastic miniature grill.

Photos of Peyton adorned the walls, some candid, and some from a birthday party. The largest was a photo of them together; Bryce's arms were outstretched, and Peyton was sailing through the air with a look of pure glee etched into her features. The happiness captured by the photographer was palpable and apparently contagious because I felt my lips tug into a smile and a warmth fill my heart.

"That was her first birthday."

I jumped at the sound of Bryce's voice right beside me, unaware that he'd already set down my bags in the kitchen and come back.

"It's a great shot. She seems like a really happy baby."

"She is. Mostly. Colic was a special kind of torture for both of us when she was younger, but now she's sleeping like a champ, and we've got a good routine going. I'm not sure that will still be the case when she gets back from Washington, though."

"I'm sure you'll both adjust back into your routine once she's home. How much longer will she be up there?"

"Couple more weeks. That's the plan, anyway."

"Having doubts?"

"I'd be lying if I said no, but I know this is good for both of us. I just wasn't expecting my separation anxiety to be worse than hers. Every time we FaceTime she's happy, and I know she's having a good time. David and Louise live on a farm; I really can't compete with that. Yesterday she ran away from the camera while we were talking because she saw the pig outside. She's obsessed with him. Never thought I'd be replaced by swine."

I laughed, peeling my eyes away from the photos to catch Bryce's smile.

"It could be worse, Bryce. One day she'll be ditching you for a boy."

His eyes went round, like he'd never contemplated that scenario before. "Yeah, but I've got, what, like twenty years before that day comes?"

"More like fourteen. Fifteen if you're lucky."

Bryce groaned and let out a few muffled curses before following me into the kitchen. "On that note, I think it's time to bust out the wine. I've got sauvignon blanc or a cabernet; I wasn't sure which would work better with your plans for dinner."

"Let's go with the cab."

Bryce grabbed glasses and uncorked the wine while I started pulling out ingredients and asking where to find the pots and pans I'd need. We fell into an easy groove with Bryce perfectly filling the role of sous chef. He started the sauce while I got the chicken prepped and into the oven.

I plopped myself on the counter and grabbed my wine, taking a sip and watching Bryce as he finished chopping onions and garlic. His movements were rhythmic and methodical, like he was totally in his element.

"Do you cook often?" I asked, willing my brain to stop thinking about how sexy he looked in an apron. It wasn't one of those lame 'Kiss the Cook' aprons, which usually elicited an eye-roll from me; just a plain red one with a few stains that gave it authenticity.

Bryce in glasses? Hot.

Bryce in glasses *and* an apron? It's a miracle I wasn't drooling.

"Not as often as I'd like," he replied, interrupting my totally-not-sexual-at-all thoughts. I forced my eyes away from his chest to the pureed tomatoes he was pouring into the saucepan. "I enjoy cooking, but it's not easy to do it alone with a toddler. Occasionally I'll cook for myself after Peyton goes to sleep though. What about you?"

"I love it. It's one of the first things I remember doing with Nana and Pops when we were little. I'd get a whiff of whatever Nana was cooking, and, at first, Sophia and I would watch her and Pops from a distance. But when they realized we were curious, Pops found kid-friendly recipes so we could help. Eventually, it became a big deal for us to all cook as a family on Sundays. I could ask if they still have the recipes if you want them. For when Peyton's older."

Bryce looked up, and I couldn't read his expression. A smile slowly spread across his face. "I'd like that. Thanks, El."

A comfortable silence settled between us while Bryce set the table and I finished the sauce and threw a salad together. (*I guess he's lucky after all.)* Soft music drifted into the kitchen from the small dining room, and I smiled as recognition dawned. I'd only mentioned my love for Ed Sheeran's music in passing the night we played Mario Kart, and I wasn't even sure Bryce had been listening.

After filling our plates and refilling our glasses, Bryce picked his up and held it out. "To being lucky," he declared with a smirk that was equal parts smug and sexy.

"To blank slates," I countered. We both let the words hang in the air for a few seconds. His smirk softened into something apologetic, so I quickly added, "And to *getting lucky.*"

He laughed, the sound dispelling any remaining tension. "You said it, not me."

We dug into the food, and as soon as the first bite of crispy, golden deliciousness hit my tongue I realized I couldn't remember the last time I had sat down to a homemade dinner outside of work with someone other than Milo or my family. These days it was protein bar breakfasts and too-tired-to-bother-with-it microwavable dinners.

But as I looked around and saw a high chair with one of those rubber bibs hooked on the side, I realized Bryce probably *only* did sit-down dinners. *Just one of the ways our lives are so different.*

I shook the thought off, determined not to over-analyze things.

"Actually, there's something else we should also toast," I said after a few minutes of eating in silence. "I talked to Sophia and my grandparents about the idea for adding a venue to the property, and they all loved it. I can't believe it's really going to happen!"

He leaned forward and covered my free hand with his, his eyes bright with the same excitement I felt. "El, are you serious? That's amazing! I told you they'd all be supportive."

We clinked our glasses, and I waited until he was mid-sip to ask, "Think you can handle being under me a little longer than we originally thought?" Bryce choked on his wine, and I didn't even try to contain my grin. "Professionally, that is."

He coughed to clear his throat, and I almost felt guilty for my little game.

But then he said, "I'm prepared to be under you for as long as it takes, El." He paused to scan my face so slowly that my cheeks flooded with heat. "Professionally, of course."

I opened my mouth to hit him with a witty comeback, but my brain chose this moment to focus entirely on the image of his abs. *Of what they'd look like under me.*

"The question is," he mused, smirking as I finally refocused my attention on his face. "Can *you* handle *me*? I mean, longer hours might mean some late nights together. And you know what late nights can lead to…"

My mouth gaped. "Wha…uh, what's that?"

"Mario Kart showdowns. And definitely a pool rematch."

"Oh."

"Oh?" he echoed, tilting his head to the left. "What did you think I was going to say?"

"I don't know. Something…else. Inappropriate. Dirty." I tried—and failed—to keep the lust out of my voice. I'd never been big on innuendo or dirty talking. But with Bryce…everything was different. I craved it with him. It was like the tiny glimpses he'd given me of that side of him were just enough to make me want more.

"Who's the gutter-minded perv now?"

"Guess you're rubbing off on me."

He arched a brow and shook his head before leaning forward to narrow the gap between us. I sucked in a breath and locked my eyes onto his lips. "Nah, El. There will be no guessing about it when I'm rubbing off on you."

That. That's what I wanted from Bryce. *Is classy dirty-talking a thing? Because I think Bryce is an expert at it.*

"Noted. Hey, speaking of things you're humble about…" I trailed off and jumped up, remembering the surprise I had in my purse for him.

A few seconds later I made it back to the table and handed Bryce a white 8"x11" frame.

His lips parted into a grin that practically encompassed his entire handsome face as he scanned the certificate. "El, you didn't have to do this."

"Bryce, I know I didn't *have to*. I wanted to. I told you, I feel bad about how we left things. Especially since we forgot about your certificate."

"Well, I love it and appreciate the gesture. Thank you."

"And, about that night…I want you to know I'm sorry for how I handled things. I—"

"No, El," he interjected, quickly shaking his head. "Your reaction was entirely justified. I should've told you about Peyton sooner, and *I'm* sorry for implying you wouldn't have been able to handle the situation. The truth is, the more I think about it, the more I hate that I didn't call you after I moved back."

"We both could've done things differently. Hindsight's a tricky thing. But you know I didn't run because you told me about Peyton, right?"

"I do now. I wasn't sure what to think at first; my thoughts were all over the place. But I knew something was up by the way you reacted to that call. Everything okay with Soph?"

"Yeah. She just…it's complicated. But she's fine." I stopped myself from explaining the situation with Helen because she was the last person I wanted to talk about right now.

Especially considering the fact that Bryce had been right to try and convince me not to go through with meeting Helen five years ago. *"Trust is earned, not granted freely,"* he'd said.

Funny how those words held so much more weight now.

"Glad she's okay."

I nodded and refilled my wine glass, searching for my next words.

"Stop," Bryce ordered, though it was more of a plea than a demand.

"Stop what?"

"Worrying. Overthinking. Stressing. Doing whatever it is that's causing these lines," he explained, reaching out to run his fingertips over my forehead.

I hadn't even realized I'd knitted my brows, but they softened at his touch.

"Sorry. Am I that obvious? I just can't seem to turn my brain off. A month ago, my life was basically on cruise control. Now it's more like a game of Mario Kart, and I'm on the damn rainbow road course."

"What are you most stressed about?"

Figuring out the next steps for the venue.

The potential for failure.

The future in general, and all the variables it held.

Meeting my mother. Being anything like her.

Wait, what?

"Well, the most immediate stress, I suppose, would be the inn and venue and what comes next."

"That's an easy one, Uno."

I arched a brow. "How so?"

"Are you forgetting who your badass architect is? Or that he also has a business degree?"

"Badass, huh? And here I thought you were just a pretty face with a knack for drawing straight lines."

He tried to look offended, but couldn't hold back a laugh. "Psh. I'm a pretty face who can draw straight lines *and* come up with a solid business plan. Among other talents."

I crossed my arms and studied his pretty face. His tone was flirty and teasing, but his eyes were sincere. "You're serious? You'd really help with the business logistics too?"

"Would that lower your stress level?"

"Yeah, but—"

"Then yes." He heaved a sigh, like my confusion about his willingness to help confused *him*. "I've got more free time on my hands than I know what to do with while Peyt's gone. And you've got more than enough on your plate. Let me lighten the load, El."

"I don't know, Bryce. Won't that make things a little too…complicated?"

He shrugged and gave me a tight smile. "Maybe. But I'm willing to give it a shot. You and I are taking things day by day, yeah? Take the same approach with the inn. There's no urgency, no reason for a self induced deadline that only stresses you out. Okay?"

"Day by day," I repeated, nodding my head mechanically while I contemplated his suggestion. "I can do that."

"That's the spirit."

And just like that, Bryce McKnight managed to take a tiny bit of the weight off my shoulders. This feeling—this trust tickling my heart—was risky. Dangerous. It was either laying the foundation for something stable and long-lasting, or it was setting me up for one hell of a fall.

We'd both finished eating, so Bryce leaned over the table to pick up my plate. I gripped his wrist and stopped him.

"Bryce?"

"Yeah?"

"Thank you," I replied, edging forward in my seat to peck his cheek.

His lips curled into a smile as he slowly pulled back and took my plate with him. "Any time, El."

I gathered the rest of our dishes and followed him into the kitchen to help, but he wouldn't have it. He insisted he was just going to rinse them off and would finish later. I acquiesced and wandered into the living room while he rinsed because Nana taught me to never argue with a man offering to do dishes.

"All done," he called a couple minutes later, rounding the corner at the same time I traced my fingers along the strings of a guitar.

I jumped back and smiled sheepishly. "Sorry. It was open, and I was curious. You play?"

"A little. Started teaching myself when I was seventeen. I needed an outlet for my anger about being shipped off to Washington, and it was either this or drag racing."

"Drag racing? Really?"

"It was an all-boys prep school. Options were limited."

"Why that school, Bryce?"

"My father grew up with the head master, and I guess he thought it was his best shot at making me 'see the light' or some shit like that. Back then my parents and I butted heads about everything, especially my future. They meant well, but I didn't see that at the time. I refused to listen when they tried to teach me the ins and outs of winemaking, and they shut down any of my attempts to talk about alternative careers. The only reason I was able to study architecture was because I double-majored."

"Wow. I knew you didn't always see eye-to-eye with your parents, but I guess I never realized how…challenging your adolescence was."

"That's probably because, with you, I never had to think about those expectations. I got to live in our 'B and E' bubble. Plus, you were, what, fourteen when I left? Things were different then."

"Things are different now, too," I countered.

Everything about the look in his aqua eyes echoed my words as he studied me. It was as if he was seeing me for the first time—like he wasn't the boy who taught me how to pop a wheelie when I was eight. "You're right, they are."

When I couldn't handle the intensity of Bryce's gaze, I dropped my eyes back down to the guitar and tried to convince my heart to go back to its normal rhythm. I wanted to ask him to play something for me, but that felt too intimate. *Maybe someday…*

"So, should—"

"Do you wan—"

"I should probably go," I said, shifting on my feet and twisting my fingers together.

Bryce looked down at his watch and frowned. "It's barely eight."

"I know, but I have some work I should get done tonight."

Bryce disappeared into the kitchen and came back out a second later with his hands behind his back. "That's too bad. Guess I'll just have to eat this all myself then," he said, pulling a pint of cookies n' cream ice cream out from behind his back.

My favorite flavor.

I'd have been impressed about him remembering that, but we'd debated the merits of cookies n' cream versus chocolate chip cookie dough on more than one occasion as kids.

"You don't play fair, Wario."

He smirked at the moniker. "Never claimed to. *I like it dirty, remember?*"

He wiggled his eyebrows and bit his bottom lip, and I was pretty sure I'd never seen anything sexier than the sight in front of me. *I think I like it dirty, too.*

"You keep saying that, and yet…here I am, still waiting for you to prove it." I took the extra spoon and dipped it into the carton, making a show of slowly licking the ice cream off and batting my eyelashes.

He reached out and tucked a chunk of hair behind my ear, letting his hand linger, waiting for me to react to the contact. "Oh, Uno," he trailed off with a *tsk-tsk-tsk* sound. He leaned in, his lips brushing the outer edge of my ear. "Just you wait. You'll see."

He pulled back, but stayed within the perimeter of my personal space.

I let out the breath I'd been holding, meeting his eyes. "You, Bryce McKnight, get way too much satisfaction out of this little game we're playing."

"I've always loved the games we play, El, but if you think *this* is true satisfaction, clearly you've never been properly fucked."

At that, my jaw practically hit the floor.

It should've alarmed me, the way Bryce took the simmering sexual tension between us and effortlessly escalated it to a boiling point. The implication in his words floated between us, a silent promise that he could easily rectify that situation.

"That so?" I asked. The words were breathy and awed so I cleared my throat. "Is this the part where you say you're just the man to fix that?"

He slowly lifted his spoon, dipping it in the ice cream and lapping it off in a blatantly suggestive way. "Nope. This is the part where we watch Dateline and eat ice cream on the couch. C'mon."

"Seriously?"

Bryce paused halfway to the couch and turned back, searching my face and reading the confusion there. He retraced the handful of steps separating us and put the ice cream down before grabbing my hands and pulling me close. "Seriously. Of course I want to 'fix' that, El. I can't look at you without wanting to *fix it* immediately. In case you didn't already know, I'm wildly attracted to you, Uno," he said, brushing his fingers along my jaw and down my neck, pausing over the galloping beat of my pulse. "But we agreed that we'd take this slow and see where things go, and I know how far out of your comfort zone it is to not have a plan. I might not know everything about you, but I know you're not the type to jump into bed with a guy without knowing where things stand or are going between you. As strange as this is going to sound...I won't use sex to influence where things go with us. Does that mean I'm going to be the perfect gentleman? Abso-fuck-ing-lutely not. But it does mean I'm going to do whatever it takes to make sure we do this right."

Emotion clogged my throat and threatened to blur my vision. Still, knowing Bryce was right didn't mean my body was on board with the idea of the slow track. I lifted a hand to travel over his shoulder and rest against the nape of his neck. "So...you're saying you think I'm hot?"

A groan in Bryce's throat sent a vibration through my palm and made my smile impossible to keep in check. "*That* is all you got out of my sincere, well-intentioned speech?"

"No. But it's either focus on that part, or focus on the part where you told me you don't want to have sex with me and it was incredibly sweet and only made me like you more."

"I think you misheard, El. I *want* to fuck you from now until Christmas. But you…we…aren't there yet. And I respect that."

His confession was startling—another taste of the dirty-talker-Jekyll hidden beneath the gentleman-Hyde.

I gazed up at him, studying the dark dirty blonde lashes framing his aqua eyes. "You're a rare breed, Bryce. A perfect balance of sinner and saint wrapped in one alarmingly hot package."

He grinned and pecked my lips before putting space between us. "The only saint-like thing about me is my patience. Now come on, the ice cream's melting."

Despite the fact I really did need to get some work done, I couldn't resist cookies-and-cream. Or Bryce. We split the pint and watched a couple episodes of Dateline, making a competition out of predicting the endings.

He was wrong about one thing; his self-restraint was also saint-like. Other than a PG-13 make-out session at my car when I was leaving, we managed to keep our hands to ourselves.

I knew going slow was the right move, at least until we had a better idea of where things were going between us. It would be incredibly reckless not to consider Peyton, not to prioritize her above all else. Bryce made it clear that we're heading toward the more-than-friends zone, but dating him means being a part of her life too, and I had to wonder if he realized what a massive step that was.

CHAPTER 14
ELLIOT

"Tell me about your childhood," Mr. Adams requested, taking me by surprise as he set his drink on the table and slipped back into the seat across from me.

I had just gotten my latte when I spotted Mr. Adams studying the menu from the back of the line. I gestured for him to join me after he got his drink, and we'd spent the last half-hour talking about Serenity—how my grandparents ran it, their philosophy behind its operation, even the origin of the name.

I expected that line of questioning. This? Not so much.

"My childhood? Why?"

"You were raised by some pretty extraordinary people, and I'm betting you've got lots of stories. I'd love to hear some of them."

"How'd you know they raised me?" I asked, crossing my arms. I was certain I hadn't said anything that would've given him that impression.

Adams picked up his tea and took a sip, unfazed by my confusion. "There are photos of you and your sister throughout your grandfather's office. He spoke as if you were his children, calling you two his 'pride and joy.' It wasn't hard to put the pieces together."

"Oh." I sank back in my chair, feeling a little dumb for not realizing that myself. *Come on, Elliot, he's just trying to get a clearer picture of the people who built the business he wants to buy. People like Adams look into every minor detail before making major financial decisions. Nana and Pops said they really like him. Stop being weird.*

"I consider it part of my job to familiarize myself with anyone I do business with, Ms. Kincaid," he said, reading my mind. "Personal life included. How a person treats their flesh and blood speaks a lot to their character. Wouldn't you agree?"

His gray storm-cloud eyes studied me intensely, and I couldn't discern what it was they held. Intensity came with the territory of his job title, which he had in spades; but this was different. Intimidating. Like he was trying to see inside my head and unlock the answer to his question with his stare alone.

I got the feeling he'd ask about my favorite cereal with equal intensity.

"I guess. But if that's the case, it seems only fair that you tell me about your family too."

He pursed his lips together and twirled the gold band adorning his left ring finger before momentarily shifting his attention to a pair of women passing by outside, his posture rigid and cold. "I don't have a family anymore. I lost my wife and son to complications during birth."

"I'm so sorry, Mr. Adams. I didn't mean…"

He turned back to me and waved his hand dismissively, shedding all traces of ice in his demeanor. "That was another life. Though I suppose you could say they're why I have somewhat of a soft spot for family-oriented businesses."

I had a feeling that was about as close as Greg Adams ever came to sharing personal information. The man was still a complete mystery, but I figured the most important thing was his interest in maintaining the principles Serenity was built upon.

"Well, Serenity is definitely rooted in family values. The majority of guests are repeats, which is something my grandparents take immense pride in. Every summer when I was growing up, George and Millie would tell us to pick a state, and we'd make a big road trip out of it and find things to see along the way. We'd get quality family time by traveling in an RV, and they also got to ensure firsthand that the staff at each Serenity property was upholding their standards. They taught my sister and me a little about the business in the process as well. I know using guest feedback to enhance the experience at a hotel isn't innovative or uncommon, but Pops prided himself on doing so on a personal level. Think Undercover Boss style."

"Sounds like George knows how to kill multiple birds with one stone. Impressive."

I nodded. "He is. They both are. I'm lucky to have grown up with them as my role models. So many times—"

An alert from Mr. Adams's phone cut me off, and he looked down and frowned. "I'm sorry, Ms. Kincaid, something's come up that requires my immediate attention."

He stood, and I stuttered at his abrupt urgency.

"Oh. Um, okay, no problem."

He thanked me for the help, and I'd barely had a second to respond before he rushed out the door.

Huh. Weird.

I shrugged off his hurried departure and headed to the counter to order another drink. My last appointment of the afternoon had canceled this morning, so I decided to stick around the coffee shop and do some of the behind-the-scenes grunt work like drafting contracts and sorting through emails.

I had my headphones in, letting Ed Sheeran serenade me in the background, when the ping of an iMessage over the music caught my attention.

BRYCE: MORE coffee??? Are you aware of potential heart issues caused by an increased caffeine intake?

My head jerked up, instinctively looking for hair the shade of dark honey. He sat across the room at a tiny table with his laptop out. Smiling eyes behind black-rimmed glasses met mine before he shot me a wink. I smiled and turned back to my computer.

ELLIOT: *Are YOU aware of the term 'restraining order'??? Exactly how long have you been watching me, McStalks-a-lot?*

BRYCE: *Never heard of it. And…long enough. This is MY coffee shop, remember? Also, if you're expanding the potential nicknames to Mc-somethings, I prefer McDreamy.*

ELLIOT: *So humble. Too bad that one's already taken. But feel free to keep the suggestions coming.*

BRYCE: *Ask and you shall receive…*

BRYCE: *McDreamboat. McHotBody. McLicious. McMagicDick.*

I spewed iced coffee onto my laptop screen and keyboard. Grabbing a napkin, I wiped up the mess.

ELLIOT: *McLicious? What are you, some kind of McDonald's dessert? I'm thinking McCock…y seems highly fitting.*

ELLIOT: *Also, my fingers are now sticky, thanks to you.*

BRYCE: *If we're about to swap confessions about masturbating after you went home last night, we should move this conversation somewhere more private.*

BRYCE: *Then again, I do love the idea of making you squirm in public…*

ELLIOT: *??????*

BRYCE: *El. Reread your text.*

I did, and my face immediately burst into flames of mortification. Other parts of me also burst to life at Bryce's words.

Also, he wasn't wrong about what I'd done after I got home last night.

ELLIOT: You wouldn't.

ELLIOT: Besides, even if that was remotely true, how do you know *you* were the reason behind it?

BRYCE: I can see you blushing from here. That's how.

BRYCE: It's adorable, by the way. But now picturing you touching yourself is giving me very NSFW thoughts and ideas.

ELLIOT: Such as?

BRYCE: Elliot Kincaid...are you trying to get me to sext you...from across the room, while we're both on the clock?

I leaned back in my chair and bit my lip, refusing to look his way. Crap. *Is that what I'm doing? I can't do that while we're both supposed to be working.* While part of me worried he actually would try to sext me right now, the idea of seeing how far I could push Bryce was too tempting to pass up.

ELLIOT: Maybe.

BRYCE: Dirty girl. I'm coming over there.

ELLIOT: No!

ELLIOT: Not yet. I actually do need to work. And you coming over here right now would probably make that impossible.

I swore I heard him sigh from across the room, but when I looked over, his eyes were on his screen.

BRYCE: I'll make you a deal. We both work—no distractions—for a solid hour, a 'power hour' if you will, and then I'm coming over there.

ELLIOT: Deal.

I closed out of Messages and successfully resisted the urge to turn and look at Bryce.

No distractions.

Right.

Easier said than done when he was in my vicinity, hijacking my thoughts every other minute.

CHAPTER 15

BRYCE

Note to self: Mental images of Elliot Kincaid, flushed and naked, writhing under me while I finger-fuck her is the definition of distraction.

Why does she have to be so damn cute when she blushes?

Why did the sight of said blush—and knowing I was actually right about last night—immediately get me hard?

Last night.

My complete honesty with her was impulsive, but not a mistake.

A mistake would've been ignoring the questions and confusion I saw in her eyes.

Previously, I'd kept the sexual undertones and insinuations to a minimum because treading lightly seemed like the best option while we figured out where we fit in each other's worlds.

But subtlety was overrated. I refused to be another question mark, another unknown in her life.

In a sea of chaos, I'd be the anchor she needed.

Logically, I knew it was risky to make that kind of promise when the truth about my role in Helen's vanishing act five years ago loomed over me like a dark cloud. A ticking time bomb that threatened to blow everything between us to bits.

But this was Elliot. *My Elliot.*

And I'll keep us in our 'B and E' bubble for as long as she'll let me.

Weeks ago, I'd asked El if she thought certain people come into our lives at a specific time for a reason. Last night, when I saw her anxiety about everything going on in her life, something changed, shifted inside of me. The same way it had the first time that question was posed to me. I'd never really believed in fate or destiny or cosmic forces bringing people together, but as soon as I'd considered it, I knew Peyton was my *yes.*

And in her own way, I was starting to think El was another yes.

I felt it in the way my heart became lighter, less hollow when she was around. In the way it seemed to soar inside my chest each time I made her smile. In the way our first kiss dulled the pain and anger my heart still harbored from Bridgette's betrayal.

I'd spent the last two years feigning apathy toward Bridgette, convincing myself that the only reason I hadn't considered asking a woman out was because Peyton needed one-hundred percent of my attention.

Denial was my shield.

But with El, one smile was all it took to completely unravel my defenses. It should've unnerved me, the way she so casually disarmed me. Instead, it brought me comfort. Peace. Clarity.

Since the day we met, El was the one person in my life who had never let me down. I'd already fucked up by not reaching out to her sooner. *And by going behind her back five years ago.* I had no intention of continuing that streak.

A look in El's direction told me she was totally wrapped up in her work. She twisted her hair around her fingers before flipping it over one shoulder and resting her chin in her hand, exposing the slant of her neck and a part of her collar bone peeking out from her shirt. As if that little glimpse wasn't enough to re-summon those NSFW visions, she bit down on her lip and narrowed her gaze at something on the screen.

So damn sexy.

And she has no idea.

Seriously, the girl was completely clueless about the kind of effect she had on dicks.

Yeah, there's no way in hell she lives with a dude and he doesn't beat off to thoughts of her at night.

I still didn't quite know what to make of her living arrangements. Milo seemed nice enough, but I'd barely exchanged words with the guy. Platonic friendships are like four-leaf clovers; you know they exist, but for every one you find, there are ninety-nine that turn out to be three-leafed ones. I believed El when she said she thought of Milo as a brother, but how could *he* not be attracted to *her*?

Maybe he's gay?

Shoving those thoughts away and refocusing on my computer screen, I minimized the Safari window and pulled up Messages.

Our 'power hour' was over, and unlike myself, it seemed Elliot had concentrated on work the entire time.

BRYCE: *Thinking you need a drink. And after watching you chew on your lip like that, I sure as hell do too. You almost ready to call it quits?*

Her head swiveled my direction, and she released her lip to give me a wicked little smile.

I returned her smile and threw in a wink for good measure.

ELLIOT: *Oh, really? Good to know what butters your biscuit.*

BRYCE: *Butters my biscuit??? Good god, that's awful, Uno. Truly.*

ELLIOT: *Strikes your match?*

BRYCE: *Worse.*

ELLIOT: *Revs your engine?*

BRYCE: …just no. How much longer is this torture going to last?

ELLIOT: At least one more. Tickles your pickle?

With that, I burst into laughter, garnering stares from a couple at the table next to me.

BRYCE: I'm starting to wonder if you're familiar with the actual terminology.

ELLIOT: Maybe I'm saving my best material for a more…intimate setting.

I looked up and caught her biting her lip while raking her gaze over me. She met my eyes and winked.

Damn.

That definitely buttered my biscuit, struck my match, revved my engine, tickled my pickle, and whatever other dorky euphemism she wanted to use.

Also…I actually believed her.

Which only reminded me how much more there was to learn about my little Uno.

BRYCE: I'd love nothing more than to hit you with a clever euphemism right now, but that was hotter than hell, and redirected all blood away from my brain. So, for the sake of all the dicks in your vicinity, quit. Biting. Your. Lip.

BRYCE: And please, FOR THE LOVE OF SANITY, tell me you're finished with work.

Instead of answering, she plopped into the seat across from me seconds later.

"I'm finished."

"But…?" I asked, knowing by her tone that a 'but' was coming.

"But I was sort of hoping we could go over stuff for the inn, and maybe swap and brainstorm ideas about a reception hall?"

The way she posed the question, somehow striking a balance of hesitancy and eagerness, was equal parts cute and admirable.

That, combined with the way she nervously twirled a chunk of blonde hair around her fingers while her eyes studied mine with unmatched intensity, was heart-kryptonite. *Right now, she could ask me to strip down to my birthday suit and recite the Pledge of Allegiance, and I'd oblige.*

Just to be the reason behind her smile.

I started scanning her body, making a blatant show of it. "Hmm. You've gotta have an off button somewhere. 'Hello. My name is Elliot Kincaid. I do not know how to relax'," I mimicked in a robotic voice, continuing with my perusal until she leaned forward and smacked my arm.

"That's not true!"

"Really? When was the last time you did something non-work-related for fun *on a weekday*?"

"Last night."

I closed my laptop and arched a brow. "Uh, while it *was* fun, that's called *dinner*, and it's something most people do on a regular basis."

She rolled her eyes and crossed her arms, making an equally dramatic show of annoyance. "Fine. But isn't this like the pot calling the kettle black? Weren't you a super-workaholic early in your career?"

She had a point, but I wasn't going to admit it. Instead, I ran my fingers through my hair—knowing it would put that lust-filled look in her eyes—and said, "We can talk shop. On two conditions."

"I'm listening."

"One—this shop talk takes place at Sipology while we drink. And two, afterward, we do something *fun,* and you're not allowed to talk or even think about work or the inn. Do we have a deal?"

"You drive a hard bargain, Caesar, but we've got a deal," she said, extending her hand for a shake.

I groaned, but took her hand all the same.

"Sorry, would you prefer Princess Peach?"

"Real cute, El." I leaned in, bringing one hand up to tuck her hair behind her ear so she'd feel my lips brush her lobe. "You can give me a million different nicknames, as long as the name you scream in my bed is the real one."

I pulled back slowly, relishing the sight of her widened eyes.

She continued to stare while I finished packing up.

"If you're going to keep staring at me like that, can you at least do it at the bar? I need a stiff drink right about now."

To go along with the part of me that El's stare is steadily stiffening with each passing second.

She blinked and shook her head, like she was just now coming back from a daydream. "Great! Yes, liquor. That's a great idea." She stood up but paused, narrowing her eyes at me and putting a hand on her hip. "You know, if I'm not allowed to bite my lip, then you're not allowed to wear your Superman 'sex-me-up' glasses. It's only fair."

My lips twitched. "I'm sorry, my what?"

She made a sweeping gesture across my whole face. "The glasses, Bryce."

"You mean the things that allow me to *see clearly*?"

"You know what else allows you to see clearly? *Contacts*. And they get the job done without making you look like freaking Clark Kent's sexier, dirty blonde twin."

I leaned back in my chair and grinned.

"What're you...? Why are you looking at me like that?" she huffed.

"Just letting myself savor the moment. This feels like a momentous occasion."

"What does?"

"The discovery of what *butters Elliot Kincaid's biscuit.*"

~

AFTER DARYL, the newest Sipology bartender, made our drinks, we headed toward my usual booth in the corner.

We slid into opposite sides of the booth, and the question I'd forgotten to ask El earlier resurfaced in my mind. "Hey, who was that guy you were with at the coffee shop?"

"Uh, his name is Greg Adams. It's kinda crazy; he was sitting across from me at the same coffee place a couple weeks ago, looking at Serenity's website. We started talking about the hotel and my grandparents. Turns out he's one of the people trying to buy it."

"And he just happened to run into you at the coffee shop again? That's quite the coincidence, El."

She lifted a brow in question and shifted to free herself of the purse hanging across her body. "Why, because he likes your coffee shop too? Don't worry, I did my due diligence and asked Nana and Pops about him after the first run-in. They had nothing but great things to say about him, and I think they're probably going to sell Serenity to him."

"Okay, fair enough." I didn't want to press the issue, so I let it go and made a mental note to check into the guy later. "Gotta say, Uno, I'm a little surprised you're a whiskey drinker," I said, nodding my head toward the tumbler in her hand.

"Why, because I don't have a penis?"

"Uh, no." I laughed and shook my head. "Because whiskey is Satan's beverage of choice. Then again, your taste buds are clearly confused; no other way to explain your love of pickles."

"Have you tried a pickle recently? Taste buds evolve over time, y'know." She picked up a menu, tapping a finger against the card-stock where fried pickles were listed. *Damn, she's almost as hot when she smirks as she is when she blushes.*

But not even her sexy little pout was enough to make me want to try pickles. From texture to taste, everything about them repulsed me.

"Don't even ask, El. Not gonna happen."

"Okay, fine. Can we compromise with mozzarella sticks? I only had a protein bar for lunch, so it's probably not a good idea to throw back the whiskey without eating. Unless you want a front row seat to the Drunk Elliot Show."

"I can always get on board with mozzarella sticks. Though the idea of seeing you relaxed and carefree is appealing."

Sipping the amber liquid in her glass, she shook her head and scoffed. "I can be carefree while sober!"

"Prove it."

"Okay. How?"

I hesitated, considering my proposal. I scanned her features, committing the shape of her lips and her high cheekbones to memory. She was holding her breath, tapping her fingers together and eagerly awaiting my response as if it was the most important answer she'd ever receive.

"Nah, I don't know. You're not going to like it," I said, carefully laying the groundwork for my plan.

She crossed her arms, subtly shifting her breasts together in a way that was impossible not to notice thanks to the cleavage now viewable through her button-down shirt.

"Try me."

I opened my mouth to reply, but Xander's voice cut me off.

"An old-fashioned? Damn. Just my type of woman," he called, sauntering up to our booth with his signature smirk that had melted panties on more than one occasion, according to him.

El's brows lifted as she turned to survey my cousin with a semi-annoyed look. Xander ran a hand along the back of his head, his smirk remaining in place—basically his default facial expression any time he met a female.

"I thought breathing was your type of woman," I countered. "Breathing and legal."

He rolled his eyes, but kept them locked on Elliot. Since she was with me, I wasn't actually worried he'd hit on her. Then again, this was the same guy who'd once slept with his roommate's girlfriend hours after they broke up. *And he wonders why he doesn't have any friends...*

"While it's true that I don't restrict myself to one specific type of woman, I actually have pretty fucking high standards, thank you very much. I'm Xander, by the way. Bryce's cousin. And you must be Elliot. It's about time Bryce stopped hiding you from me," he said, offering her his hand.

Her expression softened when she learned Xander's connection to me. She nodded and placed her hand in his while further surveying his appearance. I wasn't an idiot—I'd have to be blind not to notice the way women looked at Xander. But El didn't give him the heart-eye emoji look when he smiled at her or seem interested in his sleeve of tattoos. "It's nice to finally put a face with the name. Bryce has mentioned you a time or two."

"I assure you, whatever he told you was entirely false."

"Oh no," she quickly asserted, smiling. "I have a feeling it was all true. If anything, his descriptions were probably a little lenient."

He chuckled, rubbing his jaw and looking at me with amusement. "That I don't doubt. He fucking sugarcoats everything. Always looking for the best in people."

I shrugged. "Can't help it. Kinda comes with the territory of parenthood."

El's eyes found mine, and she offered me a smile, reaching under the booth to squeeze my knee. I grasped her hand in mine and returned her squeeze.

"Exactly. That's why you're more suited to fatherhood than I am. I'll stick with being the fun uncle that Peyton comes to for beer and sage wisdom down the line."

Elliot laughed. "*That* is why he's more suited to fatherhood? Gee, but it seems like you've got such a sunny disposition that would otherwise be so well-suited to raising children," she chided sarcastically. Her tone was light and teasing, and I kind of loved seeing this side of her. A quick glance at her drink told me she'd almost finished it. Which reminded me we needed to get some food into her, ASAP.

Xander returned her laughter, shaking his head in admiration. "Damn, Bry. She's feisty. I like her. Tell me, Elliot, do you have any equally feisty friends or sisters that might be more susceptible to my charms than you?"

I snorted at the thought. No way in hell El would ever do that to her friends or Sophia.

"Most of my female friends are married—quite happily. And my sister? Ha. I'm not positive what exactly her type is, but I'm pretty sure it's not you. And she definitely isn't *your* type. She's smart and sweet and shy and would never fall for whatever panty-dropping moves you've stored away in your arsenal."

I couldn't help but chime in. "Plus, Sophia's actually got a brain, Xander. Which means she's already out of your league."

One of his eyebrows lifted, and his mouth formed a small frown. "So, you're telling me she's one of those 'but she's got a great personality' chicks? Got it."

I sighed and shook my head, exasperated and done letting Xander hijack our conversation. "You're such a dick."

He shrugged. "Not the first time I've been given the label. Not even the first time today, in fact."

"Shocking," I said with unmistakable sarcasm. "Think you could make yourself useful and grab us some mozzarella sticks? I'd go order, but you're already here. Plus I've learned the kitchen puts a rush on it if the order comes from their manager. They're terrified of you, by the way."

"As they should be. I don't do bullshit handholding or accept excuses. But yeah, I've actually gotta go back there anyway and deal with a major inventory fuck-up. I'll have Laci bring them out as soon as they're done."

"Appreciate it."

He met my outreached fist with his and turned to El. "Elliot. It's been...weirdly refreshing to have a woman call me out like you have. If I'm ever in a pussy-drought, I have a feeling you'd make a spectacular wing-woman. Fortunately and unfortunately, I've never needed help in that department. Should that day ever occur, you'll be my first call. For multiple reasons."

He waggled his eyebrows playfully in true Xander fashion, and Elliot snorted a laugh—one of those that would've had her spraying whiskey if she'd been mid-sip.

"Easy, Casanova. I'm not above kicking your ass in front of your staff."

"You make it too damn easy, Bryce." He held his hands up and laughed before offering El a wink and quickly striding toward the kitchen.

Elliot just shook her head and turned back to me. "Is it weird that I can't decide if he's actually kinda likable, or if he's just good at tricking women into thinking he's likable long enough to get in their pants?"

"Nah, not weird. Somewhere underneath his playboy persona, there's a decent guy in there, but it'd take one hell of a woman to put up with and see past all his bullshit. I love him like a brother, but he's basically incapable of having a functioning relationship. He's a heartbreaker through and through."

She frowned. "That's kind of sad, even if he acts like he's perfectly happy with that title."

"Xander's a big boy; don't feel sorry for him."

El's shoulders snapped up, and she clapped her hands together. "Okay, so you were about to tell me what it would take to prove that I can be carefree."

Right.

"What's your schedule like tomorrow?"

"I've got a morning meeting at 9:30 and an appointment with a client at three. I was planning to do some venue research in-between. Why?" she asked, narrowing her eyes skeptically.

"That's perfect. If I come meet you at the office or at the inn after your morning meeting, give me the rest of tonight without thinking about work." She opened her mouth, but I continued before she could protest. "And I promise we will be extra-productive tomorrow. Come on, Uno, let go and live a little tonight."

A smiling blonde quickly set down a basket of mozzarella sticks while Elliot considered my offer. She wasted no time picking up the fried goodness and biting into it, letting out a little moan.

"Well?" I prompted, mostly to put a stop to the food-moans.

"One condition—after, if I'm not *satisfied*."

She paused, hitting me with a wink in case I missed her insinuation (I didn't), and the urge to clarify that she'd always be *satisfied* after being with me was almost too strong to resist.

"If I'm not satisfied with our *progress*," she added with a grin, "we reconvene after my afternoon meeting."

"Deal. Told you, El, I'm not opposed to working late nights together."

CHAPTER 16

BRYCE

ANOTHER BASKET OF MOZZARELLA STICKS LATER, WE'D SUCCESSFULLY avoided talking about anything work-related. Instead, we swapped stories from our respective college experiences. If it had been a Friday or a Saturday night, the music would've been pumping through the speakers at an obnoxiously high volume. But as it was, we sat across from each other and could converse without straining to hear.

"You did not!" she shrieked with a mixture of shock and humor. "Bryce. You actually tried to climb the rec center? After how many games of beer pong?"

"Somewhere between three and fourteen. I went a little nuts that year. But that's what freshman year is for, right? To make all the stupid mistakes you'll eventually learn and grow from?"

"I guess so. But now that I think about it, I never really had a nuts phase. Do you think that makes me boring? Am I lame for spending freshman year studying instead of allowing myself a 'real' college experience?"

She lifted a hand and drummed her fingers against her lips as her brows knitted in contemplation, and I fought the urge to run my fingers over the lines along her forehead like I had last night.

"Actually, no," she continued. "I don't regret that I spent more time at the library than at house parties. I studied a lot, but I also had fun. Sometimes. My lack of regrettable experiences isn't what made me lame back then. It was…"

Her eyes fell, and she started fidgeting with the foil that lined the empty basket between us.

"El? It was what?"

"You know what's funny?" she asked abruptly, directing her gaze back up to me. "The way we use the word 'nuts' to mean crazy. I've never understood that. How did that start? Who is this person with a nut vendetta? What did nuts ever do to them? They must have had a nut allergy. But to most of the population, they're perfectly normal, delicious treats. I happen to love nuts. If we're going to use a food as a synonym for crazy, it should be something like 'pluot' because really, whoever thought to cross plums and apricots is the crazy one."

I arched a brow and lost the battle to contain my grin. "Okay, I think that's enough whiskey for you," I said, sliding her glass over to my side of the booth. I was half-joking, but also didn't want to be responsible for her dealing with the hangover from hell tomorrow.

She crossed her arms and huffed in mock-annoyance. "That wasn't drunken rambling, Bryce! Buzzed at best. It was a perfectly relevant tangent."

"I know you're not drunk, El. But that was a blatant attempt to distract me from what you were about to say. You teed up the 'deez nuts' joke too well with the 'I happen to love nuts' comment. What were you going to say?"

She bit her lip and squeezed her eyes shut. "I don't remember."

"Elliot, look at me. Whatever it is, you don't have to tell me. But you can. You can tell me anything, Uno. No judgment, remember?" I nudged her leg with mine.

She slowly lifted her eyes, raising the curtain of long lashes blocking my view of her beautiful blues. *There she is.*

"Full disclosure," I added. "There will be a *tiny* bit of judgment if your confession is that you still squeezed into your pink Power Ranger Halloween costume from second grade. Though, I'm not opposed to seeing you in an adult version of it. Preferably of the slutty variety."

Her soft laughter filled the air, and a familiar warmth seeped into my heart, further soothing the scars it bore.

"Definitely not what I was going to say, but I'll be sure to add that to my list of ideas for Halloween costumes. If you're lucky," she said with a wink. Before I could make any kind of remark, she cleared her throat and lost all traces of humor. With her fingers woven together in front of her, she spoke her next words softly. "I was going to say what made me lame freshman year was the fact that I was so freaking terrified of becoming Helen that I avoided all remotely risky situations and played it safe with a mediocre, moderately boring boyfriend whose idea of a good time was watching documentaries on Netflix and chilling...and not the kind where chilling is a euphemism for sex. I didn't let myself live, Bryce. At least not the way I should've. I was convinced that the only way to ensure I wouldn't turn into her was to cling to anything and everything around me that was stable. It took me until a year ago to realize I could create my own stability."

"That doesn't mean you were lame. That's something plenty of people don't ever understand, much less realize at twenty-three. Everyone paves their own path, travels their own journey into adulthood; there's not a one-size-fits-all way. Helen made horrible choices, but they were *her choices*, El." I pushed aside the drinks and basket to reach across the table and pull her hands into mine. "Whose choice was it to learn how to swim when you were six?"

"Mine."

"And whose choice was it to take dance classes?"

"Mine."

"Whose brilliant choice was it to watch the movie *Scream* when we were in middle school?"

She grinned. "Mine."

"And your career? Whose idea was that?"

"Mine. Okay, I get it, Bryce—"

"Do you? Because you, Elliot Kincaid, don't give yourself enough credit. These choices you've made are just a tiny fraction of what *you* have done for yourself. Not even Millie and George, who absolutely contributed to your overall awesomeness, can take all the credit for the resilient, strong, brilliant, capable woman sitting in front of me. *Your* choices are the ones that have molded you into who you are today."

"How do you do that?"

"Do what?"

She opened her mouth, then closed it on a sigh. "I'm not sure how to explain it, really. It's just...you. It's how you've always been."

"Okay, now I'm really gonna need you to elaborate."

"When we were little, you didn't see a broken girl, you just saw me for me. When we met, you made me smile and laugh when humor was basically a foreign concept to me. You made me feel normal, taught me how to be a regular kid. It seems like every time I've needed to hear it most, you're there, reminding me in one way or another that DNA doesn't determine someone's worth. It's like you take a flashlight and illuminate the parts and pieces of me that I sometimes fail to see myself."

The weight and sincerity of her words were unexpected, and I sat paralyzed for a second while my brain committed El's explanation to memory. *Will she still feel that way if I tell her the truth about what happened five years ago? Or will she hate me?*

No. I refused to entertain that possibility.

"You're right; when we first met I didn't see a broken girl. I saw a girl who needed a friend, and I wanted to be that friend. All I ever wanted was to be someone you could count on, El."

"What about now? What do you want to be now, Bryce?" she asked. I expected her to break our eye-contact, to avoid looking at me, but she didn't. She searched my eyes like they held the key to my answer.

Surveying her for the fiftieth time today, I let myself truly study her face. If I had to create a checklist for what physical features qualify a person as beautiful, I'd start with Elliot's. A mouth with full lips to frame a smile so bright it'd outshine the moon. Almond-shaped eyes with a hint of an upward slant each time she smiled. Cheekbones that were high and round and always sported a unique shade of pink when she blushed. Expressive eyebrows that lifted into matching, inverted Vs when something surprised her.

I put a stop to my perusal before my eyes could wander south because thinking about other parts of her right now was asking for trouble. I'd stopped drinking already, but had consumed enough that the liquor flowing through my system drowned out reason and dared me to throw logic out the window.

I want to be the reason behind all your biggest smiles.

I want to be the only one who makes you blush.

I want to be whatever you need me to be.

"I still want to be someone you can count on. That's not changing, El."

She exhaled a breath and flashed another one of her dazzling smiles. "I want to be that for you too, Bryce. Do you think…" Her words dangled in the air while she shifted in her seat and played out some kind of internal debate about whether or not she should continue.

"Would we be crazy to risk what could potentially be the best friendship in history by venturing into the more-than-friends zone?"

"You mean would we be pluots?"

She rolled her eyes and laughed. "Bryce, I'm serious. What if we're making a mistake? What if we ruin *us* by crossing that line?"

I reached under the table and found her hands in her lap. She twined her fingers around mine, and I seriously doubted the possibility of a day when this—we—didn't feel right. "Hate to break it to you, but what we're doing now crosses that line, even if we're only slowly dipping our toes into the 'more-than-friends' zone. I know the timing is less than ideal, but there's no such thing as the 'right time' when it comes to this. That's not the way life works, Uno. I also know you've got at least a dozen more 'what ifs' bubbling up in that overworked brain of yours. Thing is…the wrong kind of *what if* questions are the reason people settle. For mediocrity instead of excellence. For stability instead of passion. For status quo instead of striving for more. Consider the alternative; what if we create an even better *us* by crossing that line?"

That particular *what if* was the lifeline I held on to each time the doubt and uncertainty tried to creep in.

This was *Elliot*. She was nothing like Bridgette. *Nothing like Helen.* There was no way she'd do what they did.

"I see your point," she agreed with a nod. "But some of those what ifs are worth at least some consideration."

"Like what?"

"What if we have disagreements in the professional aspect of our relationship?"

"Then we work them out and find a way to leave work out of our personal lives. People maintain a separation between business and pleasure all the time."

She leaned forward and dropped her voice. "What if we, uh, have no chemistry in bed?"

A loud snort of laughter erupted from me, and it took me a full six seconds to get it under control. El crossed her arms and stared at me. "Is that seriously a question you have? Because I'm pretty sure it's more likely that the sparks between us will set the bed on fire."

"Oh, right, I forgot I was talking to *McMagicDick*."

"I'd be offended you forgot, but I know you're actually dying to get me naked. You let a little drool slip yesterday when I opened the door."

Her mouth fell into a little 'o' shape, but she quickly snapped it shut and smacked my leg. "Did not! And whatever, we both know your state of undress was deliberate. Guys with bodies like yours are well aware of the effect they have on the female brain. Don't deny it."

"What exactly do you mean, *bodies like yours*?"

"I am so not padding your ego, *McHotBod*. But I will say that you definitely give the term 'dad bod' a way better meaning."

"Too late, you already padded it when I caught you gawking." I grinned, loving that two soft-pink stains on her cheeks totally contradicted the fake annoyance she tried to sell with an eye roll. "So, is that it for the what ifs plaguing you?"

She shook her head. "What if...Bryce, what if Peyton hates me?"

"El, she's not going to hate you. And if she does...well, sometimes she hates me for putting shoes on her feet. Or for putting the *wrong* shoes on her feet. Toddlers are mercurial like that. Think of it like Texas weather—don't like her mood? Stick around, it'll change soon enough."

She bit her lip and shook her head, resting her crossed arms on the table and drumming her pink nails against her biceps. "How can you be so sure? The last small child I was around was Sophia. I have no idea how to handle them. *You* will hate me when I screw something up."

"Two years ago, I could count on one hand the number of times I'd held a baby. I'd never touched a diaper. Hadn't so much as thought about things like teething rings or formula. When it comes to kids, screwing up is inevitable. There's not a parent in the world with a magic formula for how to perfectly raise kids. Take it from the king of parental screw-ups—all we can do is give it our best and learn from trial and error."

I didn't fault Elliot for having concerns; I'd have been shocked if she didn't have those kinds of questions. But what she didn't understand—yet—was that her having those kinds of questions was exactly how I knew she'd be just fine when it came to her relationship with Peyton.

"I highly doubt that you're the king of parental screw-ups, Bryce, but you're right. Hypotheticals breed unnecessary doubt, and I thought the point of tonight was for me to be carefree and fun, not a Debbie-downer."

"Good point. What'd you have in mind? Shots?" I asked, truly curious about the plan I practically felt her forming as she searched the bar. Her smile shifted from sweet to pure mischief when her eyes stopped roaming, and it sent a jolt of excitement straight through me. Well, straight through a certain part of me.

"Better!" she exclaimed, jumping up and running across the room.

A group of people hovering around the bar blocked my view of what she was doing, but I didn't have to wait long before she reappeared, both hands behind her back and trouble dancing in her eyes.

"Did you know there's a bucket of random games by the door?" She brought her arm around and set a deck of playing cards on the table. "I'm thinking we pick a game and the loser has to do winner's choice of shots."

"I'm in. But, to make it fair, I think we should each get to choose a game, then pick a third one we both agree on. Best out of three. That way there's no way one of us can claim the other 'cheated' their way to victory."

She gasped dramatically. "I would never!"

"Yeah, okay. And denial is just a river in Egypt."

"I'm glad you've got a solid supply of dad jokes, Bryce. Those will come in handy when you're trying to find the humor in defeat."

She pulled the cards out and started shuffling, briefly looking up to put her smirk on full display. A groan slipped from my throat at the sight of her, but she either chose to ignore it or was taking her shuffling way too seriously.

Shit. How am I ever going to focus on a card game when a few taunting words from her makes my dick twitch? Add in her smirk, and I'm seconds from contemplating the logistics of somehow jerking off right here.

"So, what's your game of choice? Mine's slapjack. It's a great way to keep the old reflexes sharp, don't you think? Gotta make sure those brain-to-hand synapses are all firing." She paused to lean across the table, simultaneously getting within whispering range and giving me a close-up of her modest cleavage. "But I should probably warn you, Bryce...*I'm really good with my hands.*"

Her voice was raspy and coated in seduction, and I was certain I'd never been more turned on by a fully-clothed woman before in my life. But that's just it. When it came to El, our banter and her brain turned me on as much as her body did. It's how I knew she was different—this was different.

"I'm on to you, Kincaid," I said, forcing my brain to focus on winning our games and not on how desperate I was to pin her up against the nearest hard surface. "You're good. But I'm better. I choose crazy eights for mine, and I think it's only fitting that we make war the third one."

"I can live with war. You know, some people call crazy eights 'screw your neighbor.'"

"Huh. I guess *some people* like to call it what it is." I adjusted my glasses and gave her a smirk. "That's the name of the game, after all... *screwing* your neighbor, I mean."

"Not if she screws you first," she replied coolly, but the flush that crept over her cheeks and into her neck gave away my effect on her.

I buried a smile.

Touché, Uno.

An impartial coin toss decided the first game—crazy eights. For the sake of time, we agreed eights would be worth twenty points instead of fifty, and the first person to get to fifty points won.

It only took a few rounds for me to hit fifty.

"How do you feel about kamikaze shots?" I asked, collecting the cards to shuffle. "Or maybe tequila. I do love the idea of you doing a body shot off me."

"Don't get excited yet, McCocky. I don't want you to say you only lost slapjack because you were distracted by that idea."

Turned out she was right to warn me about her skills. In the span of minutes she'd hoarded most of the cards.

I frowned at my thin collection of remaining cards and contemplated my odds of turning my fate around. *Not favorable.*

Right after I played my second to last card, she played a jack and beat me to it (of course). By now we both knew my last card was a jack. I flipped my card over and we slapped it simultaneously.

"Shit," I muttered, reluctantly accepting the inevitability of my defeat.

"Ha! Magic hands, remember?"

"Oh, I remember. Not something a guy forgets hearing, El."

War didn't do me any favors either. It was close at first, but she somehow ended up with three face cards in a row when my last cards were a five, nine, and two.

The fact that Elliot hardly gave it any thought before making a beeline for the bar should've been my first clue I wouldn't like whatever shot she chose.

Carrying a tray with four shot glasses, she carefully navigated her way back to the table a few minutes later.

I stared, putting the pieces together as soon as I caught a whiff of the drinks. "Picklebacks? You're going to make me drink whiskey *and* pickle juice? Shit, El, you really do play dirty."

"Just hear me out…I'm doing one with you, and if you really hate it I'll let you pick a shot for me to do."

I lifted a brow, suddenly less resistant to the idea of pickle juice.

"In that case, let's do this," I said, picking up Lucifer's poison in one hand and pickle juice in the other.

"To pluots," she toasted, making me laugh as we both downed the Jameson.

My first reaction after chasing it was that it wasn't *as bad* as I expected. But I didn't want her to know that.

"Well?"

My eyes stayed glued to her throat, where they'd been since the second her lips touched the shot glass.

"What?" I blinked, peeling my eyes away and refocusing on her face. "Oh, uh, the jury's still out."

"All right, well, I'm going to the bathroom while the jury deliberates. Be right back."

I watched her disappear down the hallway in the back that led to Xander's office and the bathrooms.

Slow. We're taking things slow.

Except no matter how many times I repeated the sentiment to myself, my dick refused to listen.

'Slow' is subjective, right? Open to varying interpretations?

After a minute, I slid out of the booth and headed to the bathroom to splash some water on my face and get the party in my pants under control.

The men's room was directly across from the women's, so when we swung the doors open simultaneously, I came face-to-face with El. She froze and slid her eyes up my body, making no effort to move or speak.

I didn't either.

I was too mesmerized by the subtle rise and fall of her chest. By the roll of her throat as she swallowed slowly. By the tiny flare of her nostrils. By the desire dancing in her eyes. I recognized it because it's the same hunger I felt down to the marrow of my bones.

I'd beg the highest power who'd listen if it meant they could suspend this moment in time and let me keep her here like this a little longer.

"Bryce." Her whisper was a question, an answer, and a plea at the same time.

I brought my eyes back up to hers, and we both stepped forward. Before logic could stop me, I reached out at the same time she lunged for me, crashing our bodies together a split-second before our mouths found each other.

Gone was any trace of saint-like Bryce.

Holding her flush against me, I stepped back into the bathroom and closed the door, pressing her up against it while I flipped the lock. El's arms fused together around my neck while her body melted into mine, and I was torn between wanting to step back to see and explore all of her and never wanting this kiss —this electrifying, desperate, earth-shattering kiss—to end.

As soon as I peeled my lips off El's, her hips pulsed forward, slowly grinding against me. I groaned into her neck and dug my fingers into the curves of her ass, internally cursing the layers separating me from the heat of her skin.

My lips trailed down until I was buried in the swell of her breasts, kissing every inch of skin along the way.

Her soft moans spurred me on, and her fingers twined through the strands of my hair made me desperate for more.

"God, Elliot. You're killing me."

"I want this. So much," she confessed between pants, slipping one hand down the back of my shirt.

I brought a hand up to her side and grazed my thumb over her breast while my other hand fumbled with the buttons of her shirt. She realized my intent and quickly joined in, furiously pulling at buttons until her shirt hung open and revealed a lace-trimmed red bra. My gaze flickered between her face and her breasts, catching the wicked grin she flashed when I realized her bra hooked in the front.

"What do you want, Uno?" I asked, grazing the pad of my index finger under the lace of her bra. Goosebumps sprang to life under my touch, and I followed the trail with my tongue.

She lowered a hand until her palm rested on the unmistakable outline of my cock. "You, Bryce. I want all of you. Right now."

"Shit, El. Don't say those words unless you mean them. I'm barely hanging on here."

"I'd never tease a man about getting lucky." She slid down my body until her knees met the ground with a quiet thud. "*This* is how much I mean those words," she muttered before unzipping my fly.

One layer of cotton and a few inches was all that separated her mouth from my cock.

Too bad my brain chose this moment to think clearly.

"El, wait." I gripped her shoulders, and she immediately tilted her head back to give me a questioning look. "I don't have a condom. And you deserve more than a quickie in a bar bathroom. I want to take my time with you."

"You can worship me later, Bryce. I don't need a condom for this."

Before I could blink, much less form any kind of thought about her intention, she pulled my cock out and swirled her tongue around the tip, making me groan and roll my hips forward.

"*Oh, fuck,*" I hissed as soon as she wrapped her lips around me completely.

In recent weeks, I'd had more than a few fantasies about what this moment would be like.

The reality was so much better.

Until it wasn't.

Bang. Bang. Bang. "Hello? Someone in there?"

"Just—just a minute," I barked hoarsely.

"Bryce? That you?"

Elliot pulled back and looked up at me.

"Xander?" I replied, registering the urgency in his voice. "I need a minute."

"The hell are you doing in there? And why aren't you answering your phone? Louise is trying to get a hold of you, man. It's Peyton."

"*Shit.* I'll be right there." Guilt immediately flooded through me, followed quickly by panic.

Something's wrong. Really fucking wrong, if she's calling Xander.

I hurriedly adjusted myself while Elliot scrambled to re-button her shirt.

"I'm so sorry, El—"

"Bryce, don't. I completely understand. Go," she said, nodding her head toward the door as she fixed the last button.

I stepped toward her and pressed a quick kiss to her forehead.

I couldn't afford to think about the look on her face—a mixture of concern and uncertainty—right now.

All I could think about was the fact that I was the world's worst parent for silencing my phone so I wouldn't be distracted with Elliot.

Because of that selfishness, I had no idea what was going on with my little girl.

What the fuck was I thinking?

CHAPTER 17

ELLIOT

Bryce called me the next day and explained that Peyton had eaten a peanut butter cookie, and it made her sick and lethargic and caused her tongue to swell up. Fortunately, Louise had already given her some Benadryl earlier in the day, so her symptoms weren't as bad as they could've been. Still, it scared the hell out of them, and Bryce caught a red eye to Seattle straight from the bar.

He'd decided to stay there instead of coming home to see a doctor because the husband of Peyton's former pediatrician was an allergist and was able to squeeze them in a few days later. After their appointment, the test results came back and confirmed Peyton's peanut allergy.

I practically felt the guilt emanating from Bryce through the phone when he called to tell me. He blamed himself for not being with her when it happened, for not doing more to introduce her to peanuts before now. All of it. Which was absurd, but parental guilt apparently doesn't live within the lines of logic.

For the past eight days, since that night at the bar, all of our conversations via phone calls or FaceTime revolved around Peyton or work. I didn't mind; when I told him I wanted to be someone he could count on, I meant it. I just hoped his guilt didn't bleed into regret about what happened between us.

Because I didn't regret it at all.

And the possibility that he might sent tiny little daggers into my heart.

Guess I'll find out soon enough.

His flight back—with Peyton—was scheduled to land at 8:45 pm. I'd already stopped by Sipology and asked Xander to borrow his copy of Bryce's house key, knowing Bryce wouldn't sleep a wink until every last trace of peanuts was out of the place.

After meeting clients for a cake tasting, I rushed over to Bryce's house and was a few blocks away when my phone rang. Sophia and Carleigh were supposed to be getting dinner together, so I was surprised to see my sister's name.

"What's up, Soph? I'm kinda in a hurry. My meeting at the bakery went long, and Bryce will probably be home in an hour."

"El, check your email. I forwarded you a message Helen just sent me."

My grip tightened on the steering wheel, and I pressed my tongue against my teeth in an effort to keep from clenching my jaw. *Deep breaths. You agreed to hear her out.*

"I'm driving; can you give me the CliffsNotes version?"

"She wants to meet us. As soon as possible."

"Meet us? Why? I mean...I thought we agreed to wait, we aren't ready to meet her yet."

"I know," she said with a heavy sigh. "She just said it was urgent, and to please seriously consider it."

I slowed to a stop at the curb in front of Bryce's, killed the engine, and released a breath. "I don't know. I don't have an answer for her—for you yet. Just...don't reply until we can sit down and talk about this, okay?"

"Okay."

A silence filled with her unspoken questions and my underlying fears dragged on for what felt like minutes. I looked up and caught the last traces of daylight slip past the trees as the street-lights flickered on in unison.

I'd never jumped on the pumpkin spice bandwagon, but this time of year was my favorite. Temperatures dropped (some days), work slowed down a little, and my love of scary movies became seasonally appropriate. Plus, October meant Thanksgiving was just around the corner, and that was my favorite holiday.

"…Home after my class? El? Are you there?" Sophia called in that way that told me she'd been talking for a while, and I'd totally spaced out.

"Uh, yeah. Listen, I have to go if I'm going to make Bryce's house nut-free before he gets here. Talk later?"

"FYI, I don't need to ever hear the words 'Bryce's' and 'nut' that close together again. Some things can't be unheard."

"Oh, please, smarts, you know what I meant." Smarts was the nickname we'd used for each other since we were little and got in trouble for trying to casually slip 'smart ass' into our vocabulary. Nana was not a fan.

"Wait, didn't you say you were just at a bakery? Aren't those places like nut city?"

"Crap! Yes, I was, and yes they are full of nuts." I glanced at the clock and groaned. Definitely not enough time to go home and shower. "Uh, okay, I'll figure something out. I gotta go," I said and hung up without waiting for a response.

I let myself into the house, ran back to Bryce's bedroom, and took a lightning-quick shower.

I knew I was probably being dramatic, but I figured it was better to err on the side of caution since I had no idea how severe her allergy was or what the protocol was for potential peanut contamination.

After upside-down towel-drying my hair and throwing on one of Bryce's shirts, I got to work in the kitchen. I started by surveying and weeding out the obvious suspects: peanut butter, trail mix, store-bought cookies, granola. I found a package of Reese's cups and instantly lamented the fact that Peyton would never get to enjoy those little cups of heaven. Or Snickers. Or peanut butter M&Ms. At least she wouldn't have to be deprived of Starbursts.

Scanning a few ingredient lists of various snacks and condiments, I realized peanuts are sneaky little bastards that apparently work their way into all kinds of foods. I never knew so many things were made with peanut oil or in facilities with peanuts. *Apparently I've taken my nut tolerance for granted all these years.*

"Well…I hope he wasn't planning on eating a full meal any time soon," I muttered to myself before grabbing a bag of egg rolls out of the freezer. Between the produce that had spoiled since he left and the high-peanut-risk foods now sitting in a garbage bag, Bryce barely had anything edible left in his house.

In a panic, I grabbed my purse and scurried to the door to make a quick trip to the grocery store around the corner. I couldn't just leave them stranded without something to have for breakfast. Right before my hand reached the knob, the door creaked open and scared the bejesus out of me. I leapt back as something between a gasp and a squeal tore from my throat, startling Bryce in turn. He jerked back, and for a split-second I worried he'd stumble and drop Peyton. But he didn't. His quiet gasp was enough to make Peyton stir in his arms, but not enough to wake her.

"Elliot?!" he blurted. Dropping his voice to a whisper, he continued, "What are you doing here? How'd you get in?"

Instead of replying right away, I just stared at him. At her. At the two of them.

Peyton was dressed in a white shirt with a blue floral print and jeggings, a sliver of her diaper peeking out in the gap between the two. On her feet were the cutest, tiniest pair of glittery pink Toms I'd ever seen. Two bronze-colored pigtails pointed to the ceiling atop the sides of her head, and from this angle I had a profile view of her sweet face where it rested against Bryce's chest. Long, dark lashes fanned out, grazing the tops of her cheekbones. Her tiny mouth was open with her lips forming a little 'o' and vibrating with each steady breath she took.

Then there was Bryce.

One arm was hooked under Peyton and held her in place, making his bicep flex and those unreasonably sexy veins ripple across his forearm. His other hand was pressed to Peyton's back with his fingers lightly patting her in that soothing, comforting gesture I assumed came naturally to all parents. Well, most parents. His hair was a disheveled mess, and he was wearing those glasses that did stupid things to my body. A layer of scruff covered his jaw, cloaking the sharp angles I loved to admire. While his mouth curved into a smile, his eyes gave away his exhaustion. They were heavily lidded and lined with dark circles.

"I, uh, got the key from Xander. I thought I'd help you purge the house of all things peanuts. Then I got carried away and sort of threw out half your food. Sorry. But you didn't really have much to begin with. I was about to go get you guys something to have for breakfast."

Bryce's eyes scanned over my body, and through the heavy fog of exhaustion I saw them spark to life when they reached the hem of my (his) shirt and he fully registered my appearance.

"Without pants?" he asked, pointedly staring at my bare legs before slowly lifting his gaze. "Or a bra?"

I looked down and realized my nipples were hard and highly visible through the fabric of Bryce's shirt. I scrambled to fold my arms over my chest. Not that it did any good at this point; they were practically a neon sign, broadcasting how much the sight of Bryce in his dad element turned me on.

Huh. Good to know.

I was prepared for the sight of Bryce with Peyton to make me smile and maybe give me that same warm, tingly feeling in my heart that I got from seeing photos of them. Call me an idiot, but I was *not* prepared for the sight to make my ovaries sing and dance. Or for it to make my thighs clench together.

"Um, there's actually a really great explanation for this," I started, waving my hands up and down my body.

He glided past me and headed toward the hallway that lead to the bedrooms. "Oh, I'm sure there is. You can tell me all about it after I put her down," he whispered over his shoulder.

They disappeared into Peyton's room; I knew because I'd taken a quick peek into it after my shower. I hadn't really thought about her room or what I'd expected it to look like, but it was perfect. The walls were a soft gray with framed photos of wild animals all around. Her crib was painted white and had pink and white polka dotted sheets. A changing table-slash-dresser sat on the wall adjacent to her crib, with a gray glider in the corner. Toys in buckets and books lined a bookshelf on the opposite wall. I could easily picture Bryce rocking Peyton to sleep or sprawled out on the carpet playing with her.

In the minute that Bryce was in there, my mind ran wild. I had no business picturing the images that my brain conjured up. It was one thing to imagine what their life looked like from the outside, the two of them playing and laughing together. It was another thing to imagine what being a part of that life would be like.

For the first time in, well, ever, the idea of parenthood didn't send my heart rate soaring through the roof.

For the first time, the image of my own mother wasn't tethered to the notion of parenthood.

For the first time, I didn't rip out the seed of hope the word planted in my heart. *Instead, I let it take root.*

And yet...this persistent voice in my head continuously pointed out that whatever Bryce and I were doing was a far cry from making me a part of this life—their life.

And what happens when whatever it is that we're doing comes to an end? What then?

One single look at Peyton and I already loathed the possibility of ever being the source of her pain and heartache.

I sighed and leaned a shoulder against the wall, suddenly aware of my own exhaustion that had crept in.

"What's wrong, Uno?" Bryce asked from behind me as he scooped the hair off my neck and leaned down to kiss my shoulder.

His warmth and crisp, clean scent enveloped me as he wrapped his arms around my waist from behind. I lifted my hand to trace my fingertip over the veins in his forearm and breathed him in. We'd taken our time to be more than fleetingly physical with each other, but now that the floodgates had opened, I craved his touch, reveled in his proximity, and ached to feel him inside me. *Guess he really does have a magic dick.*

"How can something feel so right and so terrifying at the same time?"

Bryce's lips pressed a slow kiss into the valley between my neck and shoulder.

"I think the terrifying part is what makes something real, gives it value. For the record, I'm scared too, El."

I turned in his arms, and he linked his hands together on top of my butt. I laid my hands against his chest, tilting my head back to meet his warm gaze. "Bryce, I almost made you drop your sleeping daughter. Safe to say I'm already screwing things up."

"No. You're not. Trust me, nothing about you standing half-naked in my house when I get home is remotely close to screwing things up. Speaking of..." he trailed off, reaching down to slip his hand under the shirt. His fingers slowly skimmed back up, the heat of his touch branding me with every inch he covered. "What's the story?"

I yelp-gasped when his touch turned into a squeeze and brought me close enough to feel his erection press into my stomach. Slinging my hands around his neck, I brought us even closer and rolled my hips against him to relay my own need.

"Actually," he whispered huskily against my ear before shifting his mouth to my jaw then to my neck. "I couldn't care less what the story is right now. Come to bed with me. Let me worship you."

Oh holy hell.

I hesitated and darted a glance at Peyton's door. "Are you sure?"

"Positive," he assured me, nipping the patch of skin he'd just been kissing.

My 'okay' turned into a moan when he removed his hand from my butt to swipe his fingertips across the front of my panties. His touch was so light I wouldn't have felt it anywhere else, but his precision was exact and intentional, grazing the most sensitive spot.

"You know, I'm really tempted to see just how wet my words alone can get you. But that'll have to wait for another time because I need to know what you feel like. What you taste like."

"Bryce." In my head the word came out a stern warning not to tease me right now, but in reality it came out breathy and desperate.

He tugged me forward and into his bedroom, not even bothering to turn the living room light off or his bedroom light on. Before my eyes could adjust to the darkness, Bryce's hands were at my thighs and lifted me up for the sake of throwing me on the bed. It was technically more of a toss, but he could throw me around like a damn rag doll if he wanted for all I cared right now.

Bryce pulled his shirt off, tossing it to the ground before stripping his pants off. Left only in what I could now make out as boxer briefs, he crawled his way up my body, bringing the shirt with him until it was completely off of me. I was certain my heart could be heard from any room in the house—hell, probably from any house on the block. *Is this really happening? I can't believe the boy who taught me how to play Uno and rollerblade and how to multiply is now the man who's about to school me in a whole new way.*

Bryce muttered a *hmm,* but before I could decipher its meaning he leaned over the side of his bed and plugged something into a nearby outlet. A soft glow illuminated the room, just enough to see each other clearly.

"Much better." He scooted back to where he'd been before, propped above me with his knees on either side of my hips and studied my body like it was a map that led him to lost treasure.

Coincidentally, the two indentions that formed a V at the base of his core did lead to a treasure; this I already knew for certain. A treasure that was begging to get reacquainted with my mouth.

"Christ, I should've known," he groaned.

"Known what?" I huffed, peeling my attention away from his McMagicDick.

He leaned forward onto his elbows and started slowly grinding against me.

"That you'd be so fucking perfect. So beautiful." His hot mouth started a trail along my neck, alternating between kisses and little nips on his way down. "Do you know that I haven't stopped thinking about what your lips felt like around my cock?" Kiss. "About having your body under mine, completely at my mercy?" Lick. "How many times I've wondered what your pussy tastes like?" His nip at the swell of my breast made me moan and writhe, generating a delicious friction against his erection. "How many times I've imagined you riding my cock?" *Bite.* "How it would feel to make you fall apart only to put you back together?"

Yesyesyesyesyes.

"I've dreamt of that—of all of it, Bryce," I said, his bold confessions giving me the courage to shine a light on my own. His head popped up, meeting my eyes through the dim glow. I cupped his unshaven cheek in a gesture far too sweet considering the filthy words coming out of his mouth. Or the ones about to spill from mine. "I've imagined it all. Every night. Before, when you made that masturbating comment? You weren't wrong. It's been this way since the day you came over and played Mario Kart. At this point, my vibrator should be renamed in your honor."

"Vibrator?" The question was barely out of his mouth before he scooted down and grabbed my panties with his teeth. Once they were off, he looked up and wiggled his eyebrows playfully, a dangerously seductive smile crawling from one side of his mouth to the other. "Better brace yourself, Uno, 'cause I'm about to ruin vibrator-Bryce for you. You won't even be able to look at it without knowing it's a shitty substitute for the real thing."

Okay, I only *thought* I liked Bryce's (relatively) tasteful dirty talking.

Turned out the real deal was a thousand times better than I ever could've imagined.

And then it got even better.

His fingers slid up my leg until they were *there*, pushing into the wetness, into me.

"So wet," he commented, sinking his fingers deeper. "What do you want, El? Hard and fast? Sweet and slow? Tell me."

Before I could register his question, he snaked his tongue out and over my clit.

His words...his mouth...his fingers...independently they would've rendered me breathless. Together, they drew a loud moan out of me and made me forget how to make decisions.

"Yes and yes," I panted, nodding frantically. "I want both. Either. Just don't stop, whatever you do."

"Believe me; stopping is the last thing I want right now. Not when you taste even better than I imagined. Sweeter," he said, the stubble on his cheeks tickling the inside of my thighs with each mumbled word.

His fingers started moving in sync with his mouth, a blissful torture, and I pressed the back of my hand to my mouth in an effort to contain the wild, desperate sounds Bryce's handiwork elicited.

Without breaking his concentration, he reached up and batted my arm away from my face. "No. Let me hear you, Elliot."

I complied, not even trying to contain my volume as I moaned his name while I fell apart seconds later.

The sound of foil ripping yanked my head out of the orgasm-clouds and crashed me right into a wave of greedy desire. I propped myself up on my elbows in time to catch Bryce's abs constrict while he rolled the condom on, and it took me a second to realize the foreign, needy whimpers were coming from me.

I hooked my legs together behind him and urged him forward. He looked up but didn't budge.

His hand wrapped around his cock, gripping the base. "This what you want?"

"God, yes," I cried desperately.

But it was drowned out by the sounds of *real* crying.

Loud and piercing.

From the baby monitor on Bryce's dresser.

We both froze and looked over at the screen that was now lit up with a black and white feed.

Peyton was standing in her crib, her cries on the verge of hysteria.

Bryce groaned and muttered something about her weird sixth sense and that his dick was about to hate him.

Reluctantly, he rolled off me and tugged on a pair of sweats.

"Um...should I...?" I gestured toward my clothes, suddenly feeling exposed and awkward.

"No, don't. This shouldn't take long."

"Okay."

Ten minutes and two failed attempts at sneaking out of her room later, I started to worry he'd never get her back to sleep.

On the plus side, watching him with her through the monitor, hearing him comfort her in a gentle, soothing tone brought the biggest smile to my face.

Just when I didn't think it could possibly get sweeter, he started humming then singing quietly.

Bryce freaking McKnight was singing Elton John's 'Tiny Dancer,' and I suddenly wanted him to sing *me* to sleep.

Swoon.

The next thing I knew, arms wrapped around me as a hard body pressed into me from behind, and a sharp stubble grazed the side of my neck, vibrating with the hum of a soft melody.

"Bryce?" I mumbled, trying to pull myself out of slumber.

He kissed my temple. "Shh, go back to sleep, El."

"But—"

"Later, Uno. I'm not going anywhere."

As I settled into his embrace and let myself fall back to sleep, I only had one thought.

Please don't let this be a dream.

CHAPTER 18

ELLIOT

After a night that felt like a dream, the following morning definitely wasn't.

Peyton's "Dada!" chants woke us up, and I realized how impulsive sleeping over had been. We didn't have a plan, hadn't discussed how to handle introductions. When I mentioned that to Bryce, he looked at me like I'd asked him how to defuse a bomb.

"She's a toddler, not an FBI agent, El. Her limited vocabulary makes interrogations a breeze, anyway."

Toddler or not, I was right to be wary of first-thing-in-the-morning introductions. Bryce brought Peyton to the couch where I was waiting for them, and she immediately tightened her grip on him and buried her face in his neck. It would've been a precious sight if not for the fact that it meant she was hiding from me.

"Baby, it's okay. This is Elliot. You'll like her, I promise," he said gently. He tried to pry her arms away, but she wouldn't have it.

I had no clue how to react.

Maybe if I sit really still she won't feel threatened.

I immediately gave myself a mental face-palm.

She's not a wild animal, Elliot.

"She's not a fan of mornings. At least not until after she has some milk," Bryce explained, rubbing her back. She peeked out from behind his neck, just long enough to meet my eyes for a second.

I offered her a smile, but all it seemed to do was scare her back into the crook of his neck. "I can relate. It usually takes me a cup or two of coffee or tea before I function properly."

"See; you two already have something in common."

He stood and set her down before walking into the kitchen. Naturally, she scurried after him and clung to his legs.

"Peyton," he chided with a sigh.

"Dada up! Dada up!" she cried, slapping his thighs.

"Shi—oot," he corrected quickly. "I forgot that I'm out of milk. And basically everything else. Guess we're going out for breakfast. Wanna come?" He paused, long enough to make me look up and catch his smirk. "To breakfast?"

I narrowed my eyes but didn't stop the smile stretching across my lips as I joined him in the kitchen. "You think you're so cute, don't you?"

"No, *you* think I'm cute."

"Oh, you're definitely something, McKnight."

He picked Peyton back up, and this time she didn't hide completely. She looked at me through her long lashes with reluctant curiosity.

I took this opportunity to catalog their similarities. Peyton's eyes were a deep shade of green, but they were the same shape as her dad's. Her nose was a miniature version of his, and they wore matching smiles.

She looked at Bryce and pressed her little hands against each of his cheeks. "Milk! Peas!"

Peas?

Oh. *Please. Well that's the cutest thing I've ever heard.* Cute enough to make something foreign pinch inside my chest.

He leaned in and brushed his nose against hers, making her giggle before bending to pick up the little pink blanket thing she'd dropped. "We don't have any milk, baby girl. But look, here's your pig!"

She grabbed it, a smile instantly lighting up her sweet face.

Bryce's comment triggered a memory, and suddenly Helen's face flashed in my mind—eyes dilated and jaw clenched in annoyance.

"Milk isn't cheap, Elliot. You can drink water or nothing at all."

"But Mommy, Sophia—"

"Sophia is fine. You don't hear her whining like an ungrateful little brat, do you?"

"El? Breakfast?" Bryce called. He shifted Peyton to his other arm, his brows wrinkling with concern, and for a second I thought he might question where my mind had gone.

Which would've been valid because...*where the hell did that come from?*

Nowhere good, that's for sure.

"Bryce, I don't know," I answered, shifting my eyes to Peyton. "She's not hiding from me anymore. Maybe we shouldn't push our luck. Plus, I'm not exactly dressed for going out in public at the moment."

He eyed my bare legs and smirked. "Good point. There's a kolache shop a couple blocks away. How about you two stay here, and I'll run to grab us some food."

"You want to leave her with me? Alone?" I asked, eyes wide. "Are you sure that's a good idea?"

He set Peyton down and closed the gap separating us, cupping my face in his hands. "El, it'll be fine. I promise." He leaned in and pressed his lips against mine for a quick kiss. "If you put on *Frozen* for her, you'll probably become her favorite person. And I'll be back in ten minutes. She might not even notice I'm gone."

Ten minutes.

I could handle that.

I slung my arms around his waist and sighed. "Okay. But don't forget the coffee. And make it a large."

"You got it." He turned and nodded toward Peyton where she

stood, playing with her pretend grill. "I'm gonna duck out while she's preoccupied. You got this."

Peyton must have had a sixth sense about Bryce, because ten seconds after his car pulled out of the driveway, she looked around and immediately noticed his absence.

She ran around, calling for him, each plea more panic-filled than the last.

"It's okay, Peyton, Daddy will be right back! He went to get food," I explained, following behind her.

She stopped and stared at me, confusion written all over her sweet little face. In a flash, her confusion morphed back into panic, and she burst into tears.

Shit.

"How about we watch *Frozen*? I hear it's your favorite."

That got her attention.

She followed me back into the living room, and I quickly searched for the TV remote. Except...it was nowhere to be found.

I dug around in the crevices of the couch and looked under it. Pulled cushions off and kept searching. Nothing.

"Peyton, do you know where the remote is?" I asked, not really expecting an answer.

But I wasn't expecting dead silence either.

I lifted my head up from under the coffee table and looked around. The second I realized she wasn't in the room, I heard a clicking sound from the hallway.

"Peyton?" I shouted, desperately hoping for her to magically pop out from behind the couch.

I pushed off the ground like it had turned into lava and ran toward the hallway bathroom, panic crashing over me as soon as I realized what had happened.

Oh my god. No. Please don't be in there.

I gripped the knob and twisted, but the door didn't budge.

My mother's voice echoed somewhere in the back of my mind. *"I should've known you'd be nothing but a screw-up."*

I froze.

No.

I shoved that voice back into its box and knocked on the bathroom door. "Peyton? Are you in there?"

She didn't respond, but a banging sound from inside told me she was there. The cabinets had childproof locks, but that didn't stop me from panicking. *Shit. What if Little Miss Houdini gets them open? Who knows what she'll get into.*

I tried the knob again. Definitely locked.

How the fuck did she lock the door?

I looked down and studied the lock. *Maybe I can pick it.* But I didn't have any bobby pins and had no idea if that trick even worked.

I took a second to calm my racing heart so my voice didn't relay my total panic. "Peyton, honey, I need you to come to the door and turn the lock."

Right. Because she totally knows how to follow those instructions at the ripe age of twenty months old.

I ran into the living room and grabbed my phone.

Peyton babbled gibberish and pulled on the doorknob from inside the bathroom, and I got the feeling she was seconds away from a meltdown.

Bryce finally answered after six torturous rings. "Hey. Just ordered our food. What's up?"

Words and tears poured out of me simultaneously. "Bryce, oh my god," I wailed. "I'm so sorry! I turned around for one second to find the remote and now she's locked in the bathroom and I can't get her out! I'm sorry! You shouldn't have trusted me!"

"El, whoa, whoa, whoa. Slow down. It's okay. Take a breath," he commanded.

"Bryce! How is this okay?" I screeched, not understanding how he could be so calm while I was freaking the hell out. "What if she swallows something or hurts herself?"

"El, there's a key to the bathroom on top of the door frame."

I immediately pushed up on my toes and ran my fingers along the frame. A small silver key tumbled to the ground.

"Oh my god. I feel like such an idiot," I mumbled, sliding the key into the lock.

"You're not an idiot, Uno. Just a little unpracticed."

I pushed the door open and dropped the phone, sweeping a sobbing Peyton into my arms. She latched on to me like I was her hero, and I honestly wasn't sure which one of us was more relieved.

With one arm hooked under Peyton, I picked the phone back up. "Okay, we're good. Sorry. I guess I might have overreacted."

"Don't worry about it. Really. She's stealthy as hell. I should've warned you."

I couldn't help but chuckle. "Noted."

A few minutes later, Bryce found us sprawled out in her room, reading a book about farm animals. He cleared his throat and held out her milk in one hand and my coffee in the other. Peyton shot out of my lap to run toward him.

Bryce scooped her up and pressed a kiss to the top of her head. "I'm sorry she gave you such a scare," he said, concern etched into his features.

I took the coffee and shrugged. "Nothing like a mini-heart attack to get the blood pumping before seven a.m."

"If it helps, not *every* morning is this dramatic. Plus, it seems like it wasn't all bad; she looked pretty cozy in your lap."

"Yeah; I think it actually helped us bond in a weird, round-about way."

One silver lining of Peyton waking us up at the crack of dawn was that we finished breakfast and I still had an hour before I needed to be at work.

"Hey," Bryce called from the kitchen. "There's a 'Boo at the Zoo' Halloween thing tomorrow evening. Have you been before? I'm not sure how long Peyton will last, but I think she'd enjoy it. Want to come with us?"

"I've heard of it, but I've never been. I'd love to go with you guys." I smiled, both at the thought of Peyton's excitement at seeing the animals and at my own memories of time spent at the zoo as a kid. "As long as you promise not to get any crazy ideas. Last time we went to the zoo together, you spent a month trying to convince your parents to let you get a ball python."

He laughed. "El, I was, what, twelve? Now I'm trying to hold off on pets for as long as possible considering this one will probably ask for a pig as soon as she's speaking in complete sentences. Plus, there's already a python in the house, and two's a crowd."

"Did you seriously just mention your daughter in one breath and your...c-o-c-k...the next?" I asked, dropping my voice.

He handed Peyton her sippy cup before walking over and sitting beside me on the couch. "She's not even two; she has no idea what I was talking about. Did you seriously just spell out the word cock? Because that was weirdly hot."

He leaned in, kissed my neck, and I groaned.

"Bryce. I really do need to run home and shower. And Peyton is staring at us." I tilted my head at her. She was sitting on her *Frozen* plastic ride-on car, munching on her crackers and watching us like a hawk.

He swiveled his head around to see Peyton's scowl and sighed. "My daughter, the eternal c-o-c-k blocker."

I couldn't help but giggle, pushing against his chest to stand. "You poor, poor thing. I think you'll survive."

"Easy for you to say." He stood and followed me to the laundry room. "In all seriousness, El, I'm sorry about last night, that things got...derailed. Again."

"Don't be. Maybe the third time'll be the charm," I quipped, pressing up on my toes to give him a quick peck. Before he got any ideas about taking things further, I pulled back and grabbed my purse then headed for the door. I turned back and gave Peyton a smile that morphed into a smirk when I looked at her dad. "Until then, I guess vibrator-Bryce will just have to do."

I blew him a kiss and reached for the door handle.

"Really? You're just going to give me that mental picture and leave?"

"Yeah, I think I am."

"Game on, Uno," he called, reaching for the back of his shirt as he made his way to the door. I froze and watched him pull it off in what felt like slow motion. Bryce and his ridiculously lickable abs came to a stop and leaned against the door frame. "Game. Fucking. On."

Well that backfired in a big, WTF-was-I-thinking way.

WHEN BRYCE SAID 'GAME ON' what he meant was 'I'm going to torture you with visuals of my own.'

All. Damn. Day.

I had back-to-back meetings with clients until mid-afternoon, but every glance at my phone made me regret ever walking out of Bryce's house.

An hour after I left, he sent me a shirtless selfie wearing his sex-me-up glasses and a smug smirk.

Two hours after that, another selfie, this time at the park licking ice cream from a cone.

Later, the mirror selfie to end all mirror selfies—Bryce post-shower, a towel hanging wickedly low around his hips. And the glasses. Always the glasses.

The fact that I got any work done was a testament to how dedicated I was to FMK and my job.

Even a day later, sitting in the conference room with Jasmine, Jade, and Carleigh, talking about plans for the venue, my mind kept wandering back to Bryce and this wicked little game of foreplay.

The four of us had spent a solid two hours making plans and going over the sketches Bryce had emailed from Seattle, and I only retained fifty percent of what was said. *Great.*

"Hello? Earth to Elliot," Jade called from across the table.

"What? Sorry," I said, whipping my head up and away from Bryce's text.

Jasmine sat between us at the head of the table and eyed me

suspiciously. "You were just smiling at your phone like it had turned into a magic lamp and was about to grant you three wishes. You've got a serious blush working its way up your neck. And you're so antsy to bolt out of here you wouldn't have batted an eyelash if I'd just suggested naming the venue after my second favorite porno. Spill it, Kincaid."

I swallowed and wracked my brain for a denial, but Jas was right. My mind was totally not in the game. "Uh, I...crap," I muttered, trailing my hands over my neck in a futile effort to hide my blush.

Jasmine gasped and slapped the table.

"Holy fucking shit! You slept with Bryce! I knew it," she exclaimed, looking totally confident in her assumption. "Good for you. I'm betting your history with him only made it hotter. Am I right? Of course I'm right, otherwise you wouldn't be trying to hide it from us."

Jade and Carleigh both gasped on cue and stared at me from the opposite side of the table.

"Oh my god, Jas is right, isn't she?" Carleigh mused, her smile wide and knowing, and her blue eyes studying me closely. She flipped her red mane over her shoulder and scooted closer to the table, propping her elbows on the surface and resting her chin in her hands. "You've been way too tight-lipped about things with him lately, which means things are more serious than you're letting on. I mean, we all know you were channeling your sexual frustration into your work while he was gone. And you're totally blushing like a teenager. It makes so much sense now."

I sighed and accepted the fact that there was no getting out of this conversation. "All right, Nancy Drew one and two, relax. Yes, I like him. A lot. Other than that, though, I don't have much to tell you." Jade lifted a brow. Carleigh's eyes narrowed. Jas pursed her lips. The three of them remained silent, staring at me. "Look," I said, flustered, "Our circumstances aren't exactly normal. Things ended on a high note with Peyton yesterday, but only after I let her freaking lock herself in a bathroom. I have no idea if I'll ever be able to fully win her over. On top of that hurdle, you guys know how delicate and complicated things are given his involvement with the inn and now the venue. We're not rushing to label anything, and I'm perfectly okay with that. All I know is spending time with him makes me happy, and that's enough."

"If you're happy, I'm happy for you," Carleigh offered.

Jade nodded in agreement. "We're curious because we care, El." She leaned across the table and gave my arm a squeeze, her reassuring smile echoing her words. "You've been so one-track-minded with work for a while now. Just promise me that you'll remember to let yourself have a life outside of FMK and the inn and the venue. You're twenty-four; you've got a lifetime to spend at work, but how often does a Bryce McKnight come along?"

Twice in the last decade, if we're keeping track.

Jas was suspiciously quiet, choosing this moment to go refill her coffee cup. Jas was never quiet; her thoughts were practically loud enough to hear most of the time. When she came back to the table, the three of us stared at her expectantly.

"What?" she asked, shrugging. "I mean, ditto what Jade and Carleigh said. I'm happy you're happy, El."

We all continued to stare at her, collectively waiting for the 'but' that we knew was burning on the tip of Jasmine's tongue.

She sipped her coffee and diverted her gaze to the piles of notes in front of her.

I reached out and pulled her notebook away. "Jas, what the hell? I know there's something else you're not saying. Spit it out."

She shifted in her seat, keeping her eyes down before sighing and looking up to meet my gaze. "Fine. It's just…I can't help but wonder if you'd be less reluctant to label things with Bryce if you had true closure with Helen. I've known you through two different boyfriends and through your dating hiatus, and I've never seen you anywhere near as happy as you were even when you were still trying to convince yourself he belonged in the 'strictly friends' category. It's so obvious that you two belong in each other's lives. I'm not saying you're destined to ride off into the sunset with him, but maybe you are. Maybe he's 'it' for you, or maybe not. But I know you, Elliot, and I know you won't hesitate to break your own damn heart if you think there's even a chance you'll do to Peyton what Helen did to you."

For a moment, nobody dared to speak or move. Maybe even breathe.

I forced air into my lungs and willed my heart to keep beating, even though processing Jas's words was enough to stop it cold.

God, the truth is a harsh mistress.

Finally, Jas broke the silence of her own creation, continuing, "I love and adore and admire you, El. For so many reasons. But you've never seen yourself clearly when it comes to the scars Helen left in you. I know what the absence of a parent can do," she said softly, reaching over to cover my hand with hers. "The scars and the havoc they wreak can lay dormant for years, just waiting to strike when you're least expecting it. Listen, you can say no, tell me to fuck off, whatever, but hear me out. Let me ask Dean to use his resources at work to find whatever information he can on Helen. You can do whatever you want with the information, whether that's speaking with her in person or just using that information to give you closure. Just say the word and I'll ask."

Jas's mom passed away when she was thirteen, so our experiences and losses were vastly different, but she understood more than most what it was like to go through life without a mother. Her offer was sincere and heart-felt, and I wasn't sure she'd ever know how much I appreciated it.

"I'll think about it," I promised, squeezing her hand in turn.

Maybe she was right.

Getting answers from Helen wasn't going to magically fix everything, but maybe...just maybe, it would bring me enough peace to quiet the doubts and fears that had crept into the crevices of my mind.

CHAPTER 19
ELLIOT

My phone buzzed against my desk while I packed up for my next meeting, and when I saw Bryce's name I quickly dropped the stack of paperwork in favor of reading his text. I planned to meet him and Peyton in a few hours, but that didn't stop butterflies from fluttering to life at the sight of his name on my phone screen.

BRYCE: Peyton is going to be in her costume tonight, so feel free to come in one too. I'd be happy to make some suggestions if you can't think of one… ;)

ELLIOT: Oh, you'd love that. Let me guess…slutty nurse?

BRYCE: I'm a little offended you don't think I'm more creative than that.

ELLIOT: Yeah, ohhhhhhkay. What's Peyton's costume?

A photo of a fluffy pink blob came through, and I zoomed in on the picture to see that it was a little pig.

ELLIOT: Oh my god! That's adorable. I wish I had more time. We could've all gone as animals!

BRYCE: *Good thing you're already a fox.*

ELLIOT: *Wow, Bryce. That was so cheesy, you should be a goat tonight.*

BRYCE: *Oh, I'm the goat alright. As in, 'greatest of all time'…if you know what I mean. *Smirking emoji**

ELLIOT: *Starting to wish I didn't.*

BRYCE: *You're lion.*

ELLIOT: *Stop. I don't think I can bear another dad-pun.*

BRYCE: *Whale, I can't say that doesn't hurt.*

ELLIOT: *OMG.*

BRYCE: *I'm not kitten.*

ELLIOT: *You are officially the dorkiest person I know.*

BRYCE: *Strange…I've never seen a phone autocorrect 'sexiest' that dramatically.*

ELLIOT: *…still proving my point. I'll see you soon, punny man.*

It should've been weird that a brief, flirty text conversation with Bryce made me feel like a giddy schoolgirl. The same Bryce who used to play with me in the rain and once offered to beat up the first boy who broke my heart. The same Bryce who camped out with me under the stars long ago and gave me one of the walkie talkies he got for Christmas one year, just so I could call him if I had a nightmare.

But it wasn't weird.

It was actually sorta wonderful.

Our friendship was innocent back then, but there was nothing innocent about the way Bryce McKnight made me feel now. The ease I always felt with him, the comfort from our friendship, the trust between us, had come rushing back, only now I didn't just look at him and see my old friend. The boy I'd spent my childhood playing with had become the man I couldn't stop thinking about.

And, for once, I wasn't obsessing over the future. I wasn't trying to plan and label and categorize exactly what we were doing.

For once...I was happy to just *be*. In the moment. With him.

In our '*B and E*' bubble.

The thing about bubbles though? Sooner or later, they always pop.

A FEW HOURS LATER, I drove to Bryce's house sporting the same smile I'd had since I read his first terrible pun. Not even an 'emergency' meeting with a bridezilla from hell was enough to bring me down. Instead of stressing about the five last minute, over-the-top changes she requested for her upcoming wedding, I pictured how freaking adorable I knew Peyton would be in her costume. Instead of letting my mind run wild thinking about all the work I could be doing, I focused solely on how much fun tonight would be.

Unlike the last time I showed up at his house, Bryce was (merci)fully clothed when he opened the front door. But Peyton was propped on his hip, so the swoon-factor was still perfectly intact. The sight drew a smile from my lips and sent that same rush of warmth through my veins.

"Hey, you."

"Hey, you two," I replied, giving Peyton what I hoped was a

non-creepy smile. She swung her pink-tight-clad legs back and forth and leaned into Bryce, but didn't hide completely this time, instead flashing me a tentative smile in return. *I'll take what I can get.*

Bryce adjusted her position so I could see the whole costume, then flipped up her hood to give me the full effect. With the hood up, she was covered in soft chenille tendrils with pointy ears and a round nose. Holes at the tops of her thighs allowed her legs to poke out, and little plastic hooves covered her shoes.

I'd never seen anything cuter in my life.

"Oh my god! She's going to be the cutest animal of all!"

Bryce grinned and grabbed a bag off the hook behind the door. "That she is. Ready to take this little piggy to the zoo?"

"Do you mind if I change first? I'll be fast." I held up my duffel bag. "Pretty sure silk and zoos don't mix."

"Sure, I'll get her buckled while you change. We'll wait for you in the car."

I sped off toward the bathroom and traded my dress for skinny jeans and an off-the-shoulder top I had stolen from Sophia, swapping my heels for booties.

Satisfied, I hurried out to Bryce's SUV and hopped into the passenger seat. As I clicked my seatbelt into place, he hit the brakes; we hadn't even made it out of the driveway.

I paused and looked over at him, confused. "Did you forget something?"

"Yeah. This," he said, shifting into park and leaning across the center console to frame my face with his hands. Before I could react, his mouth pressed to mine, freezing the smile splayed on my lips. I melted into the kiss, into him, gripping his wrists in my hands like I needed them to keep me grounded. I didn't know how he did it, how it was possible for a simple kiss from Bryce to simultaneously reduce me to a mess of lust and desperation and fill me with happiness and peace. But that's exactly what his kisses did. Every. Single. Time.

I blinked him back into focus after our kiss broke and met his heavily-lidded eyes. "Maybe you should forget that more often," I teased.

His thumb brushed along my bottom lip, freeing it from under my teeth before he pulled his gaze away. "Or maybe I'll just kiss you more often."

"Eh, maybe."

"Maybe?! Funny, there was no 'maybe' when my mouth was on a different part of your anatomy the other night," he countered, tapping his index finger against my lips with a smirk.

"Hmm, that's not ringing a bell. Must've been a fluke." I tried to keep my smile in check, but it refused to be contained.

"Careful, El. You know I love a good challenge."

I spent the rest of the drive to the zoo actively trying not to think about the little thrill his words sent racing through me.

THE AUSTIN ZOO was located on about fifteen acres of land at the outskirts of the city, allowing guests to enjoy the animals and the beauty of hill country simultaneously. To me, what made this zoo special was the fact that the animals were all rescues—some retired from other facilities or from laboratory testing, some seized in animal cruelty cases, and some surrendered by owners who couldn't keep up with the care required for exotic pets. Knowing these animals had been given a second chance at life, even if it was within the confines of a zoo, was heartbreakingly beautiful.

The first time Nana and Pops brought me here, I burst into tears when Nana explained that all of this zoo's animals were rescued from bad places or from other zoos who wanted to make room for younger animals. While I still found it sad that these majestic creatures were forced to live out their lives in captivity, I also felt a sense of connection with them. I knew what it was like to be uprooted from the only home you knew and dropped into a new world.

Every October, the zoo hosted several nights like this one.

Guests came after hours wearing costumes and enjoyed the haunted house or a train ride along a spooky, Halloween-themed trail. They also had the opportunity to see the nocturnal animals.

It was a perfect fall night for a stroll through the park, which was a good thing considering Peyton's disinterest in the children's show. The girl was an animal lover, through and through.

I didn't realize I'd spaced out until I looked over and saw that Bryce had walked around to the other side of the black bear enclosure, hip propped against the railing as he pointed at the little cubs wrestling on the other side of the enclosure. So far, we'd seen a tiger, a lion, and a serval. Bryce had purposely put off the potbellied pig, knowing Peyton would probably want to stay there indefinitely. Fortunately, the bears held her interest now. She clapped her hands together and squealed in delight as they rolled off the deck. Her reactions to the animals were quickly becoming my favorite part of our zoo visit. I pulled out my phone and snapped a picture of her before joining them.

"Bryce, in case I haven't said it yet, you're an incredible dad. You really are a natural; you make it look so easy," I said, nudging his shoulder with mine. "Total DILF material."

He laughed, and I could've sworn the faint color creeping into his cheeks was a blush. "You know, it's funny. She's going to be two in a few months, and I still wake up amazed that I get to be her dad. I know it sounds cheesy as hell, but it's true. I was completely and utterly unprepared for parenthood, and I was so afraid I wouldn't be enough. But when I consider what would've happened if Bridgette had kept her, the kind of life Peyton would've had..." He trailed off, then visibly stiffened, as if his words had only just registered. "God, El, I'm sorry. I wasn't thinking—"

I shook my head and covered his hand with mine. "Bryce, no. It's okay. You're allowed to make that connection. I hate that abandonment is something Peyton and I have in common, but at the same time I don't want it to be something the three of us can't or don't talk about. I know our situations aren't the same in a lot of ways, but I don't want Peyton to grow up with the same anxiety about her mom that I had, feeling like it's wrong to have questions about her. And I want *you* to know that if she does ask questions or wants to know about Bridgette one day, it doesn't mean she loves you any less."

Bryce wrapped his free arm over my shoulders and pulled me into his side before pressing his lips against the top of my head. I leaned into him and slipped my arm around his waist, loving the way we fit together.

"What was that for?" I asked.

"You just implied there will be discussions between the three of us...as in, *future* discussions."

"Oh, god, I did, didn't I? I just meant, you know..." I sighed, pulling away enough to see his face.

"That we'll be important pieces of each other's lives down the line?" he continued. "I fu...freaking hope so, Elliot. I know, based on the past, it's easy to question it, but things are different now. *I'm* different. And I'm not going anywhere."

"But what if—"

"Hey," he interjected, tipping my chin up. "Remember what I said about the *what if* game. I know you hate uncertainty. I know planning ahead puts your mind at ease and unknowns freak you out. But the wrong *what ifs* are poisonous, El. Let's try something. Give me a *what if*— a worst case about anything—and I'll give you one in return, and we go back and forth with them. Not answering, just volleying. Sometimes just verbalizing things can help clear the negativity out of your system."

"Okay. Yeah, let's do it."

Whether it was perfect timing on his part or just good luck, I couldn't tell, but we'd ambled away from the bears and were now standing in front of the pig, much to Peyton's delight. Bryce set her down, and she quickly scurried up toward the barrier, eagerly pressing her little hands against it and straining to see inside.

"Okay, we're good for at least ten minutes. I'll go first. What if

Peyton never outgrows her pig obsession and refuses to eat bacon?"

I laughed and slapped his arm. "I think you'll manage."

"Hey, it's a real concern." He smiled, but then it melted into neutrality. "Okay. No answering, El. Just back and forth."

I took a breath and released the *what if* I kept coming back to. "What if the inn or venue fails?"

Bryce's eyes softened, and I knew he wanted to address my question, but he'd just reminded me of the rules. "What if David and Louise eventually resent me for moving their only grandchild across the country?"

"What if my grandparents' retirement means they take off and I only see them once or twice a year?"

"What if you hate the way the venue plans turn out?" he asked with complete sincerity.

"Bryce." My face pinched into disbelief, but I didn't elaborate. "What if you leave again?"

"El." His hand moved to cup my face, his thumb gently stroking my cheek. "What if I don't?"

"What if we…" *What if we fall in love and things fall apart?*

Bryce stepped closer, skating his fingers over the skin of my neck before weaving them into my hair and holding me in place. "What if," he leaned in and kissed my cheek. "I." Down my jawline. "Make." Up the other side. "You." Cheek. "Mine."

Oh my god.

I couldn't decide which I craved more—his lips or his words.

But then his mouth crashed into mine and made the decision for me. I welcomed his kiss as if it held the answers to all my *what ifs*. In this moment, it did. Each swipe of his tongue against mine silenced my brain and turned those *what ifs* into hopeful *maybes*.

Mindful of where we were, Bryce pulled back before our display ventured into indecent territory. The look in his eyes was an echo of his last *what if*—a heady mixture of desire and possession. "Stay the night, Uno. Stay with me."

I nodded without hesitation, grinning like a crazy person

thanks to the way my stomach flipped at the implication behind his plea. "Okay."

"I'd say I hope you packed pajamas in that duffel bag, but I'd be lying. In fact, I'm tempted to light the bag on fire just in case you did bring pjs."

"You didn't have this little proclivity for pyrotechnics last time I slept over."

"I learn from my mistakes."

I arched a brow at him. "What if they're sexy pajamas?"

He playfully swatted my ass with a smooth subtlety. "Then they'll be *ripped* sexy pajamas."

"Promises, promises, Toad…" I trailed off into a smirk, backing away toward Peyton while my eyes roamed Bryce's body.

His laugh at my newest nickname (his least-favorite Mario Kart character) was a mixture of disbelief and warning. *I'm probably going to pay for that one.*

I crouched down next to Peyton, and she immediately began babbling animatedly about her new pot-bellied friend. My phone buzzed in my back pocket, and I smiled at the photo from Bryce—Peyton positioned between my legs where I knelt, one hand patting my leg and the other pointing toward the pig with a huge smile encompassing her face.

> BRYCE: *I'm going to run to the restroom, then I'll go buy some goat food. I figure our best shot at getting P to willingly ditch the pig is distraction. You good?*

I swiveled around and shook my head, trying not to panic at the thought of being alone with her again.

He gestured to his phone before quickly typing another message.

> BRYCE: *You'll be fine, El. I promise. She's happy.*

> ELLIOT: *What if she realizes you're gone and freaks out?!*

BRYCE: *What if she eats a handful of the goat food?*

ELLIOT: *Hm. Could be worse. Assuming it's peanut-free goat food!*

He didn't reply right away, so I looked back and found him smiling before he mouthed, "See? You got this."

I sighed and gave him a thumbs up without drawing Peyton's attention.

After a few minutes, Peyton grabbed my hand and started tugging me around the enclosure so she could get a closer view. Once we were directly behind the pig, she threw her arms up and squawked, "Up! Up!"

I scooped her up into my arms and settled her onto my hip. The pig looked directly at Peyton and stopped just on the other side of the fence from us, causing Peyton to squeal with joy and wiggle her whole body against mine. He immediately plopped on to his back and started rolling around.

I let out a laugh and shook my head. "Look, Peyton, he's showing off for his number one fan!"

"Moe!" Peyton shouted.

"Aw, does this pig remind you of your Lulu's pig back in Washington?" I asked, not really expecting an answer.

Peyton continued watching the pig, completely enamored. The joy on her face was priceless, and I couldn't bring myself to care what antics the pig pulled. I only cared about soaking in the bliss of Peyton's happiness.

Her feet went into hyper speed, kicking back and forth against me. At the same time, I felt someone brush past me from behind.

"So sorry about that," I said, turning to a white-haired woman who looked to be a few years older than Nana.

She smiled and waved me off. "It's not a problem, dear. Your daughter sure is adorable."

"She's..." I paused and glanced at Peyton. She tightened her grip on my shirt and pressed her head against my shoulder, sliding right into shy mode. "Thank you. I couldn't agree more."

I had intended to clarify the situation, but the words felt wrong and wouldn't leave my throat. I told myself it didn't matter what a complete stranger thought; going with her assumption was certainly easier than offering an explanation.

I also told myself it didn't matter that her words floated through my veins and into my heart, making a home there.

CHAPTER 20
BRYCE

I'M GOING TO HELL.

Bringing Peyton to the zoo was mostly selfish. I knew she'd love seeing all the animals, but I also knew it would wear her out. So, really, it was a win-win for us both.

She was so exhausted by the time we got home that I was able to put her to bed in record time.

Slipping out of Peyton's room without making a sound, I pulled the door closed and followed the sound of random notes from my guitar.

The sight of El curled up on the couch, running her fingers over the strings made me smile. Then again, the sight of Elliot always made me smile. It didn't matter if she was rolling her eyes at one of my lame jokes or gloating because she beat me at Mario Kart or if she was giving me a look that spelled out exactly how much she wanted me; every second I spent with her filled me with a happiness I'd only ever felt when around her. The feeling was addicting, and I found myself craving her presence every time we were apart.

"Are you gonna come over here or just keep staring at me like a true stalker?" she asked without looking up.

My smile pulled wider, but I made no attempt to push off the wall. "Not sure. I'm pretty fond of the view from here."

It was the truth. From this angle I had a straight-on, unobstructed view of her. Legs curled up and tucked under her, shirt hanging off to expose one shoulder, blonde hair falling across part of her face. So damn perfect.

"You know, Bryce," she started, still plucking at strings while finally looking up to meet my gaze. "When you asked me to sleep over, I just assumed you had something a little more...hands-on in mind."

The wink she shot me instantly made my dick twitch.

Fuck. Could she be any sexier?

"That so? Like what?"

"Hmm. I seem to recall something about late night Mario Kart races and a pool rematch."

"Oh, trust me, a pool rematch is definitely in our future, Elliot. But for now we'll have to get a little more creative than that."

"What about this?" she asked, gesturing toward the guitar by her side. "Will you play something for me?"

I walked over and picked up the guitar then sat on the couch next to El. "Y'know, when I started learning how to play, I didn't realize how much of a chick magnet it would be. Seriously. It works every time."

Elliot eyed me from beneath her pinched down eyebrows. "Bryce. If you're about to tell me about how much ass you got in college, so help me..."

I couldn't help but smirk at her reaction.

Green was a good shade on El.

I halfway considered seeing how much of a rise I could get out of her, but the truth fell from my tongue before I realized what I was saying.

I propped the guitar up in my lap and plucked a couple strings before looking back at Elliot. "Peyton's the only person I've ever played for."

Her eyes went round before softening and filling with warmth.

"Bryce," she whispered, reaching over to stop my hands from

playing. "I didn't realize...you don't have to play for me. That's your daddy-daughter thing."

"I've only played for Peyton because I've only *wanted* to play for Peyton. You..." *You make me want a lot of things I've never wanted with anyone else.* "Are the only other person I'll do this for."

I quickly searched my mental playlist of songs I knew by heart and turned to face her when I made a decision. Elton John songs were Peyton's favorite, and "Your Song" jumped out at me. For some reason, it just felt right in that moment.

As soon as I sang the first line, El's hand flew to her mouth, where it stayed until I finished. After a few seconds, I stopped, and her hand dropped to her lap. Her eyes, still round and wide, locked onto me like she had no intention of ever looking away.

"Thank god you haven't done that for anyone other than Peyton."

My lips twitched while I flickered my eyes away just long enough to settle the guitar back on its stand beside the couch. "Oh, come on. I don't sound *that* bad, do I?" I turned to her again, only to find she'd closed the already-narrow gap between our bodies. Subtle hints of vanilla and honey floated over me, a tease of the lotion I knew for a fact she used *all over her body.*

A handful of memories from last time flashed through my mind, waking my dick right the hell up.

She shook her head and bit the nail of her other thumb, eyes still trained on me. "No. Because you're right."

"Can you be more specific? I'm right about a lot of stuff, Uno."

As soon as the words left my mouth, she pushed up and crawled onto my lap, straddling my hips and looping her arms around my neck. I slid my hands from her thighs, up to her hips, and held her there.

"You're so...damn...cocky," she murmured, licking her lips and failing miserably at making that statement sound remotely chastising.

No, El wasn't scolding my arrogance at all. Seeing her pulse jump in her neck and the way her chest moved in quick little bursts, coupled with the way she'd perfectly aligned her body with mine gave me the truth her words hadn't.

But still, I wanted her vocal.

I wanted to pry the words out of her almost as much as I wanted to peel the clothes off her body.

"Tell me," I urged, my fingers squeezing into the highest part of her perfectly sculpted ass. I watched her swallow and fought the urge to devour the exposed column of her neck.

"Before, you weren't wrong about me dying to see you naked, but this just took it to a whole new level. Watching you play, hearing you sing...I swear I've never been this turned on. This wet. *God, I want you, Bryce.*"

Her voice dropped at the end of her confession, and my dick immediately reacted. I pulled her flush against my body until our mouths crashed into each other.

"Off," I growled, hooking my pointer fingers through her belt loops and pulling on her jeans. Just to give her a little extra incentive, I slipped my hand beneath the band of her jeans and felt my way down the silk material of her panties before hooking a finger inside.

"*Bryce,*" she rasped, sucking in a breath and widening her legs as much as her restricting jeans would allow. *Holy shit.* My intrusion was met by the most exquisite mixture of warmth and wetness, and we both groaned as I sank two fingers into her.

She arched into me, into the rhythm of my fingers. When she started rocking her hips into it, I stopped, and her eyes flew open, her chest heaving.

"Take. Them. Off," I said, dipping a finger into her and pulling it back to emphasize each word. "Top, too."

She fumbled with the button of her jeans before popping it open and ripping the zipper down. I rubbed her clit to encourage her along.

"*Mmm,*" she moaned, swaying a little as she stood. With my free hand I helped pull down the denim and silk combo until she stepped out of both, baring her lower half completely for me. *Jesus. Just the sight of her glistening pussy makes me wanna come.*

Keeping two of my fingers working inside her, I urged her closer, erasing a little of the gap she'd just put between us. "Elliot. Shirt. Now. I want to have access to every single inch of you."

She slipped the wine-colored top over her head and let it fall to the floor before reaching back to unhook her strapless bra. I sucked in a breath at the sight of her, completely bare and looking at me with the same hunger in her eyes that I felt in my bones. I'd seen her like this last time—laying open and eager on my bed— but this might as well have been the first time based on the way my dick reacted.

For a split-second, I was almost grateful that our friendship unraveled; if it hadn't, and we were still just casual friends who only did *friendly* activities…yeah, I definitely didn't let my mind linger on that possibility.

"Fair's fair, Bryce. Yours off, too." She plucked at my shirt, breaking me free of wayward thoughts.

Grinning, I used my free hand to reach back. I pulled the shirt over my head without hesitation. Her eyes instantly roamed my chest, taking stock of each muscle, one by one. "Yeah, you've got an okay body, I guess."

Her little laugh cut off when I gripped her hips and tugged her forward.

I couldn't decide between pulling her back down on top of me or burying my face between her legs. While I debated, she slid back onto my lap, and somehow my fingers found their way back into her pussy of their own accord. She slowly rocked her hips, and I let her movements dictate the pace for now. "Don't be afraid to tell me what you want."

"Keep going," she urged, and I felt her walls squeeze tighter. "Faster."

"Good girl," I praised, granting her request.

She started to smile, but it quickly fell as a moan slipped past her lips and she rocked her hips faster, chasing the orgasm I knew was rapidly building.

The sounds of her arousal filled the air as my fingers pumped in and out of her at a furious pace. "Pretty sure I'll never get enough of you. Of this."

"I'll never…this is…ohhhhhh, god, Bryce, I'm gonna come," she warned, digging her fingertips into my traps while she tightened around my fingers and rode out her orgasm.

I withdrew from her, licking my fingers like they held the last traces of the world's sweetest dessert before shifting our bodies so she was splayed out on the couch.

"I want you for so much more than just the way you look, El, but this body? I'd sell my fucking soul for this view." I flashed her a heated, hungry look and licked my lips. "If you only knew all the wicked fantasies your body has summoned recently…"

She pushed up on her elbows and hooked a leg behind mine, pulling me toward her. "Show me."

"Careful what you wish for."

I dropped to my knees at the side of the couch, threw her leg over my shoulder and drew my tongue up her hot center. My lips tugged into a smile when she moaned and sprouted tiny goosebumps across her stomach. Another languid swipe of my tongue across her clit made her thighs clench around me, and I had to apply actual pressure to keep her legs open.

Jerking my head up, I gave her a warning look before thrusting two fingers into her. She gasped and arched off the couch. *So fucking hot.*

I reached my free hand over to the side table where her cup sat and moved it to the floor, fishing out a piece of ice along the way. Holding it between my index, middle finger, and thumb, I brought it up to her most sensitive part and slowly dragged it in every direction.

"Ah! What the fuck?!" she yelped, flying into an almost sitting position.

I smirked and quickly withdrew the melting ice to replace it with my tongue.

"Oh. *Oh. Ohhhh, fuck, Bryce,*" El groaned. I felt her loosen back up and ease her legs wider.

"That's it, El. Just relax." I popped the ice cube between my lips and lowered my head, tracing it along the outer edges of her folds. This time when she clenched it wasn't out of surprise.

Until I gently slid the ice cube inside her.

She squealed, but a moan followed quickly behind.

"Can I still be considered an ice-virgin if it's just the tip?" she asked breathlessly, a mischievous grin pulling at the corners of her mouth.

I laughed, letting the ice cube fall out of my mouth. *God, she's something else.* If it was weird that joking and sharing a laugh came easily in the midst of one of the hottest nights of my life...I never wanted to experience normal again.

"You're a*dork*able," I teased, giving her a wink.

She faux-glared at me with a tilted brow. "And you are a tease," she countered, reaching down to pull me up by my jeans. "You wanted me to voice my own desires? What I want is *you,* Bryce. I want *this.*" Once in striking distance, her hand rubbed my shaft through the fabric, and I felt everything below my waist tense up. "I'm done waiting. Condom. In my bag," she instructed, jerking her head in its direction.

"So bossy, Uno. Not gonna lie, it's pretty damn hot."

I bent over to dig through her bag and felt a biting *smack* on my ass, right before her body pressed against mine from behind while her hands worked my jeans down my legs. With them around my ankles, she wasted no time slipping her fingers into my boxer briefs and pulling my throbbing cock in her hands, sliding one palm up and down while the other migrated to my balls and handled them like she'd been their keeper her entire life.

"You know...you're not the only one with fantasies."

Elliot Kincaid...part angel, part beautifully filthy devil. Such a perfect, lethal combination.

I grabbed the foil packet and whipped around, hauling her body against mine so she'd wrap her legs around my waist. "Change of plans," I stated huskily, leaning in to nip the side of her neck.

Instead of taking the extra ten seconds to cross the house and get to my bedroom, I walked us to the corner of the living room where Peyton's giant pink teepee sat. It wasn't big enough for us to fit comfortably, but it had a soft padding on the bottom and that's exactly why it was perfect. No burn from the living room's rug and no bruises from banging on the hardwood.

Elliot craned her neck around for a second before flashing me a wicked grin and pulling me down on top of her. "Dad of the year," she murmured against my lips while I tore open the condom wrapper.

"She'll never know."

Any other time, I probably would've tried to savor the feeling, drawn out the experience of our first time together. But between the interruptions and the fact that this felt like it was *years* in the making, not weeks, the concept of 'slow' was laughable.

Condom in place, I bent El's legs at the knee and pulled them into the angle I wanted before finally thrusting into her soaked entrance.

Warm. Tight. Fucking *perfect.*

We froze at the sensation, temporarily paralyzed by the immense pleasure I knew we both felt.

In an instant, I knew this would never grow old. That I'd never get enough of her.

If I thought I was addicted to her before…*fuck.*

The intense, raw need to move, to fuck her senseless, hit me so fast it almost hurt. The tingling sensation in my balls was enough to kill me, and I'd only been inside her for seconds.

"El, is this okay? Are you okay?" I huffed, searching her face for any signs of discomfort.

"So much more than okay, Bryce." She pulled my face down to merge our lips, and I growled into her mouth.

With her green light, we started moving our bodies, slowly at first, finding our rhythm while the sounds of skin-on-skin contact and our moans filled the air around us.

And then...

We.

Were.

Chaos.

She clawed at my back and rocked into me like she was dying and I was her only chance at salvation.

I drove into her with more fervor and need than I'd ever thought a human could possess.

I was almost certain her moans were an automatic trigger for my balls to tighten almost to the point of no return. When a stretch of the teepee's fabric ripped, I pulled out and flipped her on to all fours.

"God, is it possible this feels *too* good?" she panted, craning her neck around to flash me a heated, lust-filled look. "I'm gonna need you inside me all the time now. You've created an insta-nympho."

"Yeah, well, I'm pretty sure you've got a magic pussy, so that's not gonna be a problem." I chuckled and smacked her ass before pushing my cock back into her.

I had to bite down on the inside of my cheek when the world's sexiest moan hit my ears and acted as a siren song for the orgasm I could feel on the horizon.

"Oh god, Bryce." She arched her back and pushed into me while I pumped my hips. "I'm so close," she huffed. My fingers dug into her hips to keep her steady, and I knew the second her orgasm hit when I felt her walls clamp down on me.

Feeling her fall apart wrecked me in the best way possible; it drew my balls in until the pressure at the base of my spine combusted, sending fire burning through my veins while El's tight pussy milked every last drop from me.

She collapsed into the padded floor, and I rolled to her side, catching my breath while I wrapped my head around what just happened.

After a minute, I crawled out of the tilting teepee to get rid of the condom and bring El a rag and us a blanket. Peyton turned into a little inferno at night, so I had the thermostat set a little lower than most normal people.

I was used to it by now, but I didn't want El to get any ideas about putting clothes back on.

"Will you grab my bag on your way?" she called on my way back.

I was about to ask if she was thinking what I was thinking about round two when she grabbed the bag from me and dug out a big bag of Starbursts. Not just any Starbursts, either. In the bottom right corner of the yellow and pink bag, it said, "Fave-Reds."

"It's only the pink or red flavors. Strawberry, watermelon, fruit punch, cherry."

"Life changing sex *and* a bag of pink Starbursts? Fucking marry me already."

She arched a brow and smirked. "Life changing sex?"

Instead of making light of the moment like I'd meant to do, my mouth closed in on hers, kissing her like I'd never get enough. "*Everything* changing sex, El. In the best way possible."

She smiled and cupped my face between her warm palms. "I couldn't agree more."

I wasn't sure how to feel about her questioning my sex comment instead of the impromptu mention of marriage. *Relieved, obviously.* I should've been relieved that we weren't forced to talk about plans or a future, because we'd both agreed that taking this thing between us slow and day-by-day was best.

Except...I was pretty sure a part of me knew that was complete bullshit, at least on my end.

I knew El needed time to come to the same realization—*and I knew she would*—but I also was pretty positive what we'd just done sealed my fate and stamped her name all over my heart and soul.

I *did* want her to marry me. Not today, and maybe not even for years. I could be patient. As crazy as it sounded, she was the first and only woman I'd ever imagined myself tethered to for my whole life.

Neither of us made an effort to leave the teepee, and I couldn't help but grin when I realized its haphazard state. The poles holding it up had fallen, making the top droop down, and the fabric stretched across the outside was wrinkled and pulled out of place.

El followed my gaze and let out a laugh. "Uh, I hope this thing is washable."

"It is. Like I said, she'll never know."

After a while, we finally made our way out of the teepee and into my bed, but neither of us bothered with clothes.

I figured I should take advantage of having the option of complete nudity while Peyton was still in a crib and couldn't sneak into my room at all hours of the night.

And, if I had my way, Elliot would never spend a second fully clothed while in my bed.

Smiling at how that conversation would go, I pressed my lips to the crown of her head before drifting off to sleep.

"*Psst*," she whispered against my shoulder sometime later. "Are you awake?"

"I am now." I eased my arm around her, running my fingertips along her spine. "What's on your mind, Uno?"

"I, uh, well, there's something I've been thinking about for a while now, and tonight—the past couple weeks, really—made things crystal clear for me. I'm going to meet Helen."

I immediately stiffened beneath her, and my fingers froze in place mid-pattern. I swore my heart came to a complete stop in my chest. In an instant, every single fear and doubt I had about my decision to tell George and Millie about Helen came crashing down on me. Regret sliced through me like a razor.

Maybe I heard that wrong. Please, god, let that be the case.

"Bryce?" She shifted until her chest was halfway on my torso and looked up to catch my gaze. I was certain she'd be able to feel the wild thumping of my heart from where her hand rested against my chest.

"Wh—uh, what do you mean? I don't understand."

"Sophia found her. On Facebook. She said she wants to meet us, that it's urgent we speak soon, but wouldn't elaborate further. And I know what you're thinking; why should I believe her after last time? What makes me think she won't pull another vanishing act? Trust me, I had the same initial thought. But it's different this time. She gave us her home address in Denver. I need answers, Bryce."

"El…" I searched my brain for the right words, but came up drastically short.

Fuck. How do I tell her I'm the reason she didn't get those answers five years ago? How can I ruin us before we even get to be an 'us'?

"I have to know why she walked away from us. Why she never came back. Why she got my hopes up and opened old wounds only to change her mind five years ago. I've only spent a handful of hours with Peyton, and I'm, by no means, comparing our situations, but even being a tiny part of her life…I don't know how I'd live with myself if I hurt her that way."

Those words were everything I could ever ask of Elliot. Knowing she already felt a thousand times more for Peyton than Bridgette ever did meant *everything* to me. And yet…I couldn't shake the panic that trickled down my spine with each passing second.

I have to tell her.

"Do you think…would you go with Sophia and me to meet her?" she asked, her voice barely above a whisper.

Willing my hand to keep steady, I brushed the curtain of her blonde hair aside and craned my neck forward to kiss her forehead. "I won't pretend to know what it's like to be in your shoes, but I do know you deserve answers, and I'll always support you,

El. If you want me to go with you, just say the word. My mom can keep Peyton, and we can go to Denver for a couple days. Whatever you want."

She wiggled her way up my body and cupped my face, giving me a warm smile I didn't deserve before pressing our lips together.

"I loved our friendship, Bryce, but this…this feels so much better than I ever could've imagined."

"I know exactly what you mean. If friendship was all we ever shared, I would've found a way to live with that. But I'm glad I don't have to."

"Oh, uh, *awwww-kward*. I meant…*this*," she said, sliding her hand down my torso until it wrapped around my cock, setting a record for how fast it went from half-hard to harder than steel.

Just like that, every drop of blood in my body rushed south, silencing all the thoughts vying for attention in my brain.

My dick twitched in her hand, and I groaned before gripping her hips and flipping her onto her back to hover over her. "You think you're so funny, Uno." I arched a brow and pushed my hips into her. "Admit it, El, the nickname is accurate."

"What, Toad? Uhh, I mean, kinda weird to point out, but I guess I can see that." Her lips pulled into a smirk at the same time I reached down to pull on her nipple, making her gasp.

"Ahh! Okay, okay," she squealed through her laughter. "McMagicDick is definitely accurate!"

"That's what I thought." I flexed my hips forward to brush my length against her while my mouth found the goose-bumped flesh of her nipple and kissed away the sting caused by my fingers. "Just to be sure, I think you need a reminder."

She nodded eagerly, her chest rising in sync with her nods. "I'll probably need a few reminders…you know, just to be sure I don't get confused again."

CHAPTER 21
BRYCE

I'M SERIOUSLY GOING STRAIGHT TO HELL.

I should've finally given Elliot the truth, and I almost had—but the second her hand made contact with my dick, I was gone. Lost to the high that came exclusively from being buried inside her.

After our encore (and an encore after that), El crashed and fell into a peaceful sleep while I held her in my arms.

I, on the other hand, couldn't sleep for shit.

Tonight had given me emotional whiplash, and I had no one to blame but myself.

There were times over the last several weeks when I'd almost convinced myself that my role in whatever George and Millie had said to Helen was irrelevant, that they would've found a way to stop Elliot from meeting her regardless of my interference. That Elliot wouldn't hate me when she found out.

Then, in the moments of clarity when I accepted the reality of the situation, I convinced myself that Elliot would understand and forgive me.

In reality, it was my brain's way of giving me false hope. As soon as Elliot started talking about Helen, the anguish in her voice was like a sledgehammer to my gut, and I just *knew*.

I knew everything was going to shift between us once she found out.

Slipping out of my room after making sure not to disturb Elliot, I padded down the hallway and came to a stop in front of the stairs to the attic. Before I could talk myself out of it, I trekked into the attic and dug out a worn, leather-bound journal. I'd spent months carrying it around after Peyton was born, but it had been packed away with the last of my things David and Louise shipped to me a few months ago. I wasn't even sure what I expected to find between its pages. Answers? Guidance? Reassurance?

In the days after I found out about Peyton, 'overwhelmed' is a laughable understatement for how I'd felt. The hospital gave me a pamphlet on support groups for single parents and even for single parents of preemies. Though I'd only been to a few meetings during my stay in California, I kept in touch with the group leader.

At first, I was skeptical of his insistence that journaling was therapeutic. Sometimes he gave the group a prompt or a question to work from, and sometimes we simply wrote whatever came to us. But to my surprise, it did actually help. Not always, but more often than not.

I thumbed through the pages, welcoming the onslaught of mixed emotions I always felt each time I thought back to those early days. Every day it had felt like my heart was volleying back and forth from elation and awe at what a tough fighter my daughter was to panic, to fear about all the complications we were up against.

I stopped flipping when a particular entry caught my eye.

June 9 - 10:05 pm

I can't believe Peyton's almost six months old. Sometimes it seems like it was just yesterday that I was flying to California without a clue that I was about to become a dad. Then sometimes I can barely remember a time in my life without her in it. Today was a little of both. She woke up every couple hours last night, and I think she might have an ear infection. I know since the surgery I'm overly paranoid about everything, but I think I'd be the same way had she been born perfectly healthy.

Earlier, I was talking to Erik about the timing of it all, and he asked me to consider a question that I haven't been able to stop thinking about since…Do certain people come into our lives at specific times for a reason?

To some, I suppose the answer might depend on their faith. But if you take faith out of the equation, it's a philosophical conundrum without a simple answer.

Three years ago, I would've scoffed at anyone who tried to tell me 'everything happens for a reason.' Which would lead you to believe my answer to the previous question is a resounding no.

But three years ago might as well have been a lifetime ago.

Because three years ago, she wasn't a part of my life.

In fifty years, when I look back on my life it'll be divided into two categories—before her and after her.

Before her, I thrived on chaos of my own design. After her, I'll move mountains to contain the chaos.

Before her, my only concern was making a name for myself. After her, my only concern is a life I can be proud of.

Before her, home was nothing more than a bittersweet memory. After her, home is the only place I want to be.

Before her, making plans was how I took control of my life. After her, I realize sometimes even the best laid plans can change.

She's given me the ability to see beyond the past. To embrace the present. To envision a new future.

Now, that's not to say my answer is as simple as a yes. Maybe it's all a matter of timing. Maybe there's not always a rhyme or reason for the things that happen or the people we meet. But that doesn't mean that a certain person who comes into your life and flips everything upside down wasn't always meant to be a part of your life.

I know, without a doubt, Peyton was always meant to be in mine.

I thought back to the night when I'd posed the same question to Elliot about people coming into your life for a reason. She said she thought the concept was something one could only believe if it happened to them, if someone happened to stumble upon the right person at the right time and they just *knew*.

In a way, she wasn't wrong. But only hindsight allowed me to realize that most of what I'd written about my life before and after Peyton could also describe before and after Elliot came back into my life.

There's no way I have Elliot back in my life only to lose her again.

When I flipped through a few more pages, an envelope slipped out from between the pages in the back of the journal and sailed to the floor, landing with a *thwack* on the top of my bare foot.

I picked it up and turned it over, eyeing the sticky note attached over the middle of the front. *'We weren't sure what to do with this, but couldn't bring ourselves to throw it away.'*

I peeled the note off and instantly felt my stomach fall to the floor.

My name, alongside David and Louise's home address, was written in delicate, feminine handwriting.

Familiar handwriting.

Bridgette's handwriting.

So many questions swirled in my mind. When was this written? When I was still in Seattle? Why the hell hadn't Louise or David just given it to me instead of hiding it for an unknown length of time? *Do I even want to know what the letter says?*

I was tempted to march straight to the trash without opening it, but I couldn't do it.

Instead, I walked to the couch and flipped on the lamp to my left. The wild beating of my heart and a loud ringing in my ears was almost enough to make me reconsider my decision. The mellow light from the lamp illuminated the paper in my hands, and I forced myself to read Bridgette's words before I came to my senses and set the paper on fire.

Bryce,

I'm not going to ask for your forgiveness because I know I don't deserve it. I don't think I'll ever forgive myself. I know you'll probably hate me for all of eternity, and I don't blame you. Just please, please know that I truly didn't intend to hurt you by not telling you about the pregnancy. I wasn't in a good place in my life during those months, and I was too scared to call you right after she was born. I'm not ready to be responsible for another human being. I've never wanted to have kids; you know that.

I couldn't bear the idea of having a daily reminder of how badly I'd screwed my life up. And hers.

After the doctors explained everything about her condition, I just knew she'd be better off without me. I wish I could go back in time and stop myself from living so recklessly, but I can't.

I'm not sure you'll ever read this letter, or if you'll even get it. I guess I also don't know what you decided to do. If you kept her or if you—

My grip on the paper went from tight to obliterating; I'd officially had enough of Bridgette's bullshit. The excuses were so fucking typical of her that I wasn't even surprised. When we were together, she'd constantly find ways to explain away her bad behavior, and it was one of the reasons I finally ended things.

I wasn't sure what I'd expected to get from reading her letter, but the only thing I could focus on was how incredibly different Elliot and Bridgette were. I deserved a kick to the nuts for ever entertaining the possibility Elliot could be remotely like Bridgette.

Bridgette had the gall to even think I'd turn my back on Peyton, that I wouldn't want her. That her *condition* would make me consider giving her up. We'd dated for a year, but now I wondered if she ever even knew me at all.

Elliot had known me for almost twenty years. Even with the gaps in our friendship, she just...got me. She knew me in a way that I couldn't even fully explain. With her, everything just felt easy and right.

She knew me well enough to understand that I'd only been

trying to look out for her when I told her grandparents about Helen.

That's what I was counting on, anyway.

Elliot's husky, sleep-filled voice called out and snapped my head up. "Bryce? What are you doing? It's like, not even five a.m."

She rubbed her eyes, and concern filled her features when she got close enough to register my expression.

"What's wrong?" she asked, sitting next to me on the couch and pulling my hand into hers.

"There's something I need to tell you."

Alarm flashed in her eyes, and she immediately turned toward Peyton's door. "Is it about Peyton? Is she okay?"

"She's fine, El. It's not about Peyton."

Her shoulders slumped with relief, and she gave me a sleepy smile. "Oh. Okay, good."

"It's about your mom."

"Helen? What about her? I don't understand." Her brows pulled down, and her shoulders tensed back up the second her mom's name left her lips.

"That night, when you told me about her contacting you…"

"Yeah?" she prompted, confused.

"Do you remember that I begged you to consider talking to Millie and George first before meeting up with her? That I thought you'd regret it if you didn't?"

"Yeah…" She tucked her feet under her body and crossed her arms. "Bryce, what are you getting at?"

"I went to their office before my flight the next day. I told them that you were going to meet Helen."

"*You. Told. Them.*" She repeated the words like they were from a foreign language, as if she had no understanding of what I'd said.

I quickly continued, "I was only trying to help, El. I told them because I was worried you weren't thinking things through, and I needed to know you wouldn't have to deal with it on your own once I was gone. I thought they'd talk to you, that you could come to a decision as a family. I had no idea things would fall apart like they did."

Elliot sat still, not saying a word. I wasn't even sure she'd blinked since I started speaking.

"I'm sorry. I never intended to hurt you. All these years, I thought they'd talked to you, and that you knew I'd gone to them. Until they told me recently that that wasn't the case, I had no idea…God, you have to know I'm so sorry."

"For what, exactly?" she snapped abruptly. "For striking the match, then walking away before you saw the way it burned my world to the ground? For being the reason I've spent the last five years wondering why Helen didn't show up, thinking it had to be because she decided I wasn't worth meeting after all? I spent that entire summer avoiding Nana and Pops because I was so ashamed I hadn't taken your advice and gone to them first. I thought it was *my fault* that I ruined their chance for closure too. I couldn't even tell Sophia because I hated myself for ruining her chance at meeting our mother. And then there was the fact that I had to deal with you waltzing back into my life only to vanish again. I almost convinced myself that I made up that night. That you were just a figment of my imagination, because if you had actually been there, you wouldn't have just disappeared again. So, again, what exactly are you sorry for? Shattering my world back then, or for not telling me sooner?"

Fuck.

As much as this conversation was killing me, I knew I deserved every morsel of the pain slicing through my heart right now. Even so, I would've given anything to absorb all the hurt I saw in Elliot's tear-filled eyes.

"I'm sorry for all of it, Elliot. For being a part of something that caused you so much pain. For betraying your trust back then. For waiting this long to tell you the truth. I know it doesn't make things better, but I swear I thought I was doing what was best for you. I thought I was protecting you."

"I didn't *need* your protection, Bryce! I needed my *friend*. I trusted you."

The words she left unsaid were the loudest ones inside my head—*I trusted you, but now I don't know if I can.*

"El..."

"I wish I could say your good intention is all that matters, but it's not." She shot off the couch and started pacing, swatting angrily at her cheek. "I know you couldn't have known the domino effect your actions would have. But you know what you could've done? Picked up the fucking phone and called me. Checked in to see how everything played out. You could've at least attempted to survey the damage your shit-storm caused."

"That's not fair. I thought we both agreed—"

"Agreed that we sucked at keeping in touch? You're right, we did. But that was before I knew what you did. I get that you thought you were doing the right thing, but I *don't* get how you could just walk away without giving it a second thought."

"I was an angry, conflicted twenty-two year old with my own impossible decision to make! I had to choose between following my dreams and causing a giant rift with my parents or giving up the only thing I'd ever wanted to do with my life to make them happy. It wasn't exactly a picture perfect summer for me either."

The loudest, most painful silence of my life fell over us for a few seconds while she considered what I'd said.

"What about now?" she asked softly, taking me by surprise.

"Now?"

"Five years ago, you made those decisions as an angry twenty-two year old. What about now? If you could go back in time, knowing everything you know now—as a parent, as my...friend. Not as an angry twenty-two year old with his own life-changing decisions to make—would you still have tried to interfere? To protect me?"

It was a question I'd already asked myself time and time again the last few weeks.

It was a fair question. A logical one.

But it was also one that I was pretty sure she wouldn't like the answer to.

"If I could go back in time, I'd do a lot of things differently." I paused and forced my jaw to unclench, knowing there was a chance I was about to put the last nail in the coffin of our relationship. She looked at me expectantly, her blue eyes brimming with cautious optimism. "But knowing what I know now—as a parent and as someone who cares deeply for you—there's no way I would've let you handle that situation on your own. Not telling you what I did was a mistake, but I still wouldn't have let you go through with it by yourself. I meant what I said back then—sharing DNA doesn't merit automatic trust. All the best monsters can hide their appetite for destruction until it's too late."

For a second, I could've sworn I saw something a lot like understanding in her eyes. But then it was gone, making me think it was just the dim lighting casting a shadow across her pretty face.

"But, El, there's more you should know—"

"I, uh, I have to go."

"Elliot, don't." I pleaded, not even caring if desperation seeped into my voice. "Don't go."

"I just…I can't do this, Bryce. I need you to respect that."

And just like that, I watched the woman I loved walk out of my house.

I only hoped she wasn't walking out of my life too.

CHAPTER 22
ELLIOT

My grandparents had always been early risers, but apparently they'd adopted sleeping in as part of their (almost) retired life-style. I paced around their kitchen, trying not to fall apart while I waited for them to wake up. I'd always loved this kitchen—the marble countertops, the industrial fridge, the way it always smelled like a bakery. All the memories of cooking together as a family.

Right now I wanted to bulldoze the entire place.

The hurt and anger I felt toward Helen was manageable; I'd carried it around for so long now that it was like a second skin. It lived in a compartment all its own, contained by the force of the love I had for my grandparents.

This pain was different. Like a trojan horse, it snuck in and destroyed me from the inside out. There was no compartment for this hurt, no force capable of reining it in. I couldn't reconcile my love for them with the sting of betrayal.

"Elliebelly? What in the world brought you out here this early?" Pops called, crossing the room to come to me. He stopped when he saw my face. "Honey, what's wrong?"

An angry laugh popped out of my mouth, and I stopped pacing to meet his alarmed stare. "Is there something you and

Nana want to tell me? Something you've forgotten to mention for, oh, I don't know, the last five years?"

Growing up, people would comment on how much I resembled my grandfather, with our matching eyes and identical smiles. I used to think sharing attributes gave me the ability to read him like a book. This moment definitively disproved that notion. I watched his pupils grow and his jaw clench as he took a tentative step in my direction, but I had no idea what emotion it was that I saw on his face. "Elliot, you've got to understand something. Back then she was—"

"My mother!" I wailed, throwing my hands up in exasperation. "She's my mother, and you had no right to go behind my back. If you and Nana don't want her in your life, that's *your* decision to make. But whether or not I want the same is *my* decision. I can almost understand if you had reservations about Sophia meeting her at the time, but I was nineteen and perfectly capable of making that decision for myself."

"You're right, Elliot. You deserved more from us," Nana called, crossing the room until she reached Pops' side. Her fluid movements starkly juxtaposed with the jagged edges resonating in her voice, and it would've riddled me with guilt if not for the armor of anger encasing my heart. "We should've been more forthcoming about a lot of things regarding your mother. When you girls first came to live with us, we talked and talked about how to handle the day Helen came back, *if* she came back. The truth is…"

My grandparents turned toward each other to share a look, and I folded my arms over my chest, bracing myself for another blow.

"The truth is," Pops repeated, turning back to me. "Your mother wanted to see you and Sophia several times over the years. But each time she came to us, she was…on something. Not in her right mind. So that day, when she showed up, we had no reason to believe anything she said. We had no reason to trust her."

"It doesn't matter if you're nine or nineteen or thirty-nine,

Elliot; your grandfather and I will always do what we think is best for you. That's all we've ever tried to do since the day you came into our lives. It was never our intention to hurt you, and I'm so sorry that we did."

In the last five minutes, I was pretty sure Nana had aged a whole decade. Like the full weight of this secret had finally caught up with her.

"I get that, Nana. I do. But what I need you two and Bryce to understand is that just because your intentions were good does nothing to change how it makes me feel. If there's a hurricane forming in the middle of the ocean, would you tear your house down just because there's a possibility you're in its potential path of destruction? No. You'd keep a close eye on it and wait to make a rational, informed decision. You were so consumed by the possibility that Helen would hurt me that you failed to realize *your* actions are what caused the most destruction of all."

Without waiting for a response, I practically sprinted for the door.

"Elliot," Pops called in a tone that conveyed that this conversation wasn't over.

I turned to look at them, but kept my hand firmly around the door knob and my feet planted. "I'm going to meet her. I realize you might still think that's a mistake, but it's *my* mistake to make. I know y'all were doing what you thought was best, but this isn't the kind of thing I can just magically get over. It's gonna take some time."

They both called after me, but I didn't stop. Not this time.

I had somewhere else to be.

"Milo, wake up," I said, leaning down to shake his shoulder for good measure. There was a fair chance he'd just gone to bed a few hours ago, but I didn't care. The rules of friendship clearly state that it's perfectly acceptable to wake a friend in times of crisis.

"What the hell?" he groaned, not even bothering to open his eyes or brush the shaggy brown locks out of his face. "You realize I usually sleep naked, right? You're lucky I was too tired to finish stripping down last night." He paused and squinted in the semi-darkness. "Wait. It's not even light outside. What the fuck?"

"Milo, get your head out of your ass. This is important. Please."

He must've heard the panic in my voice because he flipped over and immediately zeroed in on my face. "El, what's wrong? What happened?"

It was a fair question since I'd just busted into his room at the crack of dawn like a psycho, but as soon as I opened my mouth to answer, tears filled my eyes and I couldn't get the words out. Milo scooted into a sitting position and pulled me down to the edge of his bed.

"Just breathe."

"I need to...does your dad still have a billion frequent flyer miles?"

"I think so. Why? Oh, shit. Did you kill somebody? Are we about to go on the lam?" he asked with way too much sincerity.

"Are you high? No! My god, you and Sophia really need to stop watching the Investigation Discovery channel. And who the hell even uses that phrase?"

"People who were pulled out of a deep sleep. What's wrong, Elliot?"

"I'm pulling the best friend card and going to need you to trust me. You're off work today, right? I am too. I need you to see if your dad can get us on the next flight to Denver. Sophia too."

"Okay, now I'm actually concerned. You're not the impulsive jet-setter type. You know I'm with you in whatever this is, but what the fuck is going on?"

"It's Helen. I have to see her, Milo. Today. I had a huge fight with Bryce and with my grandparents about her, and I just...it can't wait." My resolution was absolute, but my voice still quivered.

"*Shit*," he muttered, throwing the blanket off and wrapping his arms around me. "Okay. Go wake Sophia up and I'll call my dad. We'll get to Denver, El."

"Thanks, Mi. I owe you."

"No, you don't. You're my best friend, Elliot. I know ninety percent of our friendship is joking around with each other, but you know I'd do anything for you, right? You and Soph are the sisters I never knew I wanted, and I've got your back. Always."

"You really are the best, you know that?"

He gave me a wink and reached for his phone.

I crossed the hall and stopped outside Sophia's door, searching my brain for the right words.

Do the right words even exist to gently tilt someone's entire world on its axis?

EIGHT HOURS LATER, I stared out the window of the Uber driver's SUV, studying the sights of Denver as I tried to decipher exactly what emotion gripped my heart. Twenty-four hours ago I would've sworn it wasn't possible to experience this range of emotions in a single day.

I went to sleep last night wondering if it was possible to be falling for Bryce this soon, if maybe those three little words that had been at the tip of my tongue were always meant only for Bryce. Now I wanted to exorcise the words from my vocabulary and the entire feeling from my heart.

"El? You sure you don't want to go to the hotel first? Before we see her?" Sophia asked, squeezing my hand from the seat next to me.

I still wasn't over the fact that she'd immediately forgiven me after I told her everything. She pulled me into a hug and let me cry on her shoulder for a solid ten minutes after I woke her up. *We've come a long way in the last two months.* She said she wasn't even sure if she would've wanted to meet our mother five years ago, anyway, which made sense; high school was rough for Sophia.

I nodded and squeezed her hand in return. "I'm sure. I need to do this before I talk myself out of it."

For the last few minutes of the ride, I typed a dozen different texts to Bryce, but I deleted them all without sending a single one. Nothing felt right. Every time I thought I knew what I wanted to say I'd go right back to second guessing everything.

"I think you need to forgive him, Elliot," Sophia said, bumping my shoulder and nodding at my phone. "He's been in your corner for as long as I can remember. Bryce is one of the good ones, and he fucking loves you. There's no way he would've let things play out the way they did back then if he had known in advance how much it would affect you."

"It's not black and white, Soph. If he loves me, why did it take him two months to tell me about what he did? Why wait until *right after* we've slept together?"

"That's exactly my point, El; it's *not* black and white. Bryce was living in shades of gray. Between y'all's history, Peyton, and him working on the inn and venue, the deck was already stacked against you two. And it's worth mentioning that, on top of all that, there's no way Bryce's heart isn't scarred from Peyton's mother. You said she just vanished without a word, and Bryce had to handle her fucking him over like that *and* becoming a dad? I don't care how much he trusts you, there's no way a little part of him hasn't worried you'd do the same thing. My guess is that he was scared of losing you, and for more than one reason."

I swiveled around to give her a side-eye.

"How did this happen? I'm supposed to be the wise sister who offers wisdom and life lessons. You're supposed to need my advice, not the other way around."

She shrugged and gave me a smile. "I'm going to pretend you didn't just say that like you're surprised I'm actually capable of such insight. I'm not a kid anymore, you know. Plus, as far as relationships go, what I lack in real life experience, I make up for in romance bookworm knowledge." She dug a paperback out of her purse and shook it, making us both chuckle. "And I'll always need my big sister's advice, El. Don't think you're off the hook for sisterly wisdom down the road."

Before I could reply, the car came to a stop and Milo turned to us from the front seat, his blue-gray eyes bouncing between Sophia and me. "Ready?"

Sophia and I glanced at each other and smiled before turning to Milo.

"We're ready."

CHAPTER 23
ELLIOT

Stepping out of the SUV and into the chilly fall air, I pulled my jacket a little tighter around me and surveyed my surroundings. *This is my mother's neighborhood—my mother's house.* Surreal didn't seem like a strong enough word to describe what I felt. I was seconds from meeting the woman who gave me life.

Trees sporting a kaleidoscope of red and orange and yellow leaves lined the street. A group of rowdy kids played kickball in the cul-de-sac a few lots down. The houses were all Victorian-style with fancy woodwork and bright pops of color. Each residence on the block looked like a super-sized version of a dollhouse.

I threaded my arm through Sophia's and tugged her up the sidewalk, taking in Helen's house in its three-story entirety. A beautiful stained glass bay window caught my eye first, the blue and green hues highlighting the matching trim along the gabled roof. Something about the house just felt...inviting. Which was the last thing I had expected to feel about anything Helen-related.

Realizing the reason I was so drawn to the house, I froze. "Soph..."

"I know," she agreed with a nod. "It's so much like the manor."

The house we'd grown up in was coated in warmer colors, but

the styles were eerily similar. It made me wonder if that's why Helen chose this house, this neighborhood.

Milo ascended the porch steps first and shot us a questioning glance before he reached for the door. We both nodded, and he rapped his fist against it three times before stepping aside.

It only took a few seconds for the door to swing open, and then...

She was there.

I could barely believe my eyes, could barely breathe.

Standing two feet in front of me, clad in an expensive Adrianna Papell sheath dress, was the woman I'd never expected to see again.

Before Sophia showed me Helen's picture on Facebook, I'd had only my blurry mental images of a woman half my mother's current age. The two might as well have been completely different people—the Helen in my childhood and the one standing before me; the Helen from my memories didn't even seem to exist anymore.

She was about my height but looked like an older version of Sophia—straight, dark hair brushing her shoulders, high cheekbones, small button nose, long lashes framing her dark eyes. A nervous smile pulled at the corners of her lips.

When Sophia and I failed to speak after a few seconds, Milo stepped around us and offered his hand.

"Hi, I'm Milo. The best friend."

"Helen," she replied, shaking hands with him.

"And these two are...uh...well, I guess you already know who they are," he said, rubbing the back of his neck. His face flushed red. "Gee, I'm really glad I didn't make things more awkward."

The three of us let out soft laughs, and Helen nodded.

"Of course. Please, come in," she offered, pulling the door open to gesture us inside.

I squeezed Milo's forearm and gave him a smile of appreciation while we filed in behind her.

The house's interior was a continuation of typical Victorian-style features—high ceilings, an ornate staircase, fancy woodwork throughout, and a floor-plan that flowed seamlessly from room to room. The impersonal artwork along the walls and beige color scheme were nothing like my—our—childhood home, but there was no mistaking the similarities the two shared in style.

"Can I get anyone some coffee? Tea? Water?" she asked, absently picking at a loose thread on her dress.

Huh. We might not share a lot physically, but we've got at least some habits in common.

We all went with coffee, and a couple minutes later, she returned with a tray and four steaming cups.

"You've got a beautiful home," Sophia said, letting her eyes wander around the room for the zillionth time.

Helen set her coffee down, her red-stained lips lifting as she followed Sophia's gaze. "Thank you. We knew as soon as we walked in that it was the one."

We? My eyes flew to her hand, searching for a ring, then to the walls, searching for signs of a family. I zeroed in on a cluster of photos on the mantle, but there were no children in them, only Helen and a tall, balding man with glasses.

She must've followed my gaze because she stood up and grabbed one of the photos off the mantle.

"My husband. Alvin," she said, handing me the frame.

Sophia leaned over and studied the photo with me. They were on a cruise ship, laughing and clinking cocktail glasses together. They looked blissfully happy together.

Which shouldn't have angered me, but it did.

I shoved the frame into Sophia's lap and scooted away. "I'm sorry. I can't do the whole awkward 'get to know each other' grace period. I have to know. Why? You've obviously got a wonderful life, and you're obviously not the same person you were twenty years ago. What happened five years ago? Why didn't you want to meet me?"

"El," Sophia warned, cutting her eyes at me.

"No, she's right," Helen interjected. "She's waited long

enough for an explanation. You both deserve to know." She paused and twisted her hands together in her lap, pulling in a deep breath through her nose. "Elliot, Sophia, I want you to know how sorry I am. I know those words don't even scratch the surface of what you both deserve from me, but I'm offering them anyway. Not for forgiveness, and not because I think it will fix anything, but because it's the truth. I'm so sorry for everything."

I sat perfectly still, absorbing the words I never thought I'd hear from a woman I never thought I'd see again. For a few seconds, I tried to pinpoint how I felt about her apology. My brain kept hurling clichés: *talk is cheap; actions speak louder than words; don't believe everything you're told.*

But my brain wasn't the only organ in the fight for control. *Talk is cheap, but there's value in sincerity. Actions hold the power to hurt you, but words can heal.*

"I struggled to maintain sobriety during all of my twenties," she continued, letting us off the hook for a response to her apology. "I was haunted by my failure as a parent, by the knowledge of what I'd put you both through. But then I moved to California and met a man who helped me get clean, stay sober, and even helped me get a job. We got married, and I felt like I was finally in a good enough place in my life that I could be a part of your lives. But I owed it to your grandparents to see them first, to prove to them that I deserved another chance. I knew things would be strained between us; I wasn't expecting a warm welcome, but I was hoping they'd realize how far I'd come. Let's just say they were…less than thrilled about me getting in contact with you, Elliot."

"They didn't believe that you were sober?" I asked, though it came out as a statement.

"No, they didn't. At the time, I was devastated that they didn't believe me. But I can't say I blame them; the last time they saw me I stole your grandfather's wallet. They assumed I had some kind of ulterior motive, so I offered to take a drug test, to do whatever it took. But then they started telling me about the…nightmares you had as a child, Elliot. About how, for months after I left, they'd find you curled up in a ball in your closet at night. About how you always needed to know where they were going and how long they'd be gone every time one of them left the house. About how you wouldn't let Sophia out of your sight for weeks at first…"

She trailed off and swiped away the tears that spilled onto her cheeks.

Sophia scooted closer and squeezed my hand. *You're not alone in this*, her warm grip promised.

"They also told me that you were doing really well at the time," she continued. "That night, I went back to the hotel and told my husband—now ex-husband—how it went with my parents. I started hyperventilating while telling him what they said, and then it escalated into a full-blown panic attack. I ended up spending the night in the ER. Given my condition at the time, he begged me not to go through with meeting you; he told me it would be best not to let my past ruin our future. Our family."

"Condition?" I asked, struggling to wrap my head around everything Helen was telling me. "What sort of condition?"

Helen flinched, and I was struck by an unexpected jolt of sympathy for whatever it was I saw in her eyes.

"I was…I was pregnant. Four months. Because of my age and a couple of other factors, it was considered a high-risk pregnancy. The doctors told me to avoid stress as much as possible. Between that and the onslaught of guilt I felt from hearing about your… struggles, Elliot…it was too much. I couldn't risk my health or the baby's, so I went back to California the next day."

A million questions and thoughts burst through my mind at once, and I couldn't decide which to grab on to.

How is it possible that I'm starting to understand why she did what she did? Nana and Pops wanted to talk to me about meeting her. Why didn't I let them finish explaining? I have another sibling. What if she's lying? There's no way she's not telling the truth right now. You can't fake that kind of emotion. Why didn't she come back or contact me again after the baby was born?

"I don't...I don't know what to say. That's...a lot."

When I finally brought my eyes back to Helen, she was still trying to control the tears. Her pain was palpable, and I had the strongest urge to offer her some kind of comfort. On some level, I still felt hurt, and a part of me would probably always struggle to understand some of the choices my mother made, but right now all I felt was sympathy.

Sophia shifted on the couch before clearing her throat. "Why didn't you try to get in contact with us after you had the baby?"

"For the rest of my pregnancy, I struggled with depression. It was like my trip to Texas opened the floodgates of doubt in my mind. I'd already blown my shot at being a mother; what made me think I deserved another chance? I couldn't come to terms with everything I'd done. The week before Michael's due date, I knew something wasn't right. He had stopped moving around, and I just knew. I went to the hospital and found out he was just... gone. They couldn't explain it. For a year after...he passed, I was an empty shell. I hardly ate, I barely left my bed, I couldn't even look at my husband. Eventually, I saw a therapist, and little by little, I came back to life. Things with my ex had fallen apart, but I *wanted* to live again. I knew I needed a fresh start to make that happen, so I moved here about two years ago, and then I met Alvin last year." She leaned over to pick up the photo from the coffee table and smiled through her watery gaze. "He's shown me that it's okay to forgive myself and that my past mistakes only define me if I fail to grow from them."

By the time she finished, Sophia, Milo, and I were all fighting tears and reaching for the tissue box.

For all of her faults, for all of her mistakes...she didn't deserve to have her life ripped apart and her heart shattered into oblivion.

I reached over and covered her hand with mine. "I'm so sorry...about Michael. I can't imagine how difficult that must have been. I just...I'm sorry." I squeezed my eyes shut to contain the tears, but they slipped out anyway. "But I'm glad you found someone like Alvin."

"Thank you." Helen squeezed my hand and gave me a smile. "He's brought enough sunshine into my life to brighten all my rainy days."

My lips twitched at the familiar words. It was how Pops had always described Nana.

"Excuse me," Sophia cried, jumping up and jogging toward the door.

"Soph!" I called, pushing up to follow her.

"I'll go, El. Let me," Milo said, standing quickly.

I gave him a nod, and he took off.

A stiff silence fell over the two of us as I watched through the window and saw Milo catch up to my sister. She kept walking, so he slung his arm around her shoulders.

I released a breath and slumped back into the couch when he pulled her into his body and she didn't pull away. I trusted Milo to talk her through whatever she was feeling.

"Do you have someone to brighten the rainy days, Elliot?" Helen asked, drawing my attention from the scene outside.

"I do." The words were automatic, summoned by the magic smile and blue-green eyes that filled my dreams. *In one way or another, Bryce has always been the keeper of my sunshine.* "But it's kinda complicated."

"Most parts of life are."

"He has a daughter. She's almost two."

Surprise lifted my mother's dark brows, but it was quickly replaced by a cautious curiosity. "Ah. And that's an issue for you?"

"At first I thought it could be. I mean, not an issue. More like… a concern. I never gave much thought to having kids. I wasn't sure if I had what it took to be the right kind of parent. I still don't know. But…" I pushed off the couch and wandered toward the fireplace, admiring the other photos of Helen and Alvin. "I'm pretty sure I fell for Peyton the second he showed me her picture.

She's basically impossible not to love. I just, I don't know; I always worried I'd be like…" I shrugged and let my sentence trail off without an ending because we both realized what it was.

Awkward.

"You were worried you'd be the kind of mother I was? Oh, Elliot, no. That's not possible. I was a mess back then. I was barely sixteen when I had you, and eighteen when I had Sophia. The men, the drugs, the choices I made…that was all on me. You were never destined to repeat my mistakes, Elliot; that's why I gave you to my parents."

I turned back toward her and nodded. "I know. I realize that now. I think it took coming here—meeting you—for me to fully understand and accept that, though."

"You've always been your own person. And, if you're like anyone, it's your grandmother. I see so much of her in you. I have to ask, though, what made them tell you about what happened?"

"Uh, that's actually the other part of what's complicated with Bryce. Five years ago, he was just a friend, and I confided in him about meeting you. Long story short, he's the one who told Nana and Pops about my plans. So, he's the reason they tracked you down, and I only found out this morning that he's sort of the reason things fell apart."

"Elliot, I think there's been some confusion. I went to George and Millie myself. *I'm* the reason things fell apart."

"Oh, god. I owe him an explanation. I don't even know where to begin or if it'll fix the way we left things though. I went a little crazy on him."

Helen's hand gripped my shoulder, and it wasn't until I turned to put us face-to-face that I realized I'd started pacing across her living room. "If he's truly the man you think he is, he'll understand."

I nodded, pulling in a deep breath to steady my hammering pulse. "You're right."

A knock at the door sounded, and we both whipped around to look through the window.

"It's me," Sophia called, answering our unasked question. Helen quickly opened the door, and I realized why Sophia had knocked. A Siamese cat was purring and weaving around her legs. "We, uh, made a friend. Is she yours?"

"Muffin, how did you get out there?" Helen chastised, leaning down to pick the cat up.

"Muffin here followed us down the block. When she followed us up to the door we were hoping we weren't about to have to turn her away," Sophia explained.

"Yep. This butterball is ours. Thank you."

We all walked back into the living room, and a quick nonverbal conversation with my sister confirmed that she was okay, or at least was ready to rejoin the conversation.

For the next couple hours, Sophia, Helen, and I talked about our lives—about our hobbies and jobs and even a couple stories from our childhood, though I steered clear of those once I realized how difficult they were for Helen to hear. I had more questions—like who my father was—but I couldn't bring myself to ask any of them. Yet.

Eventually, Helen's husband, Alvin, arrived and insisted we stay for dinner.

In addition to his badass cooking skills, Alvin seemed like a great guy. He was smart and funny and made sure to keep the conversation flowing. He took a genuine interest in Sophia and me, and even got Milo to give him some tips on mixing the perfect mojito.

By the time we finished dinner, I could tell Alvin and Helen were truly happy together, and that made me happy for them. As weird as it was to feel this *at ease* with my mother, I wasn't questioning it.

Alvin and Milo disappeared to find more wine when Sophia tipped the first domino that would bring everything to a screeching halt.

"Okay, so wait a second. When you messaged me on Facebook, you said it was important that we speak right away. What was that about?"

"Ah!" Helen exclaimed, jumping up to grab her phone. "I told you that things fell apart with my ex-husband, and I wasn't exaggerating. Our grief consumed us both in different ways. I blamed myself for what happened, and he…he blamed my parents. At the time, I wrote it off as his natural way of grieving; something he'd work through over time. But he only became more obsessive. When I told him I wanted a divorce, he fell apart completely. He swore he'd make things right."

Helen paused, and I mulled over her last statement. *Make things right*?

"I was trying to start my life over; I couldn't let his issues be my issues anymore, so I didn't give his rants much thought," Helen continued. "For a while, I thought he was moving on too. Then a couple months ago, when he found out I had remarried, he had some kind of breakdown. He left me a drunken voicemail swearing 'they'd be sorry' and would know his pain."

"They?" I asked.

She scrolled through her phone and pulled up a photo before handing it to us. "My parents. After the divorce, I knew he was struggling, and that, in his mind, my parents were to blame for losing Michael and for our marriage collapsing. I had no idea he was so unstable. Before that voicemail, I'd just assumed his resentment stopped at my parents. But when he mentioned you two, I knew I had to warn you both. I didn't want to believe he would try anything, but I couldn't take that chance."

We leaned in to get a closer look at her photo, and I nearly fell out of my chair when recognition dawned.

Slim build. Black hair with a handful of gray around the temples. Gray eyes.

I knew him.

The soon-to-be brand new owner of Serenity Hotel.
Greg Adams.

CHAPTER 24
ELLIOT

The next morning, I spent the entire two-hour flight home replaying every conversation and exchange I'd had with Greg, trying to figure out how I'd missed the signs.

It all made perfect sense now—how he just 'happened' to run into me that first day, why he wanted to know stories about my childhood the second time. All that bullshit about vetting people he did business with on a personal level.

He'd said all the right things. Exploited my vulnerabilities and preyed on my love for Serenity.

And it almost worked.

But I'll be damned if I let him get away with this.

The car had barely come to a stop in Serenity's parking lot before I was out and running toward the door.

"Elliot, you can't go in there! Your grandparents are in a meeting with Mr. Adams," called Nana's assistant. I ignored her and shoved the door to the conference room open anyway.

My grandparents and their longtime attorney were seated across from Greg, and all four heads immediately swiveled my direction.

"Elliot? What's going on?" Pops asked, pushing up from his chair.

"You can't sell Serenity to him," I blurted, adrenaline pumping through my veins.

"What are you talking about? Of course we can. We *are* selling to him."

I shook my head and pulled out the photos Helen had given me. "You can't. He's Helen's ex-husband, and he doesn't want to keep Serenity intact—he wants to destroy it."

"He's who?"

"Is this true?" They exclaimed in unison.

"You're too late, Ms. Kincaid," Greg said, a smug smile lifting the corner of his mouth. "The deal's already in motion."

I looked to my grandparents, whose stunned, yet defeated expressions told me he wasn't lying. Their lawyer's face was drained of all color as she desperately flipped through the paperwork in her hands.

My heart took a swan dive, and I fought the urge to leap across the table and tackle Greg to the ground.

"Don't do this. Hurting us won't absolve your pain. You have to know that."

Anger flared in his cloudy irises as he pushed his chair back and stood. "What I know is that I would be a father and a husband if not for these two," he said, looking across the table. "Instead, I fucking buried my son and watched that loss destroy my wife. My marriage. I'm supposed to just stand by and watch while they retire and happily live out their lives like they didn't rob me of everything I loved? I don't think so. I knew it was a sign when I heard that Helen's parents were planning to sell their beloved business. This pain inside me, it can't be absolved. But that doesn't mean I won't enjoy seeing you all experience even a fraction of what I've suffered."

Nana let out a sob and reached for Pops' hands, heartbreak rippling through them both before my eyes.

"I'm so sorry. But you know this won't change anything. Michael wouldn't want you to do this," I tried, swallowing down the lump in my throat summoned by my half-brother's name.

"Don't you dare say his name," he hissed, pounding his fist on the table. "You have no goddamn right to say that, and you sure as hell have no idea what he would want."

He stepped toward me, and I instinctively flinched. Pops moved in our direction, prepared to step between us.

But a voice behind me stopped both men in their tracks.

"But I do," my mother called, stepping into everyone's line of sight. "I know it's not what our son would want, Greg."

Just like that it was as if all the air had been sucked out of Greg's body. The anger in his eyes morphed into liquid pain, like seeing Helen and hearing her words were both soothing and breaking him all at once.

"How can you say that? How can you defend them? They ruined our lives. They deserve to suffer. I thought you'd understand. That you'd want this."

Helen took another step in Greg's direction. "I do understand. I understand that you're still hurting. That you'll forever have scars on your heart like the ones on mine. But I'll never want this. And it won't lessen the pain."

Greg stood and began pacing around the room.

"Could we, uh, have a moment in private?" Helen asked, looking from Nana and Pops to me.

We filed out of the conference room, and with one last look of reassurance from Helen, I pulled the door closed behind me.

My grandparents looked utterly confused as we sat on the bench outside the conference room, so I quickly started a recap of the last twenty-four hours. By the time I finished explaining everything, their expressions had morphed into complete devastation.

"We had no idea," Nana cried, close to tears.

Pops looked over at the conference room door and sighed. "She ought to hate us, and I can't say I'd blame her."

I shook my head. "She's got a good life now. I don't think she hates you."

"What about you, Elliot?" Pops asked. "Do you hate us?"

"I could never hate you. I hate what happened, but I know that, given Helen's abrupt departure, y'all had every reason to believe keeping me in the dark was the right move." I turned to them and grabbed their hands in mine. "You guys raised me. You were the only parents I ever needed, and I want you to know how grateful I am for everything you sacrificed, for everything you've done for me to give me the best life possible. I love you both so much. Always."

Their response was interrupted by the door flying open and Greg storming off without a word, though he looked less angry and more...conflicted.

Helen followed closely behind, coming to a stop in front of us. "I'm not sure how much good that did, but he said he'd think about it. I'm sorry I wasn't more successful."

Nana and Pops immediately stood and pulled her into a grateful, albeit somewhat stiff, embrace.

"We just appreciate that you tried."

"So...what now?" I asked, shifting nervously.

To say this was awkward would've been a drastic understatement.

"Now, we wait. For the lawyers to find a way to stop it...or..." Nana trailed off, and we all understood her implication. Or for Greg to pull the plug. *Or not pull the plug.*

"Will you stay?" Pops asked Helen. "Or do you have to head out now?"

"My flight back to Denver isn't until tomorrow."

"Would...would you join us for dinner?" Nana asked.

Helen gave a small smile and nodded. "I'd like that."

They all looked at me, and I swallowed the unexpected lump in my throat and nodded. "I'll, uh, call Soph. We'll be there."

THE WAITER BROUGHT out a lemon raspberry cheesecake, and Sophia and I shared a look while our grandparents rearranged the table to accommodate our dessert. The dinner had gone shock-ingly well, with only a handful of awkward moments. But after an hour and a half of small talk about mostly superficial topics, tension crept in. We'd covered the basics and exhausted all conversation routes that didn't delve too deeply or touch on our... unique family history.

My expectations for the evening had been low from the onset. I harbored no illusions that sharing a single meal would turn us into one big happy family. But it did lay the foundation for a potential path to healing. Whatever *our* version of healing would look like.

While Nana began cutting into the cake, Sophia leaned closer to me to whisper, "Is it just me or is it..."

"Weird because it's *not* that weird?" I finished, giving her a nod. "Yep."

Soph shrugged. "Guess we should be glad. I'm still in shock this is actually happening."

I started to agree, but froze when I heard Pops talking about Bryce's renovation plans for the inn.

I automatically pulled my phone out of my pocket, hoping to see his name on the screen. Instead, I had four new work emails and a text from Carleigh.

"Still haven't heard back from him?" Sophia asked, inter-preting my heavy sigh.

I just shook my head. After leaving Serenity that morning, I went on a mission to find Bryce, to do whatever it took to fix us, but a work emergency derailed my plans and kept me busy all day. So I settled for a text, asking if we could talk tonight.

"Maybe he's busy and hasn't checked his phone."

"Maybe."

By the time we finished our dessert, I could barely focus on the conversation around me. Bryce consumed my mind, and I couldn't bring myself to care what happened in any other area of my life.

"Oh, shoot, I just remembered I have a study group thing, and

I'm El's ride," Sophia said, checking her watch. "We better go or I'll be late."

"You do?" I asked, right as she kicked me under the table. "Oh, right."

Sophia and I stood, searching for the right words to say to our mother. Nothing felt right.

She seemed to be struggling too, eventually offering us a tentative smile. "Girls...I'm so glad you came to Denver, though I wish it had been under better circumstances. It was really wonderful to see you both. To...get to know you," she said awkwardly, twisting her hands together with uncertainty. "I wish I didn't have to go back so soon."

Without hesitating, I gripped her hands and returned her smile. "Thank you for coming. For everything, really."

"Would it be okay...do you think...we could keep in touch?"

I leaned in and gave her a quick, slightly awkward hug. "I'd like that."

Once we finished our goodbyes, Sophia and I spent the first few minutes of the ride in silence, digesting the last couple hours. When I realized she wasn't going to our apartment, I gave her a side-eye.

"Okay, what's with the abrupt departure? Your study group meets on Thursdays, and you just missed the turn for our place."

Checking her rearview mirror, Sophia switched lanes and shrugged. "We're getting a drink."

It wasn't like my sister to go out drinking during the week—or go out at all, really—but after the last forty-eight hours, I wasn't about to question it.

Still, she was suspiciously quiet the rest of the drive.

Everything clicked when she pulled into the bar's parking lot.

"Sophia," I said, slowly turning toward her with a brow raised. "This is Sipology."

"Yeah...didn't you say they have a good happy hour? I'm in the mood for a martini."

"I also said this is the bar Bryce always goes to..."

She smiled coyly. "Oh, is it? Totally forgot that part."

"Liar."

"That's a funny way to pronounce 'thank you,' but okay."

"God, you're such a smart-ass sometimes."

"You're welcome!" she called, throwing her door open and hopping out. "Now stop stalling and go get your man."

She didn't have to tell me twice.

CHAPTER 25
BRYCE

"Believe it or not, I didn't come here to watch you eye-fuck your customers, Xander," I snapped, cutting my cousin a glare over the rim of my beer glass. After seeing him hit on three women *simultaneously*, get their numbers, then disappear with two of them for twenty minutes, I was past the point of regretting my decision to come to Sipology.

"Maybe you should. Watch, I mean. You might learn something," he countered with a smirk.

"Like what? The art of being an asshole? No thanks."

He shrugged, unaffected by the insult. "Suit yourself. Look, man, I get that you're all hung up on Elliot and 'it's complicated,' or whatever. But it's not like y'all are *together* together. Who says you can't have some *un*complicated fun in the meantime?"

"I change my mind, go back to eye-fucking every other chick you see. At least then you won't be saying shit that's likely to get you punched."

He held up his hands and wisely walked to the other side of the bar without another word.

After a few minutes alone with my beer, I thought about checking in with my neighbor, Mrs. Spector, who was babysitting for me, but decided against it. Peyton was already down for the night before I left, so chances were that was still the case.

Plus, I'd been avoiding my phone as much as possible for the last two days. I told myself giving Elliot space was the best move, for both our sakes, but each hour that passed without seeing her tortured me.

Two shot glasses were pushed across the bar toward me, and I looked up to see Laci, Sipology's only female bartender, give me a grin.

Before I could open my mouth, the smell of pickles assaulted my nostrils. "Laci, I didn't order this," I said, pushing the shot glasses back to her.

She nodded toward the opposite side of the bar. "I know. *She* did."

I scanned the line of bodies along the bar, my eyes on the hunt for silky blonde hair and topaz-blue eyes. A mile-wide smile and a body carved straight from my wildest fantasies.

But my heart found her before my eyes could. It took control and drew me toward her before my brain even realized my feet were moving.

She abandoned her bar stool to meet me halfway and threw her arms around my neck before I could even get a word out. Her hug was crushing, like she was trying to meld our bodies together, but I didn't mind. I breathed in the scent of her fruity shampoo and brushed my lips against the shell of her ear. "El, I'm so—"

The rest of my apology was lost, trapped between our lips. With my arms woven around the small of her back, I welcomed her kiss like I'd been waiting my whole life for it. A soft moan vibrated from her mouth into mine, and I had to pull back before I escalated our kiss to something that made Xander's eye-fucking episodes look innocent.

"El, I'm sorr—"

"No, Bryce, I know it wasn't your fault," she said, cutting me off and shaking her head. "*I'm* the one who's sorry. You weren't the reason I didn't meet Helen. She went to my grandparents herself."

I frowned. "What? El, what happened?"

"I went to Denver with Sophia and Milo, and Helen explained what happened back then. Then Nana and Pops filled in the other gaps later. Bryce, I'm so sorry for not giving you a chance to explain."

"Wait. You went to Denver?! Hang on, let's...go somewhere..." I let my sentence hang, unwilling to have this conversation wedged between random Sipology customers.

I turned toward the bar, pulling El's hands into mine at the same time I caught Xander's attention. He lifted a brow and smirked at the sight of us. I nodded my head toward the back to let him know we were commandeering his office for a while.

As soon as the office door clicked shut, Elliot began pacing the small space while giving me a play-by-play of everything that happened after she left my house.

By the time she got to the part about confronting Greg at Serenity, she was practically shaking.

I gripped her shoulders mid-turn and steered her toward the couch, settling her into one side of the loveseat while I took the other.

"What was I thinking? I practically gave him a cheat sheet for how to fool my grandparents into thinking he was the perfect buyer. I should've known better than to get involved. Then again, making mistakes seems to be par for the course these days." For maybe the first time since she started talking, she stopped and took a breath, turning to me with guilt lacing her delicate features. "Bryce, I put you in an impossible situation back then; my judgment was beyond clouded, and you were thinking clearly. Then, yesterday, I should never have run out like I did. If I had stayed, we could've pieced things together and avoided the hurt. I hate that I let you think I was walking away for good. I wouldn't do that to you, Bryce. To Peyton. Not like *she* did. I'm so—"

Now it was my turn to swallow her apology. Slipping a hand

around to cradle her head at the base of her neck, I pulled her in and pressed a kiss against her lips that I hoped would smother the flames of regret raging inside her head.

"El, it's okay. *We're okay.* I hate that you had to go through so much at once, but as far as us? We're good, Uno. We're so much better than good. Couples fight—they say and do the wrong things, they act impulsively and sometimes it manifests in pain. But it's how you bounce back from the fights and the hurt that makes or breaks a relationship."

"Is that what we are? A couple?"

"Well, 'two overly friendly competitors who have amazing sex and enjoy each other's company as much as they enjoy winning against each other' is kind of a mouthful, don't you think?"

She laughed and smacked my chest. "You make a good point, Bowser."

"Finally! A character nickname I can appreciate," I said, pumping my fist.

"Don't get used to it…I'm thinking about circling back around to Toad, since you said yourself it's more accurate."

"You know damn well that's not the one that's accurate," I argued, trailing my fingers down her side and under the hem of her shirt to squeeze her hip.

She sucked in a breath at my touch and licked her lips. I grazed the pad of my fingers over her soft curves, smiling at the trail of goosebumps that greeted my touch.

"I forgot; which one was it that's accurate? McHotBody? Or is it McMagicDick?" she asked, pushing up to throw one of her legs over me. She settled onto my lap and leaned in, her breath tickling my ear. "I'm gonna need a demonstration…for research purposes."

"It's important to be thorough," I huffed, already pulling off her shirt.

She pulsed forward until her jeans rubbed against mine to create a torturous friction, making me groan. I gripped her hips and flipped her onto her back, balancing on my knees while we each raced to get the others' jeans off. I peeled hers down just enough to grant me access and wasted no time pulling her thong to the side.

"Mmm, I missed this magic pussy, Uno," I said, slipping two fingers into her with ease.

"God, Bryce," she cried, flexing into my movements. "Wait," she huffed, pushing up to her elbows a second later. "Should we...here?" she asked, gesturing at our surroundings.

I nearly laughed. "Xander isn't going to care." Though the knowledge of what had most likely just gone down on this couch earlier tonight made me hesitate.

"But, uh, not *right here*. Hang on," I said, shucking my clothes in two seconds flat. There was a pretty good chance Xander already knew what was happening in here, but that didn't mean I'd risk being interrupted by someone else.

Plus, fucking in Xander's office was one thing.

But sex on his little workplace fuckpad was a hard pass.

Elliot's heated gaze fell to my cock, banishing any trace of uncertainty from her features.

I pulled her into my arms and carried her across the small room, pinning her body between mine and the door.

She smiled, arching into me and tugging on the ends of my hair. "Two birds, one stone. So smart."

I pushed my hips forward, rubbing myself against her hot center. "Fuck, El...the way you feel, the way we fit together...I won't be able to hold back right now, which means you're gonna have to be quiet if you care about people hearing," I warned, pushing into her slow enough to draw a moan.

She bit her lip and looked up at me from under her long lashes. "Let them hear," she said, digging her heels into my ass and urging me forward. "I want everyone to know I'm yours."

I groaned against her lips and thrust into her at the same time.

CHAPTER 26
BRYCE

One month later

"Is she asleep yet?" Elliot whispered, giving me the signal to check so as not to disturb Peyton.

In the background, Olaf was singing about summer.

I carefully leaned forward from my spot on the other side of the couch and nodded after confirming that Peyton's eyes were in fact closed. "I'm surprised she even made it fifteen minutes into the movie. You guys were playing with those building blocks for a while."

El smiled, lifting a hand to brush the hair off of Peyton's face. "I know. The girl loves to build. A lot. Maybe she'll grow up to be an architect like Daddy."

"True, but she also loves to destroy. At this rate it's fifty-fifty between becoming an architect or becoming Godzilla."

She laughed, shaking her head and giving me a kick. "You did not just compare this sweet, precious angel to a freaking monster, Bryce!"

She turned to Peyton, and I felt my chest constrict from seeing the love in El's eyes. "Don't worry, Pey, I'll make sure he pays for that," she whispered, just loud enough for me to hear.

"Don't threaten me with a good time, Uno." I arched a brow and gave her a wink. "She's been out for a while. Want me to take her to bed?"

"No, let me. Maybe just...be on standby," she said, nodding toward the baby monitor on the coffee table.

I nodded, and El carefully pushed off the couch and scooped Peyton's little sleeping body into her arms.

I turned on the monitor as soon as they disappeared into Peyton's room. She was already changed and in pajamas, so I expected Elliot to lay her in the crib and duck out. Instead, El cradled Peyton against her chest and swayed back and forth, pressing her lips against the side of Peyton's head. She pulled away enough that I could tell she was saying something, but the monitor's mic didn't pick up her whispered words.

After a minute, El leaned over the crib and put Peyton down, tucked the little pink pig under Peyton's arm, and crept out of the room.

"What did you tell her?" I asked, nuzzling against her neck after she crawled over my body to get into the little spoon position on the couch.

She shrugged, twisting around to face me. "Top secret. Not sure if you've got that kind of clearance, McKnight. Maybe someday, if you play your cards right..."

"Uno, I'll give you all my cards." Kiss. "Starting now." I sucked in a breath and wrapped my hands around her waist, keeping her body against mine. "When Peyton was born, the doctors didn't know anything about her health because Bridgette hadn't been going to regular checkups. She told them she had been drinking off and on during the first months of her pregnancy. By some miracle, Peyton didn't have any physical characteristics of Fetal Alcohol Syndrome. Other than her low birth weight and size, she was physically perfect. But she was at risk for a long list of other possible symptoms—everything from congenital malformations of the kidneys and heart, to hearing loss, to things like a delay in developing motor and language skills. Problems with hyperactivity and impulse control were also a possibility, and difficulties with social skills. Peyton has defied the odds since day one, though, and she continues to surprise her doctors at every appointment. As a preemie, she needed a certain kind of eye exam to check the development of her retinas." I paused with a sigh, thinking back to that terrifying day. El's arms snaked around my neck, urging me to continue. "We found out that she had retinopathy of prematurity, which is a disease that can cause blindness if severe and untreated. Fortunately, her case wasn't severe. But she did have surgery to fix the issues with her retinas."

"Bryce, oh my god," Elliot whispered, shaking her head and tightening her grip around my neck.

I brought one hand around to swipe a tear off her cheek and continued, "The point of all this isn't to scare you about Peyton's health complications. It's just...me laying out all the cards in my deck. Bridgette left, mostly because she's selfish and irresponsible, but also because she couldn't handle the fact that life with Peyton wouldn't be black and white..."

Elliot's hands left my neck to cup my face. "I don't need black and white, Bryce. I need you. I want a life with you and with Peyton—no matter what that life entails. That secret I told Peyton? I told her I didn't know it was possible for a heart to fall for two people in two different ways at the same time. But that's the only way I can explain this feeling. It's the realest thing I've ever felt. I'm pretty sure I've loved her since the second she crawled into my arms at the zoo, tiny pig costume and all. And falling for you..." She paused on a hiccup and used my shirt to wipe a stray tear. "I should've realized that was inevitable."

I grinned, pressing my lips against hers. "Knew you wouldn't be able to resist the glasses for long."

She laughed and pushed against my chest. "Well it definitely wasn't the awful Mario Kart skills or dance moves that did it."

I pulled her face into my hands and held her in place. "I love you, Elliot Kincaid. Enough to overlook the fact that you just insulted my dance moves."

~

I SHOVED open the doors of Hey, Baker Baker and squinted into the bright sunlight, peeling off my sports coat and slipping on my sunglasses. *Gotta love Texas in November.* I'd just finished my consultation with Bob and Laura Baker, the owners of a popular bakery in the downtown Austin area. Their shop was small—too small for the rate at which their business was growing, which was where I came in. I'd never designed a bakery before, but the two dozen snickerdoodle cookies tucked under my arm made me wonder why the hell I hadn't gone for more food-related projects.

I walked in the direction of my SUV and fished my phone out of my coat pocket, smiling at the lock screen photo of El and Peyton from last week, curled up on the couch together while they watched *Frozen.*

Elliot wanted me to meet her and Peyton for lunch at Zilker Park after my meeting since the weather was nice, so I texted her that I was through at the bakery and heading to the park. She sent a photo of Peyton blowing a kiss and said they were already there.

Over the last few weeks, we managed to find our way into a comfortable routine. El had fewer weddings in the winter months, which meant we were able to finalize both the renovation plans for the inn and the designs for Forget Me Knot's wedding venue. Work on the inn was scheduled to start in January, and the venue would hopefully follow soon after that. Our working relationship wasn't all smooth sailing—we had disagreements and argued over the merits of certain aspects of the designs, but we always found our way through it.

Then, after work hours, we either took turns cooking, depending on our schedules, or cooked together while Peyton watched a show. El practically spent every night at my house. At this rate, she was pretty much wasting money on rent. For someone who had never really given parenthood much thought, the role certainly fit her. Elliot did it all—everything from early morning wake-up calls to bedtime book reading sessions.

I spotted Elliot's car in the parking lot and pulled into the spot next to hers. A follow-up text from her said to find them at our 'regular' spot, so I grabbed the picnic blanket from the trunk and headed their way.

When I found them, Elliot was blowing bubbles and Peyton was running in circles, giggling and frantically popping them.

"I spy Potatoes and Eggs!" I called, jogging toward them.

El's head whipped around in my direction and she flashed me a grin. "Look, Potatoes, there's Bacon!" she told Peyton. "Also known as Daddy!"

Yeah, we're now those *people who give ourselves silly nicknames. Bryce-Elliot-Peyton…Bacon-Eggs-Potatoes.*

Xander would permanently revoke my man-card if he ever found out.

Peyton ran toward me, and I threw her into the air, living for the little squeals of delight she gave me.

"Hi, beautiful," I said, setting Peyton down and leaning into El for a kiss. "What's the occasion? Are we celebrating something?"

She nodded and pulled out her phone, showing me a photo of George and Millie with a couple who looked to be in their forties. "Meet the Johnstons; they just made an offer on Serenity! They're going to finalize the deal after the holidays."

"Really?" I asked, already pulling her into a hug. "That's fantastic!"

"Mrs. Johnston's family used to vacation at a Serenity in Vermont each summer when she was young, so when she heard the sale fell through, she said she knew it was a sign. She wants to keep it exactly the same; no layoffs, no major changes. I haven't met her, but Nana and Pops are really happy, and that's enough for me."

"El, that's incredible. I'm so happy for them."

"Me too," she said, nodding and handing me a panini from our favorite sandwich spot.

We dug into our lunch, and I told her about my plans for the bakery since she knew the Bakers through work, and she told me about the fun she and Peyton had at the zoo this morning.

Eventually, Peyton got restless, so I caved and pulled up the PBS app on my phone before handing it over.

With her content and occupied, I pulled out the bag of Star-bursts and started moving them into a specific pattern on the blanket, swatting away Elliot's hand when she tried to snag one.

When I finished, it said 'B <3 E' with various shades of pinks and red.

She looked down and smiled before leaping into my lap. "That goes both ways, y'know. I love you, Bryce. So much. With you, the *what ifs*...fade away. If I lost the inn or if things fell through with the plans for the venue, I'd still be as happy as I am in this moment, as long as I had you two to come home to."

"Funny you should mention home—"

"Wait!" she yelped, practically jumping up and down in my lap. "There's actually another reason I wanted to celebrate. Do you know what today is?"

"Uh...should I?"

She turned toward Peyton. "Did you know the seventeenth of November is 'World Prematurity Day'? I was doing some research and found that out last week. I found a couple organizations that do really great work for families with premature babies and made a donation to both in Peyton's name. I also thought maybe we could start a tradition for this day, even if it's just lunch or dinner or playing a game or something. What...uh, what do you think?"

"I think..." I wrapped my arms tighter around her waist and crushed her body into mine. "El, I think that's the sweetest, most thoughtful thing anyone's ever done for me—for her. And I love you even more for it. You really are one of a kind; you know that?"

"And here I thought you always called me Uno because that's the first thing I ever beat you at."

"El, I call you Uno because it was the first word you ever said to me, and because I'll never forget how happy you were that day.

I think I loved you then, too; I just didn't know it was the once-in-a-lifetime kinda love."

She smiled, but her response was cut off by Peyton's pleas for more bubbles. She climbed out of my lap and swung a laughing Peyton into the air. "Ooooh, Peyton, let's go down the slide," Elliot said, pointing toward the playground. I was confused about the random suggestion, but realized what she was doing when I picked up the empty bottle of bubbles.

Distraction.

Peyton clapped eagerly and immediately forgot about the bubbles.

"Bryce, there's nothing I'd change about our history. Even if it did take us nineteen years to get to this part." She winked and offered a hand to help me up. "Now come on, we'll race you to the playground!"

We took off, but my head wasn't in it, and I slowed to a walk before we made it halfway there. El kept running, and I heard her cheer in celebration as soon as they reached the jungle gym.

I couldn't think about anything other than what Elliot had said, about it taking nineteen years to get here. About how crazy that felt.

By the time I caught up to my girls, Peyton had already gone down the slide once, and El was helping her climb back up to go again. The sight filled me with a happiness I'd never fully be able to explain. It just felt…right.

It felt like forever.

"Are you okay?" Elliot asked, giving me a concerned once-over as I walked up to meet her at the bottom of the slide. "If I didn't know any better I'd think you let us win."

She knelt down to greet Peyton when she came out, but I knelt down for an entirely different reason.

"Elliot, you mean more to me than I'll ever be able to express. When I was eight, you became my best friend. Fast forward nineteen years, and now you're my everything. You've become Peyton's mom in every way that counts, and I'll forever be in awe of the bond you share with her. There's never going to come a day when I don't want to wake up and see you, to make you laugh, to watch the way you love Peyton, to play you in every game known to man. It doesn't have to be today, or tomorrow, or even a year from now, but please, make me happier than I ever thought possible by marrying me."

She nodded and threw her arms around me, crying and laughing simultaneously. The second Elliot started to speak, Peyton barreled down the slide and plowed into us. We held her between our bodies, both smothering our little giggle machine with kisses. El looked up at me and smiled. "Yes. A thousand times yes, Bryce. I can't imagine any better way to spend my life than with the two people I love most in this world."

The second we started kissing, Peyton reached up and patted our cheeks. We laughed, but quickly grabbed her hands to stop the attack.

"Baby, I *just* got her to agree to keep us forever; maybe hold off on the human drum treatment until after it's official," I whispered to Peyton, just loud enough for El to hear.

Elliot giggled and pressed kisses all over Peyton's face.

Peyton launched herself into Elliot's arms and kept laughing through the onslaught of kisses.

"Hey, can I get in on this kissing action?" I asked, feigning jealousy.

Both girls turned to me, one smiling sweetly while the other licked her lips and gave me a seductive wink that made my mouth drop.

"Maybe...if you're lucky."

Oh, I'm lucky all right.

"I always get lucky, remember?"

EPILOGUE

ELLIOT

THE SECOND I FINISHED SIGNING THE DOCUMENT IN FRONT OF ME, A bottle of champagne popped behind me. I didn't need to turn around to know it was Jasmine doing the popping.

We were gathered in the conference room of FMK—Jade, her husband Emmett, Jasmine and Dean, Bryce and me, and Sophia— and we had officially signed the contract to start the construction of Serenity Oaks, our wedding venue.

Carleigh sent a text earlier saying she'd had some kind of plumbing emergency at her apartment, and wouldn't be able to make it. I wouldn't have given it a second thought, but she had been bailing on our after-hour get-togethers a lot lately. I had no idea what was going on with her.

Jade passed the glasses around the table as Jasmine poured. With the glasses distributed, Jas held hers up in a toast. "To Serenity Oaks and the four badass women who are going to make it a massive success." She turned to Dean and hung an arm around his neck before giving him a G-rated kiss (or, at least what I imagined to be Jasmine's version of G-rated). "And to the men who support us tirelessly. We love you." She gave Emmett and Bryce quick smiles, lifting her glass in Bryce's direction. "Especially you, Bryce. Without you, our vision wouldn't have come to life. We owe you. Since you refused to let us pay you in money, Elliot will pay you in orgasms."

"Jesus, babe," Dean groaned, shaking his head through a laugh.

Sophia groaned in disgust, but the rest of us laughed, not even a little surprised by her comment.

Jade lifted her glass higher and nodded. "I was going to say ditto what Jas said, but that feels weird now. Actually, there's, uh, something else I want to add anyway." She handed Emmett her glass and reached into her purse, pulling out a small, rectangular sheet of paper. "We're pregnant!" she squealed, wrapping an arm around Emmett's waist.

"Baby Sinclair is due in July," Emmett added.

We all erupted in cheers and rounded the table to congratulate them.

After a few minutes of talking details, Jade pulled back from our third group hug. "You know...you could make this a trifecta if you had a date for the wedding to toast to," she said, giving me a nudge.

"Seriously. Play calendar roulette at this point, El. You plan weddings for a living; how do you not have a date yet? Hey, actually, we don't have a wedding this weekend...how do you feel about being a December bride?" Jas asked, waggling her eyebrows.

I know she's joking, but...

Instead of answering, I turned to Bryce and actually considered the idea.

Before I could come to my senses, I marched over and grabbed Bryce's hand, dragging him into the hallway.

I looked up, meeting his aqua eyes and smiled. "Hi."

His brows scrunched in confusion. "Hi. What's up, Uno?"

"Did you mean it when you said I could pick every detail of the wedding?" He nodded. "You sure about that?" Another nod, slower this time. "Then marry me this weekend," I blurted, throwing myself into his arms.

"*This weekend?* As in…five days from now?"

I nodded, pulling away and rushing to explain that I'd take care of everything. "…I don't need the fancy decorations or a band or even a big white dress. I just want you, and I want Peyton, and I don't want to wait to start our happily ever after. Bryce, let's get married."

"El, I'd marry you on the side of a road five minutes from now if that was on the table." He paused, and I laughed, shaking my head to confirm that was definitely not an option. "Of course I'll marry you this weekend. Just tell me what I can do to help and where to show up."

I squealed and leapt into his arms again.

DESPITE THE COMPLETELY UNORTHODOX way our wedding came about, we managed to get all the important pieces checked off.

Dress? I borrowed Jasmine's, so it doubled as my 'something borrowed' too.

Cake? The Bakers came through with a nut-free red velvet masterpiece.

Music? Spotify playlist for the win.

Officiant? Milo got ordained online.

Location? *That one was easy.*

"El? Are you ready?" Jade asked, holding her grocery store rose bouquet in one hand and her clipboard in the other.

I nodded, forcing my fingers to stop tracing a pattern over the beads of Jasmine's dress. "Give me one minute."

I unfolded the note Bryce had left taped to my apartment door. It said 'open me right before the ceremony.'

So, naturally, I tore it open immediately and had read it fifty times since this morning.

El,

By now I hope you know I'll love you always. There's no way we're not meant for this.

Forever yours,
    Bryce

P.S. I can't wait to see you. I'll be the one in a suit, drooling over the hot chick walking down the aisle in a white dress.

P.P.S. Technically, I'm going to beat you to the altar, so...don't forget the Starbursts.

I walked out of the manor and found Pops, already sitting behind the wheel of the Jeep—my chariot to get us the rest of the way.

"Oh, Elliebelly," Pops gushed, shaking his head and dabbing a cloth under his eyes. "You look magnificent. Bryce is a lucky, lucky young man."

"Thank you, Pops," I replied, leaning over to peck his cheek while he drove. "I feel pretty lucky myself."

Time seemed to slow, and at the same time a thousand thoughts raced through my mind.

But it wasn't worries or fears or questions. *It was happiness.*

I was jittery and excited and thoroughly desperate to marry this man.

I was so lost in my own thoughts that I didn't realize Sophia was talking to me once we made it to the ceremony location.

"Peyton and I are about to go, then you and Pops are up. Got it?" she asked, turning around to confirm I was listening.

"Yep, got it."

A few seconds later, I finally stepped into the aisle and looked up to find my almost-husband.

If not for Pops keeping me on track, I would've sprinted to him.

When we finally got to Bryce, standing directly in front of our

'*B + E*' tree, I was positive my heart would burst. He looked like a cover model, only *better.*

"El, you're so beautiful," he whispered.

I smiled and squeezed his hand as Milo began addressing our small crowd of thirty or so guests.

For multiple reasons, we went with a 'less is more' approach, so it only took a few minutes before we exchanged rings.

Then Milo asked Bryce to recite his vows, and my eyeballs nearly fell out of their sockets.

"Milo! We're not doing vows," I whisper-yelled.

"I told him to add this part," Bryce said, squeezing my hands. "But I know we're all cold, so I'll keep it short...ish," he announced to the crowd, earning a collective laugh before turning back to me. "If I tried to list the reasons why I love you, we'd be here for...well, a really freaking long time. I know we agreed that not saying individual vows would help save time, but Elliot, I wanna start our forever with my own words of promise. I can't promise perfection, but I can promise that I'll never stop *trying.* To make you laugh, to get to know you in the details and in the big picture. To support you in success and pick you up in defeat. I promise I'll never stop trying to make you happy or trying to help you chase your dreams. I promise not to take your love for granted—not the way you love me or the way you love Peyton. Speaking of Peyton...this parenthood thing is a wild ride, but there's no one else I'd rather experience it with. But more than that, there's no one else I'd rather experience life with. I love you, El. Always."

"Bryce," I whispered, fighting the urge to fling myself against him. "That was...perfect." I cleared my throat and shook off the emotion threatening to really choke me up. "I've always thrived on plans. I thought I had to know exactly where I was going and control every aspect to ensure a certain outcome. But then you came back into my life and made me realize how much I was missing by letting my doubts dictate my decisions. You breathed life into my soul and made me see the world through a new lens.

I'd never promise perfection either; but I'd rather have *real* any day. I promise to be a team in this parenthood journey. I promise I'll love you and Peyton and our life together in the details and in the big picture."

Bryce cupped my face and brought our icy lips together.

"Uh, right; you may kiss the bride!" Milo called a half-second too late.

When we peeled apart, tiny hands reached between us and patted our legs. "Mama, up! Dada, up!"

Mama.

It had been weeks since the first time Peyton claimed me as her mom, but it still filled my heart with an indescribable kind of joy each time she said it. I knelt down and brushed our noses together in an eskimo kiss before picking her up and sandwiching her body between mine and Bryce's.

"I'm so glad you fell for my killer dance moves and expert Mario Kart skills, Uno," Bryce whispered against my ear.

So am I.

NEXT...

What happens when an unapologetic playboy crosses paths with the one girl who sees through his act?

Find out in Xander and Sophia's story, coming later this year!

Be the first to know about it and other releases by subscribing to my newsletter:

HTTP://EEPURL.COM/DXWT1T

LOVE THIS BOOK?

Please consider leaving a review on Amazon or Goodreads! Reviews are so important, and they mean the world to authors.

Be the first to know about my upcoming releases, giveaways, and sales by signing up for my newsletter:

HTTP://EEPURL.COM/DXWT1T

Come hang out in my Facebook reader group, Caitlin's Brew Crew, to chat all things books (and coffee)!

HTTPS://WWW.FACEBOOK.COM/GROUPS/CAITLINSBREWCREW/

You can find all of my books on my Amazon author page:

HTTPS://WWW.AMAZON.COM/AUTHOR/CRELLIS

WANT TO READ MORE OF THE FMK SERIES?

Read the Forget Me Knot series from the beginning, available now on Amazon and free with Kindle Unlimited!

Jade and Emmett's story: *Why Stars Chase the Sun (FMK #1)*

Jasmine and Dean's story: *When Light Leads to You (FMK #2)*

ACKNOWLEDGMENTS

Cullen, you are the real MVP, and I still can't believe I get to keep you forever, even after I made you watch Twilight the first day we met (sorry, not sorry).

Katie, Shannon, Brenda, and Brittany—I can't thank you guys enough for reading and rereading and helping me with this book. Hope y'all are ready for more because you're stuck with me now! :)

To Sarah, for always believing in me and patiently giving me encouragement when I need to hear it most. Thank you.

Jessie, I swear our texts and conversations sometimes are the only things that keep me sane in the madness of writing and publishing.

Thank you, Autumn, at Wordsmith Publicity, for everything you do, big and small.

Jenny, I don't want to know how this book would've turned out without your help. Thank you!

To all the wonderful book bloggers and bookstagrammers—you guys are incredible, and y'all are the reason the book community is as strong and awesome as it is. For everything you guys do to get your favorite authors' books out into the world—thank you!

Last, but *definitely* not least, to the readers—thank you for taking a chance on my books when I know there are a million options out there. I'm so grateful to each and every one of you.

ABOUT THE AUTHOR

C.R. Ellis is a Texas native who writes contemporary romance novels with plenty of drama and humor, and just enough heat to ignite e-readers and paperbacks everywhere. She can almost always be found attached to her laptop with coffee nearby and her two trusty canine sidekicks by her side. When she's not writing or plotting, she enjoys going to concerts with her sweet husband, dragging him along to see rom-coms at any theater that serves booze, checking off the next destination on her ever-growing travel bucket list, and trying new recipes.

Her passion for writing stems from her lifelong love of reading, and she often binge-reads entire books in a day. She's an unapologetic book hoarder, and her paperback collection is rivaled only by her massive shoe collection.

For more information about her and her upcoming releases, visit www.crellisauthor.com.

Sign up for my newsletter to receive up-to-date information about books, new releases, and promotions.

HTTP://EEPURL.COM/DXWT1T